I0599938

the ghost of black hill road

hopedale mystery series
book two

Tom Deady

GREYMORE PUBLISHING

For library kids everywhere...

Stay at home, stay at home,
Lonesome Amie will find you alone.
Stay off the road, stay off the road,
Lonesome Amie will take your soul.

prologue

Hopedale Village, October 31st, 1885

THE GIRL SITS up in bed rubbing sleep out of her eyes. Usually, if she wakes in the night, it's to use the outhouse or because she had a bad dream. She doesn't recall a nightmare, and even though she doesn't feel the urgent need to pee, she decides she may as well since she's awake.

She pads across the rough-hewn floor and out the back door. Moonlight casts an eerie blue glow on everything and she is suddenly afraid. *Maybe I did have a scary dream and just can't remember.* She does her business quickly and starts back toward the house, but something draws her toward the street despite the gnawing fear that constricts her chest.

The streets are empty, the quiet almost a physical presence. Then she hears something. A faint pop. A distant gunshot? It's hard to tell in the dead stillness but she thinks it must have come from the woods up Black Hill Road.

Her Uncle Otto is a lumberjack, and he lives up in the logging camp. He's often told her stories of the critters that

1

venture into camp looking for food. Bears, raccoons, and bushy-tailed foxes. He told her they only shoot in the air to scare the scavengers away, but she's seen a lot of the lumber-jacks wearing coonskin caps and doesn't believe him.

More faint pops, and...is that yelling? Another ripple of fear spreads through her, this one colder and darker than the first, and she considers waking her father. No, she decides, he would be angry. He works hard all week and must get up early tomorrow for church.

She stands, staring up the hill into the impenetrable dark-ness, when the idea hits her. Once formed, it grows like a bad weed. *Uncle Otto is in danger.* She shivers, wishing she'd grabbed a sweater. The October night is chilly. A cruel reminder that another long, cold winter is not far away.

Something bad is happening. The thought— no, the *knowledge* is undeniable. She is powerless to ignore it. With a long look toward the cabin, again considering waking Pa, but again deciding not to, she starts up Black Hill Road. Again wishing for a sweater against the night's chill, she also misses her dolly. Why didn't she take her when she got up?

She moves to the center of the road and follows the parallel steel tracks of the logging car. The loggers had modified an old flatbed mining car to send their hauls down the hill. A pulley-and-rope system was attached to the rear of the car and the loggers took turns hauling the car back up the tracks for another run.

Deep shadows lurk on the sides of the road, and she feels there might be eyes watching. Bright green ones, or red, perhaps. Not people, but the critters that come out at night to hunt. Better to stay where she is, smack in the middle of the road.

She puts her head down and focuses on following the tracks. The seed of dread that was planted by the thought that Uncle Otto is in danger has taken root and is growing in her belly. The popping sounds are louder as she climbs, and she is sure they are gunshots. More shouts, the words indiscernible but fraught with emotion, reach her, too. She folds her arms across her chest against a thin breeze that has stirred, and continues her trek.

To keep her mind off her fear she walks tightrope on one of the rails. She is good at it and has no trouble keeping her bare feet on the cold rails. Then she notices something odd. A humming. No, more like a vibration. Frowning, she steps off the rail and kneels, placing a hand on the steel. It feels like she has put her hand on a hornets' nest. Confused, she gets to her feet and looks down the hill, but there is only darkness and the sleeping town. When she turns, it is too late. She looks up as the fireball hurtles at her. Her last thought as the burning mine car takes her is for her Uncle Otto.

chapter
one

A LOW GROWL sounded from beside Hannah Green's bed. She sat up in bed, absently reaching down to pat Scout. "It's okay, boy," she whispered. The sound of her voice in the darkness did not allay the fear that clung to her. Her heart hammered and she felt the unnerving beat of her own pulse in her throat. A thin sheen of sweat covered her shivering body. Insane images from her nightmare flashed in her memory, but they were fading quickly. She got up to get a drink of water and was glad Scout padded at her heels.

The severed foot, she thought, *Mama Bayole.* A shudder ripped through her. That past summer, Scout had trotted out of the woods carrying a pink Converse high-top sneaker containing a decomposing foot. The events that ensued had led Hannah and her best friend Ashley into a decades-old mystery that involved a woman named Mama Bayole who had lived just down the street from Hannah in Hopedale, New Hampshire. Though she couldn't focus on the nightmare, she was sure it involved the old witch. The dreams that had plagued her since then *always* included Mama Bayole.

Hannah stood in the kitchen gulping water while Scout sniffed around at her feet. A cool breeze sent the kitchen curtains flapping, and Scout raised his head, sniffing furiously at a scent he caught riding the air. He ran to the back door and jumped, his front paws splayed on the wood, and began barking.

Hannah put the glass down on the counter and went to him, gently pulling his collar to get him off the door before he scratched it. She had never seen him do that before, and the fear that had subsided from her nightmare began to creep back. Thoughts of Mama Bayole and her followers filled her head. *Are they out there?*

She knelt next to Scout, patting him and whispering that it was okay, all the while holding his collar, feeling his tense body ready to spring. His growl was low but fierce. Hannah realized, not for the first time, how isolated they were. The closest neighbor wasn't within screaming distance, she thought with another shudder.

Part of her wanted to let Scout go outside, chase away the coyote or the deer or whatever it was, and be done with it. The other part, the part that ruled in the wee hours of the night, knew he might go out, and she might hear a pained yelp, and he might not return.

She held him until his growls subsided. Finally, he began sniffing wildly again, then, satisfied the threat was gone, drank water from his bowl and slumped to the floor. He was asleep almost instantly.

Hannah turned off the light and peered through the back door. The night was clear and a half-moon threw enough bluish light for her to see the back yard to the edge of the woods. She watched for a bit, then went back to her room, glad to hear Scout follow and take his post at the foot of her bed.

Sleep wouldn't come. Even with the windows open, the temperature in Hannah's room was uncomfortably warm for September. She listened for the sound of late-season crickets, sad that summer was over. Winter's desolate silence would soon take over the nights. Scout stirred on the floor, as if sensing her restlessness. Hannah tried to imagine that oppressive winter quiet but couldn't conjure it in her mind. Instead, she thought about other sounds that made her feel sad or lonely. A pulley clanging against a flagpole. A November leaf skittering across a deserted parking lot. Her footsteps on the pavement when she went running at night. As she finally drifted off, the sound of a conch shell was the last lonely sound she imagined.

chapter
two

"MISS GREEN!"

Hannah stared at Mr. Costello, then looked around the classroom as the snickering filled her ears. *Did I fall asleep?* She realized immediately that wasn't the case: *It's happened again.* Heat rose in her face, and she scrunched down in her seat as if she could hide from the class. From the world. She had managed to stay under the radar during her first few weeks as a Hopedale High freshman, but it seemed her streak had come to an end.

"Sorry, um, what was the question?"

Costello gave an overdramatic sigh and repeated the question, something—as he'd stated numerous times already this year—he was *loath* to do. Hannah saved face a bit by knowing the answer. Costello was one of those teachers who seemed to feed off making students uncomfortable, often to the point of public humiliation in the form of his scathing tongue. She was glad she got off easy with just a long sigh.

The whispers continued and Hannah felt eyes on her. She turned in her seat and found the piercing gaze of a girl she had never seen before. The stranger's lips began to turn up, like she was going to offer a smile, but then her head dipped toward her desk. The girl's unkempt black hair shielded her face and Hannah couldn't tell if the smile was there or not.

The spells, or whatever they were, much like the nightmares that haunted her, had started after the showdown with Mama Bayole at Champlain Park. She would simply... zone out. A few minutes of time would be lost, with no memory of it passing. She wondered, sickly, what happened to her during those minutes. Would she stare slack-jawed into space? Would she continue to interact, carrying her end of the conversation with no knowledge of what she'd just said? Was she possessed?

When the bell rang, Hannah hurried out of the room, grateful to be free of World History. The new girl disappeared into the swell of kids filling the hall, her colorful skirt billowing behind her. Hannah scanned the corridor for her best friend, Ashley, but she was probably on the far side of the building where the college prep classes were held. Hannah was in all AP courses. Freshman year, they would see very little of each other. Even their lunch periods were different. Hannah moved with the stream of students, nodding and saying "hi" to friends she hadn't seen much of lately. Hopedale was a small town, but it had been a strange summer.

"Hey, Hannah."

She felt a familiar tingling in her belly as she turned toward the voice. "Hi, Marcus. How was Algebra Two?"

"Polynomial equations are boring enough, but Mrs. Stevenson's voice makes them exponentially worse." Marcus grinned.

Hannah chuckled at his math pun as Marcus slid next to her and their hands found each other. "Yeah, she's rough. Especially first period." They both had Mr. French for English next class, and Hannah again mused at all the bad jokes the poor man must have heard over the years.

"How was Costello? Did he ruin anyone today?"

"I was almost his first-period victim," Hannah said miserably.

"You? Hannah Green of the straight-A Hannah Greens?"

She laughed. "I don't know what happened. One minute I was taking notes, the next minute he was calling my name and had to repeat his question."

"Which he is *loath* to do," Marcus mocked. He paused, then whispered, "Are you okay?"

Hannah's mind wandered back to Mama Bayole. Her fifteen minutes of fame over the summer's events had passed quickly. Even in a town as small as Hopedale, things moved fast. The internet helped focus everyone's attention on the next big, tragic thing. Still, something wasn't quite right. Hannah's mind had never strayed as much as it was these days. Marcus hadn't noticed her spells and she wanted to keep it that way.

She ignored his question as the image of the new girl's stare jolted her. "Hey, did you hear about a new kid starting?"

Marcus nodded. "Yeah, my mom said she heard something about a new family moving to town."

Marcus's mom was a devout churchgoer who also happened to be a notorious gossip. Dad had said if someone farted in church, everyone in town would know before the pew cleared, then he'd laughed himself silly over the terrible pun. Hannah wondered what Mrs. Diaz had said about her and Ashley over the summer.

"Was the new kid in your class?" Marcus asked.

"She was, I didn't catch her name or anything, just noticed a new face." She realized Mr. French would have introduced a new student. How had she missed that?

"And that's it?"

Marcus had slowed and was looking at her with a curious expression, one tinged with doubt.

"Mostly. She was kind of staring at me after I had my little episode. It creeped me out."

"Are you okay?" Marcus repeated.

Hannah wanted to scream, *No, I'm not okay! My best friend was kidnapped and there was a cult running around Hopedale. Oh, and they never caught all the members.* But they'd arrived at Mr. French's room. Their hands slipped apart, and they took their seats. Hannah watched Mr. French, who was engrossed in his notes for the class. Even though he was the brunt of so many jokes, Hannah liked him as a teacher.

He unfolded himself from his chair and began class. He was in constant motion, his long legs pacing the floor in easy strides, his hands flailing as he spoke. "Welcome, everyone. Now that the freshman year jitters are in the past, why don't we, as they say, kick it up a notch?" He smiled in spite of the groans. "Well, then, let's get started. First on the agenda is... any guesses?"

More groans: this time, Hannah had to help him out. "Summer reading?" Mr. French had let them know on the first day of class that he would be giving them a few extra weeks to catch up on their summer reading assignments. "Given the unusual summer," he'd said, and all eyes had turned to Hannah that day, too.

The groans turned into mock anger directed at her, but she laughed it off.

Mr. French aimed finger guns at Hannah. "Give the girl a Kewpie doll! Summer reading, it is."

He went back to his desk and switched his computer display so it was on the big screen at the front of the room. The list of summer reading books came up. *Did I forget to do summer reading?* Then she remembered she'd gotten it out of the way at the beginning of the summer. The *before* time.

Hannah had picked *Lord of the Flies,* which had completely freaked her out. As if being trapped on an island wasn't scary enough, the way the boys had turned so... feral, was terrifying. She looked around the room, trying to imagine her classmates in that situation. Who would be the leader like Ralph? She thought Marcus could do it. And who would be the Jack Merridew of the bunch? As Hannah was wondering what part she would play in it, she noticed Mr. French staring at her. He wore a bemused expression. *Does he know what I'm thinking?*

He opened his mouth to speak but was cut off by the shrill din of the fire alarm.

In the parking lot, the students huddled in groups while the fire engines rolled in. If there was smoke, Hannah didn't see it. Most likely, someone had pulled the fire alarm to get out of a test or something.

Marcus stayed near, a protective arm draped over her shoulder. It didn't take long to figure out that *nothing* was going on within the school. After the firemen had explained the situation to the principal and packed up their gear, the teachers began herding the students back to class.

"Hannah? You coming?"

Marcus wore a look of concern. She noticed most of the kids were well on their way across the parking lot. She'd zoned out again.

"Um, yeah, let's go." She tried to smile but it didn't feel right.

As they caught up to the slow-moving crowd, a kaleido-scope of color across the lot captured her attention. She turned and her heart thudded when she saw the new girl. She stood statue-like, staring right at Hannah. Her multi-colored skirt and silk blouse with its voluminous sleeves looked like some-thing out of an old disco movie.

"Marcus ..."

Marcus turned, his eyes narrowing as he studied her face. "What is it? Is something wrong?"

He followed her gaze to see what she was staring at, but the girl was already gone, having slipped into the tide of students.

"No, it's just ... I'm fine. Let's get back to class."

Hannah started walking but Marcus grabbed her arm gently. "Hannah, what's going on?"

She looked back across the lot, then to the group of kids jostling to get back into the school. She tried to spot a flash of color, just to prove to herself that she really had seen the new girl, but couldn't find her.

"It was that girl, the new girl. Staring at me like she did in class earlier." Hannah didn't tell him that she might have lost a few seconds of time as well.

Marcus scanned the crowd. Hannah almost laughed, since he had no idea who he was looking for.

The rest of the morning went by like most: slowly and uneventfully. Hannah sat with Marcus at lunch, both self-conscious and smug due to the stares they got. The whole boyfriend-girlfriend thing was new to them, and Hannah suspected they were just stumbling their way through it, trying it on for size. It fit pretty good, as far as she was concerned.

Kenny joined them after they'd finished eating. He'd been sitting with the band kids, like Marcus had done last year in middle school. Kenny plopped down, eyeing Hannah and Marcus, then looking around the cafeteria.

"What's up with you?" Marcus laughed.

"Did you hear about the fire alarm?" Kenny's voice was low, conspiratorial.

"Um, yeah, we heard it, we had to leave the building, remember?" Marcus was being snarky, trying to annoy Kenny into telling him whatever his big news was.

Kenny looked around again. "They took a girl to the principal's office. They think she pulled the alarm."

Hannah's jaw tightened and she clenched her teeth. She already knew what he was going to say next, but kept quiet.

"Some new girl, kind of a weirdo, I guess."

"What does that even mean, Kenny?" Hannah's tone was harsher than she intended. She felt Marcus's stare boring into the side of her face but she kept her eyes on Kenny.

He shrugged. "You know, she dresses funny, doesn't talk to anyone, kind of a loner."

Hannah's pulse quickened and her face burned. "She's new to the school, you just said so. What do you want her to do, walk around shaking hands and kissing babies, for Christ's sake?"

Conversations around them stopped. More eyes turned to them.

Why am I defending her?

"And since when are you the freaking fashion police?"

"Hannah?" Marcus reached for her hand, but she wasn't having any of it. For reasons she couldn't explain, her temper had risen and was getting the best of her. She jumped up from the table, ignoring the stares of the kids around her, just as she ignored Marcus's pleas for her to calm down.

"You guys need to grow up." Hannah slammed the rest of her lunch into the trash and stormed out of the cafeteria.

chapter
three

"SO, you had a total meltdown in the cafeteria?" Ashley tried to play it off lightheartedly, but her words were laced with worry.

"The weird thing is, I don't even know why. It wasn't like I was sticking up for a friend, the girl had creeped me out twice already, but there I was, protecting her."

They sat on the back deck of Hannah's house. She tossed a slobbery old tennis ball, and Scout dutifully fetched it. The night was warm, the girls were both in shorts and t-shirts. Dad was in the house, probably dozing off in front of the television. They had just finished dinner when Hannah dropped the bomb about what had happened at lunch.

"Who is she? This poorly-dressed weirdo?" Ash's eyes were bright, and a smirk played at the sides of her mouth.

Hannah took the tennis ball out of Scout's mouth and threw it at Ashley, fresh drool and all. She sidestepped the ball with a shriek and Scout padded over to fetch it again.

"I have no idea. I didn't even catch her name in class, and I didn't give Kenny a chance to tell me before I flipped out."

"So, you didn't hear anything about her? She just showed up?"

Scout dropped the tennis ball and rolled over onto his back, a not-so-subtle hint he was done fetching and it was belly-rub time. Hannah knelt next to him and complied.

"You know how that goes," Hannah said. "One story is she transferred here after being released from an asylum. Another one says she just got out of rehab for heroin addiction and was here for a fresh start. The real story is probably something closer to her dad got a new job around here and they had to move. Do they even have asylums anymore?"

"If they did, you'd be in one," Ashley said. "Let's go find some ice cream."

They started towards the house, the last of the daylight slipping from the sky behind them.

"So ... How was your day?"

Hannah still struggled with the new schedule, and with not seeing her best friend all day.

Ashley smiled. "It was so amazing. Our side of the school is like a carnival. We watch movies for half the day, have dance parties, there's a never-ending Coke fountain and hunky, shirtless male waiters who serve lunch."

"Ha-ha! You're such a dope."

Ashley grinned. "School is school, you know? I mean, I miss not hanging out with you guys, but what can I do?" She shrugged.

Hannah wished she had some of whatever it was that made Ashley *Ashley*. She could adapt to any situation and have a good time. She never seemed to stress about anything.

"Hey, did you and Marcus ever make up?"

At the mention of his name, Hannah felt tears sting behind her eyes. "No, we didn't have any classes in the afternoon, and he had soccer practice after school. I talked to Kenny and apologized, but ..." She trailed off. Ashley grabbed her hand and pulled her toward the back door.

"You're calling him. Right now." She yanked the door open and dragged Hannah inside.

"Ash, no. I can't."

Ashley already had her cell phone in her hand. "Yes, you can. And you will. Now."

Hannah shook her head, embarrassed by the tears leaking onto her cheeks.

Ashley looked at her cell and Hannah knew she was searching her contacts for Marcus's number. "Then I will."

"Not with that," she said. Hannah lived on the outskirts of Hopedale, one of the few places with no service. Then she heaved a disheartened sigh and picked up the landline phone.

Ashley reached over and gently wiped the tears away. "That's my girl." She turned toward the living room. Dad was asleep in the recliner, but Ashley didn't care. "Yo, Mr. G, what's up?"

Hannah dialed Marcus's number. "Hi. I wanted to say I'm sorry for the way I acted today." A lone tear slid down her cheek.

"Yeah, what was that about?"

Hannah closed her eyes and gripped the phone tighter. "Honestly, I don't know. I had a couple of weird experiences, then, it just seemed wrong for Kenny to be judging the new girl for the way she dresses. I know I overreacted and I'm sorry."

"Listen, I agree with you. That's why I was so hurt when you said, 'you guys'... I hadn't said *anything* about the girl."

Hannah thought back to the incident and felt sick when she realized he was right. "I'm so sorry. I don't know what happened, I just got so mad." *Why* did *I lash out like that?* "I apologized to Kenny this afternoon, but I never saw you after lunch."

There was a long pause, the silence filled only by the pounding of Hannah's heart.

19

"Are you okay, Hannah?"

Her breath caught in her throat. His voice was steeped in concern, and it filled her with a mixture of emotions that threatened to overwhelm her. She felt a little lightheaded and queasy, but also wonderful somehow.

"Yes ... no ... I don't know." Hannah knew she sounded childish and afraid. "I just want things to be normal," she whispered.

The laughter at the other end of the phone took her by surprise. It was so far from the reaction she was expecting that she found herself smiling. "Hey, you don't have to laugh at me!" Hannah couldn't hide the happiness in her voice.

"Sorry, I'm not laughing at you, I swear. It's just—" He broke into another fit of laughter.

This time she laughed along with him. It felt as if a dark cloud had been hanging over her since the incident at lunch, and it had finally lifted.

"I don't think things are going to be normal if I tell you what I found out today."

He was still laughing but Hannah wasn't. Her body went cold, goose bumps popping up on her arms.

"What is it?"

Marcus stopped laughing too, probably hearing the dread in her voice.

"Well, my mother, you know how she is. She talked to a bunch of people about that new girl."

Hannah didn't want to hear whatever it was he had to say. She opened her mouth to tell him as much, but no sound came out.

"She heard that the reason they moved away from their last home is because the girl killed her baby sister."

chapter
four

"HANNAH, you're not going to get all 'let's play detective' on me again, are you?"

Ashley was sitting on the bedroom floor, leaning against the wall, absently patting Scout, whose head rested in her lap. Hannah had filled her in about things being patched up between her and Marcus, but Ashley must have seen it written on her face there was more. So she'd told Ashley what Marcus's mother had said about the new girl.

Hannah grinned. "Well ..."

"Well, count me out. One near-sacrifice is enough for me. I need my beauty sleep and a stress-free existence if I'm going to break all the hearts that Hopedale High has to offer.

Hannah's grin widened. "Nice alliteration."

Ashley stuck her tongue out. "Do you think it's true?"

The story Marcus had told, who knows how many times removed from the truth, was disturbing. The new girl, Dawn Holman, had just moved to Hopedale with her father. Marcus's mom had said they'd come from Minnesota or Wisconsin or "some godforsaken midwestern tundra." Dawn's sister had apparently died under mysterious circumstances. From what Hannah understood, Dawn's mother had accused her of killing her sibling, though no charges were filed following the investigation. Dawn's father, however, had packed up and moved to Hopedale to start over and get away from the mother, who still believed their daughter to be a murderer.

"I don't know. There were a lot of holes in the story. Like, some of the obvious facts—what state they lived in, how old Dawn's sister was—that stuff should be common knowledge for anyone able to spell *Google*."

Ashley looked at her, eyebrows raised, head tilted to one side. Then she frowned. "Hannah, just drop it, okay? Enjoy your first year as a high schooler. Enjoy having a boyfriend. Enjoy not having a blood-drinking voodoo witch as a neighbor."

Hannah laughed. "Drop what?" She batted her eyelashes.

Ashley's face was lined with concern, and something else. Something that looked like fear. "I'm not kidding!"

"Hey, I'm just messing with you. Chill."

She stared at Hannah, waiting. Hannah willed herself not to look away. The shrill ring of the phone, like a scream, broke the standoff. A minute later, Dad knocked and said Ashley's mom wanted her home soon, and that he could drive her.

"Thanks, Big G," Ashley yelled.

Hannah smiled as her dad muttered something, though she could picture his half-smile while doing it. They both stood, Scout giving Ashley a look of utter inconvenience at having to move his head.

"You're going to drive that poor man crazy, my friend."

"It helps him stay young, and he needs that to keep up with Benson."

"Gross," Hannah moaned. Though she did it with little conviction. Hannah liked Rick Benson, and she was happy Dad had another adult to spend time with. But she certainly didn't want to think of him and Benson *that* way.

"So, are you going to be able to keep yourself together at school tomorrow? I don't want to spend my whole day worrying about you."

"As long as the stupid boys keep their stupid comments to themselves, we'll all get along just fine."

chapter **five**

THE NEXT DAY AT SCHOOL, Costello seemed to watch Hannah closely, waiting for her to doze off or zone out so he could pounce. She refused to give him the satisfaction.

She'd decided that she was going to talk to the new girl. So, when the bell rang, she made sure she timed it right so they would meet up at the door.

"Hi, you're new here, right?"

The girl looked at Hannah, surprise turning to curiosity, then suspicion. Her deep blue eyes held the same piercing look Hannah had seen the day before.

Finally, she said in a voice barely above a whisper, "My name is Dawn."

Hannah smiled. "I'm Hannah Green. If you don't know anyone, you're welcome to eat lunch with me and my friends. It must be hard being the new kid."

She regarded Hannah for a long time before answering, her gaze unwavering, as if she was running some kind of scan to see if Hannah was being sincere. Then she smiled. It made what Hannah had thought a rather plain face suddenly pretty.

"That would be great, thanks."

"Okay, see you at lunch." Hannah smiled and half-waved

before slipping into the stream of kids heading to the next class.

Marcus caught up with her as they approached Mr. French's room, his hand slipping into hers as if they'd been walking that way forever.

"I asked Dawn to eat lunch with us. You don't mind, do you?" Hannah glanced up, trying to read his expression.

"Dawn, as in Dawn the new girl? Hannah, you're not going to ... you know?"

Hannah glared at him. "Not going to what?" Her face heated up and her lips tightened.

"You know, start anything with Kenny?"

Hannah almost laughed but didn't want to hurt his feelings. "Of course not," she said, her voice syrupy sweet. He eyed her for a minute, but she started laughing before he could respond. "Relax, Marcus, I'm only trying to be friendly. As long as Kenny doesn't start calling her weird, we'll all get along fine."

The tension drained from his face, then he frowned. "Wait, you're not trying to get to know her because of—"

"Class is about to start," Hannah said, turning the corner into class. "We'll chat later!" She ran to her seat, ignoring his muttering.

As soon as she sat down, she felt eyes on her. Mr. French didn't let students choose their own seats, he believed in the tried-and-true grammar school logic of assigned seating. By some cruel twist of fate, Marcus was all the way across the room. The feeling of being watched was palpable. She turned to find the leering grin of Derek Campbell. He was in the next row, one seat back.

Derek, not-so-cleverly nicknamed "Soup" by those who dared call him that, was an oversized, creepy menace. He was older and bigger than the rest of the ninth-graders, courtesy of staying back twice, and used his size and strength to intimidate everyone around him. Unlike most bullies, who had an entourage of sycophants in tow, Derek was a loner. Aside from his brutish ways, his lack of hygiene was in direct proportion to his lack of friends. Derek was, in a word, gross.

Hannah didn't know why he hadn't been in class all year and didn't really care. Any day she didn't see Derek Campbell was a good day. He made no attempt to look away, to pretend he wasn't ogling her. Instead, he waggled his eyebrows at her in what was intended to be a suggestive manner. In spite of being nauseated by the two furry caterpillars dancing on his forehead, she burst out laughing.

Derek's attempt at seduction boiled over into rage instantly. "You stuck-up jerk!"

Gasps erupted around the classroom. His words should have bothered her, but Hannah couldn't get the image of the caterpillars out of her head, and she slapped her hands over her mouth trying to suppress the giggles.

Mr. French appeared, his face tight. "Mr. Campbell, when you're done apologizing to Miss Green, you can enjoy a nice stroll to the office."

Derek jumped to his feet, knocking his chair over. His face was tinged a dangerous red and his eyes burned with fury. He wasn't quite as tall as Mr. French, but probably outweighed him by fifty pounds. He seemed to loom over him, but the teacher didn't flinch. He met Derek's gaze with a sort of elated challenge, and Hannah wondered for a second if French might be a little crazy. Or maybe he'd just had enough of kids like Derek.

"Something you want to say, Campbell?" French leaned toward Derek, and suddenly the size difference didn't matter. There was something in French's eyes that even a bully like Derek couldn't ignore.

Derek turned to Hannah, his eyes narrow and his breath coming in heated gasps. "I'll see you later, sweetie."

Hannah snorted, knowing she'd regret it when Derek did see her again, but seemed incapable of containing her laughter. Mr. French glanced at her with a smirk.

Derek's eyes searched the room and settled on Marcus. "You too, Diaz." Then he stormed out of the room without another word.

Hannah's laughter died when she realized what she'd done. Derek was a creep, but he wouldn't be dumb enough to touch her. He could get to her through Marcus, though.

"Are you all right, Hannah?" Mr. French's tone was sincere, but that hint of a smile was still there.

"I'm fine, thank you."

He nodded and returned to the front of the class. Hannah turned to look at Marcus. He was staring back at her with a mixture of fear and admiration. "I'm sorry," she mouthed.

He smiled and shrugged, but the smile didn't touch his eyes. He knew the same ugly truth as Hannah: Derek would get him.

chapter
six

"LET'S REVIEW," Hannah stated, her voice dripping sarcasm, "first, I zone out in Costello's class and get the 'I am loath' speech. Second, Soup hits on me and then calls me a loser, and my childish outburst will most likely result in the death of my boyfriend."

Hannah, Marcus, Dawn, and Kenny were eating their lunches. Introductions had been made and it was a lot less awkward than Hannah thought it was going to be, even though the atmosphere seemed tenser than usual.

The others looked at her like she had three heads, evidently not picking up on her tone. "For my next trick, I can't decide if I'll challenge Principal Meadows to an arm wrestle, or just commandeer the PA system and do karaoke."

"Oh, I get it, you're joking." Kenny's deadpan tone got a chuckle out of Dawn and Marcus.

Hannah threw her hands up in mock exasperation. "Thank you, Captain Obvious." Her eyes found Marcus. *Is he still worrying about Derek?*

"Seriously, Hannah, I think Ashley is rubbing off on you," Kenny said.

"Who's Ashley?" Dawn asked, between bites of Doritos.

"Ashley is Hannah's best friend and partner in crime. Or should I say, partner in *solving* crimes."

Hannah flashed him a look, but it was too late.

"What does that mean?" Dawn asked.

Kenny spent the rest of lunch telling Dawn the *Reader's Digest* edition of how Ashley and Hannah had both been kidnapped over the summer and eventually broke up a child-killing voodoo cult. He got a lot of the facts wrong and exaggerated the ones he got right, but Hannah was not in the mood to correct him.

Dawn was enthralled, often glancing at Hannah, wide-eyed. It took Hannah a minute to realize that Kenny might be trying to hit on Dawn.

Any anger Hannah was holding about Kenny's cruel words the previous day evaporated. She even smiled at the thought of them getting together. Even though Kenny could blurt out some famously stupid comments, he had a good heart. At the very least, he had probably learned a lesson about judging people by the way they look or how they dress. He certainly didn't seem to mind Dawn's outdated skirt and blouse today.

Marcus caught Hannah's half smile. She jutted her chin toward Kenny and Dawn, then raised an eyebrow. Marcus got it and nodded slightly. If Derek didn't kill Marcus, this year might be okay after all.

For the rest of the day, Hannah kept an eye out for Derek. While they didn't have any other classes together, the brutish boy would be easy to spot lurking in the halls. When Hannah didn't see him, she knew he was probably suspended. Her stomach tightened at the thought, knowing it would only make his revenge all the worse.

When the final bell rang, she went to the usual rendezvous spot to find Marcus. Soccer practice had been canceled so he was able to hang out after school.

Kenny and Dawn were going to meet them and hang out at Champlain Park for a while. Ashley couldn't make it, as her parents were picking her up after school for some family thing.

Marcus and Hannah walked hand in hand, enjoying a companionable silence. After meeting the others and getting ice cream, they ended up at the gazebo. There was a bunch of classmates playing basketball or tossing a football and frisbees. Hopedale didn't have a mall or much of anything else to do, so other than the gamers holed up in their basements, Champlain Park was it.

They chatted about the day at school, then proceeded to regale Dawn with stories about some of the kids in their grade. A couple of boys ran up to the gazebo and cajoled Marcus and Kenny into a game of touch football. Kenny immediately jumped over the rail of the gazebo, thrilled to get away from the gossip. Marcus hesitated, however, and glanced at Hannah.

"Go," she yelled, laughing, and he was gone, over the railing and sprinting to catch up with Kenny.

Hannah's gaze found Dawn, who was bathed in the afternoon's soft rays.

For the second time, Hannah noticed that in spite of her passé clothes and her bedhead, she really was pretty. Her fair skin and deep blue eyes required no make-up. She had what Mom would have called "natural beauty." The thought brought a wave of sadness with it.

She turned quickly to Hannah, and her face hardened. "What?"

Dawn's tone had the steely edge of defiance and came out as a challenge.

"Nothing, I ..." It struck Hannah that she had done the same thing as Kenny: judged her on her looks. To a lesser degree, maybe, but it still wasn't right. "I think you're really pretty." Hannah's face burned and she looked away. "Sorry, I hope that didn't sound as weird to you as it did to me." She tried to laugh but it came out more like she was choking.

Dawn's expression softened and a shy girl suddenly stood in front of her. "Thanks. So, how long have you been going with Marcus?"

The moment passed and they fell back into a comfortable conversation while they watched the boys play what had quickly devolved into tackle football. They had just finished making plans to hang out on Saturday when a familiar voice rose over the sounds of the football game.

"Hey, guys, got room for one more?"

Derek Campbell sauntered past the gazebo and shoved his way into the middle of the game.

chapter
seven

DEREK DWARFED most of the kids on the field, and even those close to his size seemed to shrink away from him. One of the bigger kids, Jason Becht, spoke after a moment. "We kinda have even sides …"

Derek stepped toward him, and Jason's voice trailed off. They were playing shirts and skins; Marcus was a skin and Kenny a shirt.

"Driscoll, lose the shirt. Skins will have an extra player; it will still be fair."

The whole time he spoke, his eyes never left Marcus. Kenny looked around, saw no support, and stripped off his shirt.

Derek nodded, satisfied. "Right. Your ball, skins."

A knot had formed in Hannah's stomach the minute Derek had appeared. Now that she saw what he was doing, it burned from her gut into her chest, spreading like some malignant disease. She swallowed, her throat gone dry, and decided she couldn't let this happen.

"Soup!" Hannah's voice was scratchy and sounded a lot weaker than she'd intended.

Derek turned, color rising in his cheeks and murder gleaming in his eyes.

"Your problem isn't with Marcus, it's with me."

Derek's eyes narrowed and he snarled. He turned to Marcus. "Diaz, you really gonna let your little squeeze talk for you?"

Hannah closed her eyes, immediately realizing she had made things worse.

Marcus stepped toward Derek. "Let's play."

Derek turned back to Hannah, a triumphant look on his face, and blew her a kiss. Ice-cold fear settled on her like a nightmare. Hot tears formed but she blinked them away. A light touch on her shoulder made her turn. Dawn offered her a weak smile. She tried to return it but couldn't.

The first play had Marcus going out for a pass. Derek took a vicious forearm swipe at him, but Marcus was too quick. He deftly avoided the hit and sprinted past Derek, easily making the catch and scoring a touchdown for the skins. Derek's chest was heaving, his fists clenched by his sides.

Hannah couldn't see his face—she didn't want to.

Shirts had the ball next. They came out of the huddle, and the play, of course, was to Derek. He bulldozed over two skins and was barreling straight for Marcus, who stood his ground as Derek lowered his shoulder. At the last second, Marcus went low, wrapping both arms around Derek's legs, then launching out of his crouch. Derek's momentum took him up and over Marcus in an awkward flail of arms and legs. He did a half somersault and came down hard on his back. The air erupted from his lungs in a bellowing wheeze. The ball rolled out of his hands, but nobody moved to pick up the fumble.

Hannah's eyes traveled from Derek's prone figure to Marcus. He stood over Derek, his body tense, waiting for the retaliation. Derek inhaled with a coughing gasp, his face scarlet. He sat up panting, his expression a mix of pain and confusion.

"I'd give it a seven for artistry, but you really need to stick the landing." Kenny's deadpan comment was met with nervous laughter.

Hannah closed her eyes. It kept getting worse for Derek, and that meant a more severe beating for Marcus. Eventually. She made her way down the steps of the gazebo to the field, knowing she wouldn't be much help but wanting to be close to Marcus anyway. She sensed something behind her and turned to see Dawn there. Warmth replaced the icy tendrils from a moment earlier. Dawn was a good friend. This time Hannah was able to offer her a smile. She turned back to the field, then blinked in surprise. Marcus wasn't laughing. He was standing over Derek, offering him a hand.

Derek looked at him, uncomprehending. The laughter died out. Hannah's mind drifted back to memories of Derek. He had been the brunt of jokes for as long as she could remember. Kids used to call him "Dirty Derek" and a bunch of other names, until someone had come up with "Soup" and that was the one that stuck like a "kick me" sign on his back. Maybe he just needed a chance, Hannah thought, a little compassion.

Derek slapped Marcus's hand away and lumbered to his feet. He was still breathing hard and winced when he stood. Marcus didn't back off. They stood two feet apart, Derek glaring down at him.

Dawn's hand was on her shoulder again and her grip tightened until it felt like the talon of some giant bird. Nobody moved. Nobody spoke. The air seemed to go still, the calm before the storm.

Movement caught Hannah's eye. Kenny had picked up the football and was standing next to Dawn, as if he might need to protect her. "Are we playing, or are you two going to start dancing?"

Nobody laughed this time. Derek was breathing hard, his jaw clenched so tight Hannah thought she could hear his teeth grinding. The cords on his neck stood out and his shoulders tensed. *Here it comes.*

Derek's meaty arm drew back with a bellow. Marcus moved one foot back, taking a fighter's stance, fists raised to protect himself. Derek's ham-sized fist began its descent.

A dark blur moved, and Derek's head snapped back. He stumbled a few steps, then his knees crumbled, and he sat down hard. His hands shot to his face and blood poured between his fingers.

Hannah looked at Marcus, shocked he could have done so much damage with one punch, when the football bounced to the ground. Marcus hadn't thrown a punch, Kenny had thrown the football, catching Derek square in the nose. Kenny was staring at his hands and shaking his head. He looked up, catching Hannah staring at him, and shrugged. His lips mouthed the word "no."

"Oh, no," Dawn's whispered, an expression of abject terror on her face. Then she turned and ran.

Marcus had grabbed a shirt from the pile the "skins" had made and was holding it over Derek's nose. The shirt, once blue, was now purple from the blood.

Derek was cursing and threatening fates worse than death on whoever had thrown the football. His words came out nasally and muffled by the blood and the shirt, but the intent was crystal clear. Kenny was still staring at his hands, as if unable to believe what they'd done. His face was a mask of dread, and he cringed at every profanity-laced tirade of Derek's.

Some of the kids had begun to wander away, either grossed out by all the blood or the fear of having their own spilled.

Hannah bent to help Marcus tend to Derek and had to turn her head away from the odor of old sweat and fresh blood.

"Let us help you up." She tried to grasp Derek under one arm, but he slapped her hand away with a growl.

"Get away from me!"

Hannah took a step back.

Derek glared, his eyes full of black hate. "I'll get you all," he said.

chapter
eight

THEY WERE WALKING home from the park, the three of them quiet, somber, until Marcus spoke. "Kenny, you know I love you like a brother, and what I'm about to say may hurt."

Hannah bit her lower lip to hold back a smile. Whatever Marcus was about to say probably was going to hurt a little and embarrass a lot.

"How did you do it? I mean, I've seen you throw a football, friend. You couldn't hit the broad side of a barn if you were standing next to it."

Hannah snorted a laugh. Kenny looked shocked at first, then kind of thoughtful. He just shrugged.

"Hey, what happened to Dawn? Couldn't stand a little blood?"

"She bolted right after Derek got hit," Hannah replied. "I have no idea why. Maybe she *was* freaked out by all the blood."

"That is pretty weird," Marcus said.

"So, you two were getting pretty chummy up in the gazebo," Kenny said quietly. "What do you think of her?"

He does like her! It struck Hannah as odd, since he was the one talking smack about her the day before.

Hannah averted her gaze so Kenny wouldn't catch her knowing smile. "She's actually pretty cool. We're going to hang out at her house on Saturday."

"What do you think is going to happen with Derek?" Kenny's voice was low and unsteady.

"You mean his nose?" Marcus asked.

It hit Hannah like a sledgehammer. The target had just moved off Marcus's back and onto Kenny's.

Marcus put a hand on Kenny's shoulder. "Hey, don't worry about that, okay?"

Something was bothering Hannah about the whole incident, but she couldn't put her finger on it. "Marcus, when you were holding the shirt trying to stop the bleeding, did he say anything?"

"No, I don't think so." He grunted a half-laugh. "I was so relieved to still be alive that he could have recited the Gettysburg Address and I wouldn't have noticed."

"I just thought, I don't know, he looked scared?"

"Derek Campbell, scared? I don't think so. He's too stupid to know when he should be scared." Kenny sounded pissed that she would even suggest it.

"Whoa," Marcus said, holding up a hand, "Derek Campbell is a lot of things, including a sociopathic neanderthal, but one thing he's *not* is stupid."

"What are you talking about, Marcus? He stayed back twice—"

"True," Marcus interrupted, "but that just means he does bad in school."

"I rest my case," Kenny said.

"No," Marcus said, his voice rising a bit, drawing a look from Hannah. "You know how you hear about straight-A kids who bomb on the SATs? It's like that. My mom heard his IQ scores were off the charts."

For some reason, that bit of information sent a ripple of

fear through Hannah. But it made sense, since he was in her AP English class.

"Irregardless," Marcus said with a grin, knowing how much Hannah hated that word, "there was a lot of blood, and it must have hurt like hell. I don't know, who wouldn't be scared?"

Marcus's thoughtful tone made Hannah's stomach tingle. His character was part of the attraction. He was always helping out the teachers at school—not in a suck-up way, just to be nice. And last year, he'd broken up a fight in the school-yard between two big seventh graders and somehow got them to shake hands. He was a good person.

"A knuckle-dragging neanderthal with a brain the size of pea, that's who."

Hannah knew she should let it go, but Kenny shooting his mouth off was really getting on her nerves. "Why do you have to judge everybody? Marcus just told you he's not stupid. Yesterday you were calling Dawn a freak and today you're all 'what's she like', maybe you should give people a chance, Kenny. Are you so freaking perfect that you get to look down on everyone else?"

"Hey, Hannah—"

She cut Marcus off. "No, don't you stick up for him." She pinned Marcus with a glare. He opened his mouth to say something but seemed to think better of it.

"You're right, Hannah."

Hannah whirled on Kenny, waiting for some smart-ass follow-up, but the look on his face told her he meant it.

"I don't know why I say some of the things I say. Most of the time, I don't even mean them. I'm just trying to get a laugh, or, I don't know, sound tough." He gave a bitter laugh. "I guess it just makes me sound like a jerk."

Hannah softened. She knew Kenny, and he was really nice most of the time. Marcus had told her once that Kenny's home life wasn't the greatest. His dad was kind of a bully and treated him poorly. Marcus thought his wise-ass persona was partly to hide his real feelings. "I'm sorry, Kenny, I don't know why I keep snapping. I kind of felt bad for Derek for a second there."

Marcus's arm snaked around her waist, and he pulled her close as they walked. "Hannah Green, humanitarian," he joked.

chapter
nine

HANNAH GOT to school early on Friday and scanned the halls for Derek. She didn't see him but she'd know one way or another in second period if he came to school. She couldn't stop thinking about what had happened.

Costello's class was endless, and she considered making him repeat himself just for entertainment. She tried catching Dawn's eye, but she ignored her. When the bell rang, she made a beeline for the door, making sure to get there before Dawn.

"Hi, Dawn. Are we still on for tomorrow?"

Dawn looked up and Hannah nearly gasped. Her eyes were sunken in her head, surrounded by dark circles. The rest of her face was pale and drawn.

"Are you okay?"

She tried to smile but her hollow eyes made her appear haunted. "Tired. Didn't sleep well." Her voice was weak, distant.

"Dawn, why did you run away yesterday?" Hannah tried to maintain eye contact but staring into that endless void made her uneasy.

Dawn shrugged, and even that movement looked languid. Hannah dared another glance at Dawn's face and noticed a change in her eyes. Suddenly, there was something guarded about her, aware in an almost predatory way. *Am I reading too much into this?*

"I have to get to class, see you at lunch?"

Hannah smiled and nodded, watching Dawn walk in the opposite direction. She turned to look back, made another failed attempt at a smile, and walked on.

Hannah got to Mr. French's class right before the last bell rang. Derek's empty seat stared accusingly at her. She smiled at Marcus, and he gave her a nod, raising an eyebrow, as if to ask if she was okay. Hannah knew she didn't have much of a poker face; between the exchange with Dawn and Derek's absence, she felt defeated.

When the bell rang, she stood to wait for Marcus, but Mr. French asked to speak to her. Marcus left with the rest of the class and Hannah went up to his desk. He stared at her for a long moment before speaking, giving her time to imagine all kinds of scenarios.

"Is everything okay, Hannah?" His voice was gentle, filled with concern. "You seem distracted."

She started to speak but he held up a hand.

"It's no secret what you went through over the summer. If there are lingering issues that might be bothering you, I think you should consider talking to someone about it."

She'd always liked Mr. French as a teacher, but this show of compassion nearly brought her to tears.

"I'm sorry I've been a little off in class. It's not the stuff that happened over the summer, really. For some reason, that all seems like it happened a long time ago. There's just ... new weird stuff going on."

His expression was one of relief and amusement. "Is the new stuff good weird, or bad weird?"

Her face burned when she caught his meaning. He was talking about her and Marcus. Hannah didn't know why it made her blush until she realized with horror that she might have a crush on her teacher.

"Um, a little of both, I guess. There's a new girl and people are saying things about her. About her past, I mean."

He nodded slowly. "Dawn Holman. She's in my fifth period class. Smart kid, quiet." He fixed Hannah with a hard stare, not in a bad way, just serious, all the emotion gone. "I don't know anything about Dawn's past, and even if I did, I couldn't talk about it. But I've heard the rumors and I know what that kind of gossip can do to a kid." He leaned forward, glancing toward the door. His next words were spoken in a near-whisper. "You're a good person, Hannah. Kids talk and say mean things and it can snowball. Not everything, or everyone, is what they appear to be. Just keep being a good kid, and a good friend, okay? Sometimes it's harder than it sounds."

The moment felt important, as if he had dropped some profound knowledge on her, and she was too thick to get it. "Thanks, Mr. French." She wondered what else he had heard. Was this all about Dawn, or had he heard about Derek? "Do you know if Derek will be back Monday?"

His eyes changed, softened, losing their solemn formality. Hannah felt like maybe she had gotten it right.

"I'm not sure."

She didn't know if he was out because of what had happened at the park, or if he'd been expelled. She was about to ask when the late bell for third period jolted them out of their conversation and back to the reality of the school day.

"I'm so sorry to keep you, Hannah. I just wanted to make sure you were okay. Let me write you a pass for next period." He seemed embarrassed, rummaging through his drawer for the passes.

"Thank you."

He looked up from filling out the pass and offered a smile, holding the pink slip of paper out to her.

"Have a nice weekend," Hannah whispered, suddenly shy.

"You as well, Hannah. Be a good friend, right?"

She wanted to talk to Dawn and find out what was bothering her. She didn't want to just be a good friend, she wanted to be Super Friend.

She turned back to Mr. French before she left but he was already busy writing something in an assignment book. "I will," she promised, more to herself than to him.

chapter
ten

FRIDAY WAS a stay-at-home movie night with Ashley. She played freshman soccer which took up most of her afternoons, and Hannah had plans with Marcus on Saturday night, so this was the perfect time for a catch-up. Until they were separated by class schedules, she didn't realize how much she would miss Ashley.

Dad was out on a date with Rick Benson, so after playing with Scout to tire him out, it was just Hannah and Ashley, soda, a ton of snacks, and Netflix.

Hannah was ready to dig into the horror movies, but Ashley vetoed the scary stuff. Her tastes had had shifted since the summer. Hannah's hadn't, but she acquiesced. The movie was on, and they were on their second bowl of popcorn when Hannah realized Ashley wasn't up to date on all the Dawn and Derek drama that had become Hannah's life.

She paused the movie. Once she started talking, she could tell Ashley had forgotten all about the 'plastics' in their high school movie. Real-life school turmoil beat any film.

"So," Ashley said through a mouthful of popcorn, "what are you going to do?"

"Well, I have plans with Dawn tomorrow, hopefully she'll open up a little." Hannah noticed her friend's hurt look and quickly added, "I knew you had soccer when I agreed to hang out with her."

Ashley grabbed another handful of popcorn. "What about Derek? Man, I remember when he was in some of my classes in middle school, what a creep. He used to stare at me, and I swear I could *feel* him thinking creepy thoughts about me." She gave an exaggerated shudder to emphasize her point. "I was glad he ended up in all the remedial classes, so I didn't have to deal with him."

"He's not in remedial English," Hannah said. "By the way, Marcus's mom heard that Derek's IQ is like, genius level or something. Did you ever catch that he was smart when he was in your classes?"

Ashley thought about it for a long time before answering. "Now that you mention it," she said, "there were a couple of times the teachers called on him, and he kind of stumped them with his answers." Ashley's eyes were wide. "I remember old Mr. LaRoche snapped on him after he did it, actually telling Derek he had no idea what literature was. We were talking about *The Outsiders*. I remember googling what Derek had said, and it turned out he was right and LaRoche was wrong."

Hannah drained her glass of Coke and refilled it from the two-liter bottle on the coffee table. The ripple of fear she'd felt when Marcus had first mentioned Derek's IQ was turning into a tidal wave. Under her fear, the compassion she'd felt for him remained.

"What?" Ashley prodded.

"I don't know. The thing with Derek, it was weird. Maybe his home life sucks? Maybe he's never had a friend?"

Ashley chomped on more popcorn. "A lot of people's

home life sucks. It doesn't give them a license to be a creep. And maybe he's never had a friend *because* he's a creep."

Hannah countered, "What is the cause and what is the effect?"

Ashley laughed. "Wow, AP classes have changed you. You're like a cross between Mother Theresa and that Freud dude."

Hannah laughed with her. One thing about Ashley, she could always make her laugh. It wasn't always appropriate, but it always worked.

"I'm serious, Ash. I kind of felt bad for him, you know. He looked scared."

"So what? He was scared. My dad told me an old expression, 'there are no atheists in a foxhole' or something like that. It sort of applies here."

Hannah's humor wavered. Not because of what Ashley had said but the way she'd said it. Something about Ashley when she mentioned her father.

Ashley was quick to change the subject once she had the last word.

"Hey, what about Kenny suddenly being Tom Brady?"

Hannah laughed. "Yeah, that was a one-in-a-million shot."

"Remember the dunk tank?"

Hannah smiled. The school had sponsored an event to raise money for new instruments for the band, and Mr. Costello had volunteered to sit in the dunk tank. Kenny had spent half of his savings trying to dunk Costello and never came within five feet of hitting the target on the lever. Costello had finally told him to just go up and hit the lever. The funniest part was Kenny pretended not to hear him, making Costello repeat himself, and, of course, utter his catchphrase. To get him back, Costello took the mic for morning announcements the next day to personally thank Kenny for funding all the new band equipment.

"Yeah," said Hannah, "it sure makes Kenny's throw even more impossible to believe. But he did mangle Derek's face pretty good."

The conversation over, she went to the kitchen and threw another bag of popcorn in the microwave. Then it was back to the movie.

chapter
eleven

DEREK CAMPBELL STOOD STARING at his weed-infested back yard, gripping the shaky wrought iron railing until flakes of paint and rust fluttered to the ground. He could probably tear the railing from the crumbling four-by-six cement slab that passed for a porch, *wanted* to do just that, but to what end? Another beating from his mother—that was *always* the end. His anger wasn't directed at the railing — that would be crazy— it was directed at those jerks who had messed up his nose. He reached up to test the pain threshold, pushing until he could feel tendrils of agony spreading around his eyes.

Kenny Driscoll, Marcus Diaz, Hannah Green. The names floated by in his head like those banners that sometimes trailed airplanes, advertising one thing or another. Only these names were written in blood. And what about that new girl? Was she going to join their little nerd patrol? Probably. She was just as freaky as they were. He pushed on his nose again until brightly colored stars flashed in his vision, accompanying the pain that echoed through his face. *Written in blood,* he thought again, *that's the ticket.*

He removed his hand from his face and wandered down the stairs into the weedy patch of dirt he called a yard. Beyond the rusty chain-link fence lay railroad tracks, and beyond that, the abandoned parking lot of one of the old leather mills. Nature had taken back the lot. It was now overgrown with thick weeds, the occasional sapling, and even some wildflowers in the summer. He thought back to the summer, standing in this very spot at his back fence, when he had put a penny on the train tracks to see if it would flatten out. He had waited as a freight train rumbled by. But when the final car had passed, something strange had happened. The abandoned lot beyond the tracks had been teeming with fireflies. That wasn't what was unusual, it was the patterns he saw in their flashes of eerie green light.

Derek didn't understand Morse Code, but he understood what the fireflies were telling him. He had stood there, mesmerized, as the lightning bugs had told him things. Great things. When his mother had hollered at him, her voice thick with booze and her words slurred, he'd smiled to himself and gone inside. He'd never gone back for the penny.

He had read the book that had been assigned for summer reading. Not something he would normally have done, but when he'd heard some kids talking about it at the park one day, he'd been intrigued. He'd stolen the copy the kid was holding and read it in a single sitting. Derek knew everyone thought he was stupid, and he didn't care. A few nights later, after that train had rumbled by, he understood everything. The fireflies had told him what to do.

That's why the incident at Champlain Park made no sense to him. Could the fireflies have been wrong? He pondered that possibility for a long while. When he saw the dim glow of a single lightning bug in the distant field, he knew he'd gotten his answer. He was being tested, that's all. Great things don't come easy. *Shouldn't* come easy. He turned back toward his house, his resolve strengthened by the message he'd received. *Kenny Driscoll, Marcus Diaz, Hannah Green.* Yes, they would all get theirs. *Dawn Holman, too,* he thought. He was Derek Campbell. Lord of the Fireflies.

chapter
twelve

SATURDAY GREETED Hannah with cool winds and distant thunder. Her eyes opened reluctantly, a 'TV hangover,' Dad would say. After *Mean Girls*, she'd convinced Ashley to watch *Jaws* with her. Ashley dozed off not long after the first shark attack and was barely conscious when Dad returned from his date to drive her home. Dad watched the end of *Jaws* with her. He was the one who'd introduced Hannah to it a few years ago, and she shared his love for everything about the film.

After Hooper and Brody began paddling home, Dad began babbling about his date. Hannah couldn't remember the last time she'd seen him so happy. She knew he really liked Rick, and so did she. But it still seemed like they were cheating on Mom by liking someone in her place. Maybe if they'd had closure it would be different, easier. Hannah's mom had left them a couple years earlier. No note, no goodbyes. Hannah still had nightmares about the clearing and that hooded figure that moved so much like Mom.

Dad was at the kitchen table drinking coffee and staring out at the gloomy day. Somehow, Hannah knew he was thinking about Mom. She stopped in the doorway and watched him for a moment. His hair was bed-mussed, and he had the shadow of a beard, but it was the shadows in his eyes that bothered her. He turned, sensing her watching, and gave her a smile.

"Morning, Hannah. Sleep okay?"

Hannah flopped down in the seat across from him. "Okay, just not enough. Are *you* okay, Dad?"

His smile widened but it didn't light up his face the way his conversation had done the night before. "Sure, why wouldn't I be?"

It pained her to see him trying so hard for her. "You just looked ... like maybe you were thinking about Mom." She dared a glance and saw her words had struck him.

He smiled again, this one genuine, if tainted with sorrow. "Guilty as charged. Some days are harder than others, but I guess you know that."

"Dad ..." Hannah hesitated. The question had gone through her head a billion times, and though she and Ashley had talked about it, she had never dared ask him.

"I really don't know, sweetheart."

His answer jarred her, not in its simplicity, but that he had known the question. Hannah guessed it probably wasn't as shocking as it first seemed. It was probably written all over her face in neon lights.

"I've gone over all the scenarios: drugs, another man, some kind of amnesia, an accident, abduction ... but I guess we'll never know."

"But what do you *think*, in your heart?"

He looked at Hannah for a long time before answering. His eyes glistened with tears, but his gaze never wavered. "I think she realized, even before I did, that ... we weren't right together."

He chose his words carefully, but Hannah knew what he meant.

"We never talked about it, we just drifted farther apart. I think she got mixed up in something that consumed her. Changed her from the person she was into someone else. You remember how strange she was acting. Drugs are the logical answer, but ... and I know they can get a hold of anyone, but it's just not *her*, you know?"

She *did* know, but Dad was right, Mom wasn't herself before she disappeared, and drugs were the most obvious personality-altering answer. But it didn't feel right. "What about ..." Hannah struggled to put it into words, but she had to let it out.

What she had seen, or, at least, *thought* she had seen, was like a cancer inside her. It had started as a small growth that night in the clearing, and was spreading through her, ravaging her from the inside. It was poison, like a pus-filled boil that needed to be lanced.

"What if she was part of a cult? One of Mama Bayole's followers?"

Dad's eyes widened at first, then narrowed. Shock to suspicion in a blink. "Hannah?"

She held up her hand, needing a minute to collect herself. He waited, his hands growing fidgety, his foot tapping the floor, drawing Scout out of Hannah's bedroom with a yawn.

"The night I helped get Ashley; all the followers were wearing robes and hoods. One came over to the altar, close to where I was hiding. I didn't realize it then, but I had a dream about it later, after everything was over. It was the way the person moved. Do you remember the Halloween when Mom dressed up as a ghost? She moved the same way ... I can't explain it and I know it sounds crazy ..."

The dam finally burst, all the pain and confusion and *not knowing* erupted in lava-hot tears. Dad was around the table in an instant, holding her and whispering that it would be all right. The poison exited Hannah's body in soul-cleansing tears. When she got herself under control, things seemed clearer. For her, at least.

Dad grabbed his coffee and walked to the back door, staring out at the approaching storm. He half-turned, and in that queer yellow light his face held storm clouds of its own.

"Hannah, why didn't you tell me?" His voice was even, his words came slowly, clipped.

"I wasn't sure, I'm still not sure..."

He turned to her. "But it might have been. And maybe Benson could have found her."

His words hit her like a wrecking ball. Despite all the time that had passed, despite his new relationship, he still loved Mom. Wasn't *in love* with her, Hannah knew, but still wanted to tell her things, to make her understand it wasn't her fault. Maybe to share their daughter's life with her.

Hannah stood and took a tentative step toward him. "I'm sorry, Dad. I don't know what to say. Maybe I just *wanted* it to be her, you know? When I think back, it doesn't make sense that I could recognize her with the hood and the robe ... but still ..."

Dad walked past her and picked up the phone.

"Who are you calling?" But she already knew. She had opened a can of worms that could have painful repercussions.

"I'm calling Rick," he said, and Hannah's heart sank.

chapter
thirteen

THE DRIVE to Dawn's house was twenty minutes of awkward silence. Hannah couldn't talk Dad out of telling Rick about her dream—they were meeting for coffee after he dropped her off—and they were each frustrated at the other for not understanding their position.

She stared out the window as he drove, wondering miserably if every other ninth-grader's life was so complicated. Part of her wished she hadn't made plans with Dawn. She wasn't really in the mood to carry the conversation all day. Hopefully Dawn had snapped out of whatever funk she was in yesterday.

They drove through downtown Hopedale, such as it was, and into a more industrial-looking area. Hannah didn't venture this way often, and none of it looked familiar. The buildings looked more run-down as they continued. Dad turned off Commercial Street and they were in a more residential neighborhood, but not like any Hannah had been to before.

The houses were all jammed close together and most were in need of repair. Some looked abandoned, windows boarded up and yards overgrown, but she saw people on the steps of some of them.

"Dad, where are we?"

He glanced at her, and his lips tightened before he spoke. "Most people call it Cabbagetown." He shook his head. "Not like the artsy community in Atlanta, though. Basically, it's the bad part of town."

Hannah looked around, taking in the seedy surroundings and the poorly dressed people who seemed to be wandering aimlessly about the streets. "I didn't know there *was* a bad part of Hopedale."

Dad barked out a laugh. "Yeah, it's a relative term, I guess. It's not bad compared to some of the bigger cities, it's really just people who can't afford anything better."

Hannah realized just how sheltered she was in her little corner of town with her small group of friends. They'd meet at Champlain Park or hang out in the modest downtown, and Hannah had no idea this 'other side' even existed. *What else don't I know about Hopedale?*

A few turns later and Dad pulled over to the curb in front of a small brick single-family house that looked like all the other small brick house on the street. At least the tiny patch of grass that passed for a front yard was maintained, and there were no old appliances doubling as lawn ornaments. The same couldn't be said for many of the others.

She felt Dad's eyes on her and turned with a smile. "Thanks, Dad."

His eyes flicked to the house, and up and down the street. "You sure you're okay with this?"

Before she could answer, the door opened, and Dawn came bouncing down the steps.

"Hi, Hannah."

Dawn was smiling and Hannah again marveled at how different the girl looked from the serious, almost morose expressions she often wore. Not ugly, Dawn could never be ugly, just ... sad. Her good mood transformed her into something stunning.

Hannah couldn't help but smile back. "Hi, Dawn. This is my dad."

Dawn leaned in the passenger window and greeted Dad cheerfully.

"Nice to meet you, Dawn. Welcome to Hopedale. How do you like it so far?"

A cloud seemed to pass over her face, but she wiped it away with a renewed, if not sincere, smile.

"It's a lovely town, Mr. Green. Dad and I both think we're going to be very happy here."

"That's great, Dawn. If you girls need a ride anywhere, call my cell. I'll be in town for a bit then home for the afternoon."

He kissed Hannah's forehead and she got out of the car with a wave. He drove away slowly, probably checking out the rest of the neighborhood to make sure it really was okay. An inexplicable wave of anxiety hit her as soon as he turned the corner. Hannah was watching him go one second, near crippled with panic the next.

She struggled to breathe, and the corners of her vision began to darken. From miles away she heard Dawn's voice, but she couldn't make out the words. She could hear them, knew they were English, but couldn't grasp their meaning.

As her knees started to buckle, a strong arm circled her waist. In her delirium, she thought it was Marcus. Then, just as quickly as it had arrived, the panic abated. She turned to Dawn —it was *her* arm that held her up—and offered a shaky smile.

"I'm sorry, I don't know what happened. I just felt ..."

"Come inside, I'll get you something to drink and you can sit down, okay?"

Hannah was mildly surprised to find a neat, well-kept home. She immediately felt guilty for being surprised, knowing she had set her expectations based on the neighborhood, Dad's description of Cabbagetown, and the fact that Dawn had said it was only her and her dad.

The living room was modestly furnished with a couch and recliner, a large flat-screen in the corner. Photos and paintings decorated the walls, and despite the brooding brick exterior, natural light flooded the interior. They continued into the kitchen, and it was just as homey, if a bit cluttered.

Dawn ushered Hannah to a seat at the table and poured her a glass of orange juice.

"Here, no matter what's wrong, OJ fixes it."

"Unless you're Nicole Brown," Hannah quipped.

Dawn gaped at her for a second, as if she hadn't heard correctly, then burst into laughter. Her laugh was melodious and meant to be shared. The anxiety attack was already forgotten as Hannah's own laugh complemented Dawn's.

A shadow appeared on the floor and Dawn's laughter died abruptly. Hannah turned to see a man standing in the doorway. He was wearing only a dirty-looking pair of boxers, a yellowed 'wife beater' t-shirt, and a haunted scowl.

"Hi, Dad. This is my friend, Hannah."

He continued to stare, his expression unchanged. Normally, Hannah would have gotten up to shake his hand, but approaching a man in his underwear didn't seem right. Instead, she managed a nod. "Nice to meet you, Mr. Holman." She couldn't help staring at the lines of angry scars on his arm. It looked like he'd survived an animal attack.

Something in his eyes changed and his expression softened. He looked down, as if only just realizing his lack of attire, and backed out of the kitchen. "I'm sorry. Hi, Hannah."

As he scurried away, Hannah risked a glance at Dawn. Her face was scarlet, her lips pressed together so tight they looked bone-white against her fierce blush.

Hannah tried to ease her friend's embarrassment by speaking first. "It's okay, parents can be weird. Thanks for the orange juice, I feel much better."

Hannah saw what looked like relief and gratitude on Dawn's face.

"So, what do you do for fun in Hopedale?" she asked.

Hannah laughed. "We usually hang around Champlain Park or walk around downtown. I don't really know this neighborhood very well. I should have had you over to my house, maybe. It borders the woods and there's tons of trails, but ..." Hannah hadn't really done much walking in the woods since the Mama Bayole incident. The truth was, she hadn't been past the edge of her backyard at all.

Dawn waited for her to continue. When the moment stretched, she asked, "But what?"

"Well ..." The story poured out of her—the real story, not Kenny's abbreviated Hollywood version. At some point, Dawn's dad returned, dressed in shorts that were a little too short and a tie-dyed t-shirt that looked too big for him. Hannah barely noticed as she went breathlessly from Scout carrying the foot out of the woods to Ashley's kidnapping, to Big Jake and Mama Bayole. The only thing she left out was thinking she'd seen her mom. The wound from her argument with Dad was too fresh.

When Hannah came out of her storytelling fugue, all she saw were four bulging eyes and two hanging jaws. Hannah noticed something odd about Dawn's expression.

"Hannah, you're like a legend around here, I guess!"

She shook her head, but it was too late. Mr. Holman was nodding now.

"I remember when I was at the realtor's office signing the lease, people were talking about that. Wow."

Hannah's face burned. She realized it might have sounded like she was bragging, telling the story the way she did. She felt the blood drain from her face. There was something, she didn't know what, but something was off about the way they were looking at her.

"Anyway, that's why I haven't been in the woods behind my house lately."

Dawn and her dad exchanged a look, then Mr. Holman stood. "It's almost lunch time, there's a little sub shop around the corner, how about I go pick us up something before you girls get all wrapped up in your ... whatever it is you do."

Hannah shrugged. "That sounds pretty good. We could go with you, Mr. Holman. I haven't been to this part of Hopedale before."

Mr. Holman's smile faded a bit, turning sardonic. "Well, there's not much to see but I'd enjoy the company. Just let me grab a sweatshirt."

Dawn rolled her eyes and Hannah gave her a questioning look. "Sorry, my dad is a bit of a hippie. He might come back wearing a Grateful Dead sweatshirt. Or worse."

Hannah laughed, thinking about the commune story her dad had told her. "Nothing wrong with hippies," she said, "I could see my dad being one."

Dawn stood and Hannah saw another look of gratitude shining in her eyes. It made her wonder if she'd ever had friends before. Hannah didn't think she was doing anything heroic, just being polite, but Dawn's expression bordered on adoration. Mr. French's words about being a good friend seemed to have taken root.

The day hadn't cleared, but it hadn't gotten worse either. The weathermen would have called it 'unsettled'. Hannah called it yucky. Occasional thunder growled in the distance and the clouds went from gray to grayer, but the rain held off.

They walked through the neighborhood, not saying much. Hannah looked around uneasily at first, but soon relaxed and became curious. Dawn and Mr. Holman greeted the few people they saw walking or sitting on their porches, and most seemed friendly if a bit distant.

It was as though the people had begun to take on the characteristics of the neighborhood. They were listless, faded, like they'd given up. Hannah wondered if every city and town had a place like this. The thought made her sad and she knew if she lived here, *she* would begin to be assimilated, too. It was as depressing as it was terrifying.

Corner Pizza, cleverly named for its location on a corner, was like a million other pizza joints in a million other small towns. The minute she stepped inside, the heady aroma of tomato sauce, pizza crust, and grilled steak brought a smile to her face. The workers all wore red and white striped shirts, and all the younger men bore a striking resemblance to the older guy manning the giant oven.

"Lorenzo, how are you today?" Mr. Holman called.

Lorenzo smiled and wafted a hand back and forth. "You know how it is, Ned. Good days and bad days," he replied cheerfully.

They ordered lunch and decided to eat in when the first drops of rain splashed the windows. Mr. Holman paid and refused to take any money from Hannah. She felt guilty, wondering how poor they were, then felt like a jerk for thinking that way.

They settled into one of the booths and chatted about Hopedale and the first few weeks of school. Hannah took a liking to Mr. Holman, the specter of the man in dirty underwear with the haunted look already fading. He was amiable and easy to talk to, and clearly took a keen interest in his daughter's life.

One of the young men brought their pizza out a few minutes later and they attacked it with glee.

They destroyed the pizza in record time and sat back in the booth listening to the rain and drinking Cokes and singing the praises of Lorenzo's creation. Hannah was sitting across from Dawn facing the window. She never sat with her back to the door or window if she could help it—aces and eights. A figure was approaching, but through the rain-streaked glass, Hannah couldn't make out who it was. Then the figure cupped their hands, pressed their face to the window, and Hannah gasped. Dawn turned, and her expression clouded, her eyes turning to narrow slits. It was Derek Campbell, soaked to the skin, glaring in at them.

chapter
fourteen

BRIAN SAT across from Rick in a booth at May's diner. He'd just finished telling him about Hannah's suspicions and how she thought she'd seen her mother that night in the clearing. But something was off. Rick listened, and nodded when appropriate, interjected with a few questions, but ...

"So, are you going to tell me what's been eating at you all day?" He watched Rick's reaction, the way his expression fell, and he immediately wished he'd chosen his words more carefully.

Rick sighed. "That obvious, huh?"

Brian leaned in and lowered his voice. "I think we're close enough that it should be obvious when one of us is unhappy." He searched for the waitress, wanting a refill for his coffee, *not* wanting to look at Rick. Afraid of what he might see.

"I'm not unhappy," Rick said softly. "I'm concerned."

"Concerned? About us?"

Rick shook his head. He started moving his hand toward Brian's then pulled it back. Brian knew they were both comfortable with their relationship but they had agreed to keep it quiet. Rick wasn't sure how his colleagues and superiors on the police force might take it. "No, we're fine, Brian. It's Hannah. Have you noticed anything off with her lately?"

Brian felt both relieved and scared. He considered the question before responding. "Other than she's head over heels for Marcus? No, I ..." But there *was* something. Hadn't she mentioned an incident at school where she'd zoned out? And she'd slept through her alarm a couple times, but Brian had chalked that up to her being a teenager. "I'm not sure," he finally said. "Nothing serious, but ... maybe she's been a little off." The waitress floated by, topped off their mugs, and was gone again.

"I think there may be aftereffects from the incident last summer," Rick blurted out.

"That's crazy," Brian replied. Sure, she'd been through a lot, but she was a tough kid. "She's adjusting to high school—"

"Hear me out, okay?"

The room suddenly felt too hot, the air too thick, the once-pleasant aroma of grilled food now nauseating. He wiped a thin sheen of sweat from his forehead. What had he missed?

"I've been watching her closely after what happened at Champlain Park in the summer. She's displaying some mild symptoms of trauma: lack of concentration, disturbed sleep, hyper vigilance. I've taken some classes on it. I think maybe she should talk to someone."

Brian let out a shaky breath. He wanted to deny it but couldn't. The symptoms were there. As Brian replayed Rick's words, he was able to correlate them to specific examples. "I just thought—"

"It's nothing to feel guilty about. A lot of the symptoms are easy to miss, especially with kids her age. I don't want it to get worse, start impacting her school, her relationships."

Brian put his elbows on the table, head in hands. Despite Rick's words, guilt washed over him. First, he'd let his wife down, pretending to be someone he wasn't. Now, he was failing Hannah. An idea struck him. "What about thinking she saw her mother in the clearing that night? Could that be ... I don't know, her mind putting something there that wasn't?"

"To be honest, it could be part of it," Rick said. "Don't get me wrong, I'm taking her claim seriously, but it could be a false memory, yes."

Brian bit his lip. "Okay," he said after a minute. "I think you're right. Do you know someone I could call to set up an appointment?"

Rick handed Brian a business card from his pocket. "I've worked with him before on a few cases, he's very good with kids Hannah's age. I hope you don't mind; I gave him a call last night. I didn't use any names, of course."

A bolt of annoyance, just short of anger, flashed through Brian. He immediately dismissed it, knowing Rick's intentions were good. "I think it's wonderful that you're looking out for Hannah," he said. "Would you be comfortable being there when I have the conversation with her? She'd probably resist if it were just me, accuse me of overreacting."

"Of course, I'd be happy to."

"Thanks," Brian said. "She's got plans tonight and I don't want to ruin them. Tomorrow, after dinner."

chapter
fifteen

"WHAT IS HE DOING HERE, DAWN?" Seeing Derek had startled Hannah, but his staring was starting to really scare her. Crazy thoughts ran through her head. *Did Dawn lure me here? Has Derek been stalking me?*

"I ... I don't know."

Hannah quickly realized that as scared as she was, Dawn was borderline terrified. She was wide-eyed and not blinking, her face gone chalky-white. Mr. Holman picked up on their shaky voices and looked out at Derek.

"What is this?" He bolted from the booth and shot across the restaurant in three graceful strides.

"Dad, no!" Dawn yelled.

He opened the door and ran along the sidewalk. Hannah turned to see what Derek was doing but he had gone. Mr. Holman checked around the corner, turning his head this way and that in search of Derek while the rain poured down.

Dawn slumped in her seat. Her eyes were open, but not seeing anything in this world. "Dawn, are you okay?" Hannah went around to her side of the booth and sat beside her, taking her hand. Hannah gasped at the cold, rubbery feel of her skin.

"Dawn?" She touched her cheek, and it, too, was cold beneath her fingers.

The door opened and Mr. Holman stepped in, followed by a blast of cool, misty air. He shook his wet clothes off before noticing Hannah holding his daughter. His face flashed concern and he glided over to the booth.

"I don't know what happened. I was watching you chase Derek and I turned around and she was..."

Mr. Holman was perfectly calm as he slid into the booth on the other side. "It's okay, Hannah. She has ... spells. She gets like this when she's stressed. It will pass in a minute." He held Dawn's glass of Coke for her and let the straw touch her lips, softly urging her to drink.

Within a minute or two, she was sipping and blinking, then looking around, still a little dazed.

"Did I pass out?"

"You're fine, honey," her father cooed.

"Sorry, Hannah. I hope I didn't frighten you."

Hannah shook her head. She didn't trust her voice yet.

"What did that boy want, love? Why was he staring at you like that?"

Dawn's vacant stare cleared.

"He was looking at me," Hannah gave him a quick rundown of Derek's awkward creepiness and how she had laughed at him. "He kind of has it out for me and my friends now, I guess." *Had Dawn really not told her dad what had happened?*

Mr. Holman nodded, but he was watching Dawn the whole time. It was as though he expected her to say something. The moment stretched.

"What was wrong with his face?" he finally asked, his voice tight.

Hannah launched into the story of the football game and the bloody aftermath. Mr. Holman's eyes narrowed. She knew she had said too much but couldn't figure out what part of the story could get her friend into trouble with her dad. She was merely a spectator to the whole mess. Then she remembered how Dawn had disappeared that day and realized they still hadn't talked about it. Clearly, this wasn't the time. Did Mr. Holman think Dawn had thrown the football? Hannah also remembered the strong arm circling her waist when she'd had the panic attack earlier.

"Anyway," she blurted, "I'll talk to him at school Monday and try to smooth things over. I think maybe he doesn't have the best home life and takes it out on everyone else."

Mr. Holman bristled, finally unpinning Dawn from his gaze. "Doesn't give the boy the right to be disrespectful or mean. Plenty of kids have it rough at home and do just fine."

They finished their drinks in brooding silence, picking at the remaining scraps of pizza crust. The weather kept people away, or maybe the place wasn't that popular, but they mostly had the place to themselves. They waited for the rain to let up, then they all walked back to Dawn's house.

On the way, Hannah kept an eye out for Derek, but there was no sign of him. Dawn remained quiet, sullen. Just before they got back, the skies opened, and they made a run for it. They spilled into the house soaking wet, laughing, the tension broken.

Mr. Holman made himself comfortable in the recliner, flipping aimlessly through the stations as usual and finally settling on a college football game.

Dawn brought Hannah to her room, and it was as neat and well decorated as the rest of the house. Movie posters covered most of the walls, everything from *Twilight* to *The Breakfast Club*. A bookshelf crammed with paperbacks stood next to her dresser. Hannah browsed the titles and was shocked at the diversity she found. Mysteries and romance on one shelf, biographies and non-fiction tomes on sharks and shipwrecks on another. Even what looked like medical text-books. It was an impressive collection.

She noticed a collection of books on the supernatural, which looked well-read, based on their worn bindings and loose pages.

Dawn sat on the edge of her bed, put her iPhone into a dock and turned on some music. It was all instrumental and Hannah didn't recognize any of it.

"Your room is cool. I love the posters."

"My mom used to work in a movie theater." A sad smile touched her face.

"She always got me in free to see whatever I wanted and brought home posters of the movies I loved."

Hannah wanted to ask about her mom, but it felt like prying. And it was probably too soon. Instead, she returned to the books. "You read a lot. And you read just about *everything*."

Dawn laughed a little. Hannah thought she was about to say something, but instead she flopped back on her bed.

"Are you okay?" Dawn still didn't look right.

She let out an exaggerated sigh. "I don't know."

"What is it? Did seeing Derek upset you?"

Dawn burst into tears.

After a moment's hesitation, Hannah sat and placed a hand gently on Dawn's shoulder. She tensed for a second, then relaxed. Hannah wasn't sure how to respond. If this had been Ashley, it would be different, but she hardly knew Dawn.

"I'm sorry I upset you. Sometimes I talk too much. Ask too many questions."

Dawn was shaking her head but was not speaking. Her crying had subsided, but her breath was still coming in hitches. She sighed and rubbed her face, and finally sat upright. She looked sad and embarrassed and utterly lost. Without thinking,

Hannah leaned in and hugged her. It's what she would have done if Ashley was upset. There shouldn't be any minimum friendship requirement before a person can offer comfort.

"Thanks, Hannah. I have to tell you something." She paused. "I knew who you were when I started school here. I … I had heard the stories and wanted to meet you."

It made sense now, the way Dawn had been staring at her that first day. "You don't have to feel bad about it," Hannah said, "I get it."

"You're a good friend," Dawn replied.

A wave of guilt washed over Hannah, soaking her to the bone with regret. *Hadn't I started talking to her in the first place because of the rumors about her sister? That's not being a good friend, that's being a jerk.* She told herself it didn't matter, that she really was her friend, no matter how they'd got here. It would take more convincing to make her feel right about her words.

"Speaking of friends," Hannah offered, "you still have to meet Ashley. We've been friends forever and are inseparable. Or were, until we ended up in all different classes this year."

Dawn sniffed and wiped her eyes again. "That would be nice. It stinks being the new kid."

An inspiration hit Hannah. "Hey, how about you come out with us tonight? I was supposed to go on a date with Marcus, but we can all go as a group instead. Ash, Kenny, you, it will be a blast and you'll get to hang out with all of us and not feel like the new kid!"

Dawn's eyes brightened. "That would be nice. Thank you."

Hannah shrugged it off and stood up. "It's no big deal. It will be fun, they're all cool to hang out with." Hannah walked back to the bookshelf. "You really like all this supernatural stuff, huh?"

"Yeah, I'm into a lot of weird stuff, I guess." She uttered a nervous laugh.

"Nothing weirder than what I went through over the summer." Hannah shivered. "Is there anything in these books about human sacrifices and drinking blood to stay alive longer?" She was half-kidding, but curious.

Dawn moved a finger across a few of the spines, finally resting on one and pulling it from the shelf. She flipped through it, her face the picture of concentration. She found what she was looking for and snapped the book closed with a satisfied smile.

"This one has blood-drinking rituals from Haiti and parts of South America. I think one of them mentions eternal life somewhere."

Hannah took the heavy volume and read the title: *Religion, Rituals, and Unexplained Phenomena*.

"Thanks! Do you mind if I borrow it?"

A look of worry flashed across her face.

"I promise I'll be careful. And I won't bend the corners of the pages," Hannah added with a grin. She knew all too well the perils of lending books and getting them back messed up. If they ever got returned at all.

"Sure, sorry. Some of these books are kind of rare. And expensive."

Hannah regarded the book with a sort of reverence. It occurred to her that Dawn had never answered her question about Derek, but there was no way she was going to bring that up again.

"So, how are you liking school so far?"

Dawn shrugged. "It's okay, I guess. The teachers seem nice. I just ... it's hard for me to make friends sometimes."

Hannah tried to imagine herself being the new kid, thrown into a school full of strangers. Kids who had long ago established their friendships, their cliques. Images of *Mean Girls* flashed in her head. "Well, that problem is solved after tonight. I think we're all going to get along great. I really hope you like it here. Is it very different from where you moved from?"

Dawn's face darkened, like a summer sky when storm clouds move in. "It's nicer here, we lived in the city before."

Even though Hannah had asked too many questions before—or rather the wrong question—and had upset Dawn, she couldn't stop herself. "Boston?"

Dawn shook her head. Hannah could see her withdrawing, like a turtle pulling its head into its shell. "No, we were in Hartford."

So much for Mrs. Diaz being a reliable source. Hannah nodded. *Don't push it.* "I don't know anything about Hartford. Isn't it funny, it's so close but I've never been there? Dad says they used to have a hockey team, but other than that, it may as well be in Africa for all I know about it."

"There isn't much to know, really."

"What made you decide to move from the city to a place like Hopedale?" Hannah tried to keep her voice neutral. She failed. Dawn's face hardened. The summer storm had arrived.

"Are you here to interrogate me?" Her blue eyes were ice on a frozen lake.

Hannah recoiled, backing up a step. She bumped the bookshelf, sending a pile of hardcovers crashing to the floor. "Dawn, no. I just—"

She stopped talking. Dawn's face had gone slack, and she blinked slowly, then looked around as if she was unsure of where she was.

"Are you okay? Should I get your dad?"

Dawn focused on Hannah but stayed silent.

The door flew open, and Dawn's father stepped in, almost

tripping on the books that littered the floor. His eyes were full of accusations. "I think you should call for a ride now, Hannah."

chapter
sixteen

"YOU'RE KIDDING? Her dad threw you out?"

They were sitting on the swings at Champlain Park. Hannah had asked her dad to drop her off there to see Ashley after he'd fetched her from Dawn's house. The wait for him had been awkward and silent; she could feel the hostility coming off Dawn and her father in feverish waves.

"He didn't actually throw me out, just told me to call for a ride." Soccer practice had ended early because of the lightning but Ashley was still dressed in her practice jersey, her socks rolled down around her ankles.

"I hate to say I told you so, but—"

"I know, I know." Hannah cut her off. "We were really getting along, though. She seems like a good kid; I think you'd really like her. I asked her to hang out with all of us tonight, but now I don't know if she'll even talk to me." Hannah knew she sounded whiny but didn't care. She *felt* whiny. She hated when things went so wrong, especially when it was her fault.

"Wait, I thought you had a date tonight?"

"I did. I mean, I do. But I think Marcus would be cool with making it a group thing. I was going to have him ask

Kenny, and I figured you'd come and get to know her. Derek Campbell was on the list, too."

Ashley smacked her friend's shoulder with the back of her hand. "Be nice."

Hannah felt bad as soon as she'd said it. But Derek had looked so creepy staring in at them, rain dripping off him. She was afraid of him. "You're right, that was mean. Hey, do you know if he lives over there?"

Ashley kicked idly at the gravel. "You mean Cabbagetown? Yeah, I think he lives in one of the neighborhoods by the old shoe factory."

Hannah remembered her father telling her about the days when Hopedale was a mill town and bustled with clothing and shoe factories. Some of them had been converted into upscale office buildings. The one Ashley was talking about was an abandoned brick monstrosity. It was boarded up and fenced off, but it didn't stop kids from breaking in and either vandalizing it or using it as a place to party.

She tried to imagine living in the shadow of that hulking old building, feeling it looming over her. That neighborhood was a lot shabbier than Dawn's, row after row of nearly identical tenements in varying stages of decay. When the wind blew just right, there was a faint chemical smell that carried on the breeze. Even with the factory closed for so long.

"You were in his class for a year, do you know anything about him?"

Ashley pushed off with her feet to swing, the chains creaking miserably. "Not much. He was always quiet, but in a weird way, not a shy way, you know?"

Hannah nodded even though she wasn't sure if Ashley saw her.

"He would stare at you, then when you caught him, he wouldn't look away. Then he got worse, bolder. He would say things; creepy, suggestive things." She skidded to a stop, kicking up gravel dust. "I think he got kicked out of school for it."

Hannah waited as Ashley tried to coax the memory to the surface.

"It was something he said to Emma Gould. Nobody ever got the real story because it happened outside of class when they were both on bathroom passes. There were rumors, of course."

Hannah vaguely remembered hearing about it, probably from Ashley. The rumors had surfaced in two flavors. In one, Derek had made disgusting sexual comments and tried to grab Emma. The other stories were worse, describing sadistic, violent things he wanted to do to her. In both, Emma had managed to run away and find a teacher.

"Then, she moved away," Hannah said.

Ashley nodded. "She never came back to school after that. I mean, even before her parents moved."

"Hey, do you think she's on Facebook or Insta?" Ashley looked at her for a minute before answering. The look on her face said, *What are you up to?*

"Probably ..."

"Which story do you think is true?" Hannah asked. "There were two, remember?"

Ashley remembered; Hannah could see it written on her face.

"I honestly don't know. Emma was friends with Justine McElroy. I hung out with her a little bit when we played rec league basketball together. She told me that Emma never talked about it, and they were besties. But gun to my head, I'd say it was the version where Derek told her how he was going to cut her up. I don't think he understands or even cares about sex. I used to see him watching the boys with that same dead stare."

Hannah shivered, then tried to lighten the mood. "Lifeless

eyes, black eyes, like a doll's eyes." Her "Quint" impersonation wasn't good, but it got a chuckle out of Ashley.

"You know," Ashley countered, "sometimes I think you might just get along with a guy like Derek. Maybe you should give Marcus the boot and get your Soup on!"

Hannah made retching noises. The moment had passed, and it was for the better. Hannah was getting a bad feeling about Derek, but oddly, it was Dawn that troubled her. "So, what about tonight?"

"What about it?" Ashley smirked.

Hannah kicked gravel at her. "You know, going out as a group."

She considered, then said, "I didn't think you'd still want to do it if Dawn was out."

Ashley sounded nonchalant, but there was an undertone. Was she jealous that Hannah was trying to be friends with Dawn? She and Ashley had always had other friends. Kids that came and went, or who remained on the periphery.

"I'm going to call her when I get home. Either way, I'm not in a very datey mood. I'd rather be part of a crowd."

Ashley cocked her head. "You okay?"

"Sure," Hannah replied. "Why wouldn't I be?"

Ashley gave her one of those looks that said she wasn't fooling anyone.

"Hey, why don't you sleep over tonight after we go out?"

"Sure, that'll be cool. I'm certain your dad and Rick have been missing me."

"Ha! Something like that. Maybe we can troll social media and see if we can track down Justine."

Ashley groaned. "Here we go again."

chapter
seventeen

HANNAH GRIPPED the phone until the muscles in her forearm ached. She was afraid Dawn would answer, hear her voice, and hang up. It was worse.

"Hello?"

Something hard and cold formed in Hannah's belly. "Hi, uh, Mr. Holman. This is Hannah ... Dawn's friend from earlier?" She considered hanging up before he could respond.

"Hello, Hannah. I was hoping you would call. I want to apologize for my behavior."

"It's okay—"

"No," he interrupted. "It is most certainly not okay."

Hannah breathed a sigh of relief. If he wasn't mad at her, maybe Dawn wasn't, either. She waited, thinking he needed to get whatever he wanted to say off his chest.

"My daughter has been through a lot, you see. I've become ... overprotective. When I saw her so upset, I ..."

Hannah waited but it sounded like he had put his hand over the phone. *Is he crying?* "I understand—"

"Hannah?" Dawn had taken the phone from her father.

"Yes. Hi, Dawn," she said hesitantly.

No response.

"I called to apologize. I didn't mean to upset you. I know you probably think I was just pumping you for information but ... I don't know. I wanted to get to know you and I guess I was too aggressive. I'm sorry." She heard a deep sigh from the other end of the phone.

"It's okay. Maybe I overreacted."

"Is your dad okay? He sounded—"

"He's fine." Dawn laughed nervously. "He gets emotional."

"Are *you* okay?" Hannah asked.

"Yes. We're both fine."

Hannah wanted to ask about the weird fugues...spells, her father had called them. Was it the same things she, Hannah, was experiencing? No, she'd already pushed it too far once. Okay, twice. She wouldn't make that mistake again. At least, she hoped she wouldn't. "Listen, I never got a chance to finish asking you but a few of us are going out tonight and I'd really like you to come along. You've already met Marcus and Kenny, but Ashley is going, too. I think you'll like her. She comes on a little strong and she's kind of a wiseguy—"

"Wow, you're really selling her to me!" Dawn laughed.

Hannah replayed the words in her head and laughed along. "Yeah, forget all that. You're going to love her."

"So, what do the youth of Hopedale do for fun on Saturday nights?" Dawn's voice held an unmistakable note of sarcasm.

"Well," Hannah replied, "there's usually a rave out in the woods behind Champlain Park but the cops always break that up pretty early. The upperclassmen run these crazy scavenger hunts where teams of us have to get all kinds of outrageous items. Sometimes we just break into the abandoned factories and play hunters versus zombies."

"Okay, okay," Dawn said. "I get it. There has to be a bowling alley or a movie theater, at least?"

"You're not gonna believe it," Hannah said with an exaggerated gasp. "We have both!"

"Oh, my. Sensory overload. How do you choose?"

Hannah giggled. Dawn really would get along great with Ashley. "Are you up for it?" There was a pause and Hannah was sure she was going to pass.

"Just let me check with my dad, okay?"

"Sure," Hannah said. "Do you wanna call me back?"

"No. Do you mind holding on for a minute?"

"Not at all, take your time." Hannah heard the phone being put down, then muffled voices in the background. She glanced over at the clock. She had to call Ashley and Marcus, then get ready to go. The voices rose, still muffled, but it was clear they were arguing. Then came the sound of the phone being picked up.

"Hey," Dawn said, out of breath, "I'm in."

"Sweet! Do you want my dad to pick you up?"

"Is that a hassle?"

"Nah, he's pretty paranoid because of everything that happened over the summer. Marcus's mom or dad will probably drive us all home." Hannah thought for a minute, and said, "How does bowling sound? I like the movies but then you won't really get to know everyone. I promise no more inquests, okay? I feel really bad about this afternoon."

"It's okay," Dawn said, "and thanks."

"For what?"

"For being nice. I don't think I would have had the guts to call you after the way I acted, and then my dad ... and I think I would have missed out on having a good friend."

Hannah tried to swallow but a lump had suddenly appeared in her throat. She wasn't the best at accepting praise, and she didn't know what to say. Thankfully, Dawn saved her.

"So, bowling?"

Hannah cleared her throat. "Um, yeah. It will be fun. Pick you up around seven?"

"Sounds good, see you then."

Hannah said goodbye and hung up the phone. *Why am I getting so emotional?* "Hey, Dad, can you give us a ride downtown later?"

chapter **eighteen**

DAWN HUNG up the phone and took a deep breath. Now to smooth things over with her dad. He wanted her to have friends, but he also made it difficult. While she understood for the most part why he was like that, she sometimes wished things could just be normal for her. Then she thought about what Hannah and Ashley had been through and wondered if there even was such a thing as normal. *Maybe every kid has problems, just different kinds.*

She wandered into the living room, where her father was watching an old black-and-white movie. "Hey, Dad," she said softly. He turned to her, and she was shocked to see tears in his eyes. "What's wrong?"

He shook his head, wiped his eyes, then laughed. "I don't know. Just a lot on my mind, I guess."

Dawn sat down next to him and put a hand on his shoulder. "I'm sorry I make you worry so much."

"No, honey, it's not you. There's just been too much *bad* in our lives. It's nothing you've done, it's just ... I want us to be happy."

She squeezed his shoulder. Everything that had happened in Hartford *was* bad, but none of it had been her father's fault.

Or her own ... at least that's how she felt on good days. "I am happy, Dad. Aren't you? I mean, *can* you be? I know you're still grieving, but—" She raised her eyes to the ceiling, as if the right words were written there. "I think Hopedale can be good for both of us."

Mr. Holman laughed. "Do you know why we moved here?"

"Well, to get away from Hartford, for one thing. I guess I just assumed it's because you got a job here." Her father was a facilities manager. In Hartford, he had overseen facilities at a fifteen-story office building. From what she understood, he was responsible for pretty much everything that kept the building and the companies within it operating. Electrical, heat and air conditioning, cleaning, food services. Dawn found it overwhelming to think about. He would often get calls at night and on weekends, that required him to go into work. The building he oversaw in Hopedale was much smaller, and she hoped that meant he'd be home a lot more.

He was smiling, but Dawn couldn't figure out if it was a sad smile or a real one. "I picked this place *before* I had the job at the Palmer Building."

"Then, why Hopedale—" She squinted at her father, her smile growing wider. "Oh, Dad, you didn't?"

He laughed again and wiped a tear from his eye. "Yes, I did. I picked Hopedale strictly for the name. I was lost, all out of hope, so I figured ..."

Dawn leaned over and hugged him tightly. When she pulled away, her eyes were wet with tears, too. "You did good, Dad. It's going to be great; you'll see."

"Thanks, honey. Now, I suppose you're here to ask about going out with Hannah tonight?"

"Yup. Hannah and her boyfriend, Marcus. Her friend, Ashley, and another boy named Kenny. There's a bowling alley in town. Mr. Green will drive us there and either he or Marcus's parents will drive us all home."

Her father was nodding slowly but his eyes never left her. "This friend, Ashley, is she Kenny's girl?"

Dawn's face heated up and she knew she would never get anything by her father. How had he known just by her saying his name? "No, they're all just friends, except for Hannah and Marcus."

"And maybe you have a little crush on this Kenny?" He smiled again, and this time it was a sad smile.

Dawn got to her feet. "That is a definite maybe. I take this all to mean you are giving me permission to go?"

He sighed. "Yes, go make friends. Just promise—"

"I'll be careful, I promise. I'll call if I need anything, okay?" She was bouncing on the balls of her feet. Maybe this really was going to be good for both of them.

"Yes, yes," her father said, waving a dismissive hand. "Go out on the town, live it up. I'll find a deck of cards and play solitaire or something." But he was grinning, not trying to lay a guilt trip on her.

Dawn leaned forward and kissed him on the cheek. "Thanks, Dad." *Hopedale,* she thought, *my new home.*

chapter
nineteen

THE BOWLING ALLEY WAS PACKED, all sixteen lanes in use. Hannah saw a lot of families with younger kids and figured the wait wouldn't be too long. Marcus didn't seem to mind the change in plans, and Kenny was in heaven over the chance to hang out with Dawn on a Saturday night. She smiled to herself, remembering the fight they'd had on Dawn's first day at school.

"Hey," Dawn said suddenly. "What's with the tiny balls?"

Kenny giggled and Marcus punched him on the shoulder. "It's candlepin bowling," he said. "Did you play tenpin in Hartford?"

"We played with big balls," Dawn said, giving Kenny the side eye.

"Don't worry," Ashley said, "we've been bowling here forever and none of us are any good."

Kenny cleared his throat. "I object to that sweeping generality."

"Objection overruled," said Marcus, rolling his eyes. "You stink, too."

Kenny scowled at him. "Care to put a little wager on the games, big mouth?"

"Boys," Hannah said sternly, "maybe dial the testosterone back to 'normal teenager' and just have some fun?"

Holding up her palm for a high-five, Ashley hooted. Hannah complied.

A lane opened up and they were next on the waiting list. They'd already gotten their bowling shoes, so they headed over.

"Do you ever think about who wore the shoes right before you?" Kenny was looking at his two-tone shoes with an expression of comical disgust.

They were all wrinkling their noses. "I never did before," Hannah said, "but now that's all I'll think about. Thanks, Kenny."

They spent the next several minutes laughing over who might have been the worst person to have worn their shoes. When Marcus threw Derek's name out there, the joke was over.

"Okay," Hannah said, clapping her hands. "Who's up first?"

Ashley called, "I'm up first!"

"Dibs on second," Dawn said, raising her hand.

"You're third, Marcus. Then Hannah," Kenny said, rubbing his hands together in a manner Hannah thought was supposed to look diabolical. "That means I get to watch you all and design my winning strategy."

Dawn folded her arms across her chest. "What, exactly, would you do differently based on how we bowl?"

Kenny's face lit up like a fire truck siren. "You'll see."

Everyone laughed and Ashley made a show of prancing up to get a ball. She stood at the line, wiggled her butt, and rolled her first ball. "That's what I'm talking about," she cried when she knocked down seven pins.

Hannah and the others had some great laughs as the game continued. After eight frames, Kenny was winning, with

Marcus right behind him. Hannah and Ashley were tied, and Dawn was in last, but by only five pins.

Ashley grabbed a ball, did her butt-wiggle, and rolled a strike. She thrust both fists in the air and proceeded to do a little jig. Everyone laughed and clapped, including the people bowling the surrounding lanes. Ashley bowed and waved, hit the reset button and grabbed another ball. She filled the strike with eight pins, putting her ahead of Kenny. She finished with a ten.

Dawn finished with back-to-back eights. Hannah got a spare but only managed four pins on the fill, followed by a nine. Marcus spared and filled it with a six, then finished with a ten. Kenny stood, grabbed a ball, then turned back to the others. "Behold," he said, "and prepare yourself to crown me the victor."

"Hannah pointed at the overhead scoresheet. "You need nineteen to win, Kenny. That's not a lay-up."

"Not for you, my dear," he said. He rolled the ball with his customary curve and got eight pins down, leaving a relatively easy spare. He turned back to get another ball, then stopped in his tracks.

Kenny's face had lost all its color, and his whole being seemed to deflate. He sighed, grabbed a ball, and stood staring down at the pins.

"Come on, Kenny, you got this," Dawn cheered.

Kenny's sudden change in demeanor became clear when Hannah spotted Derek Campbell standing by the arcade machines, glaring over at Kenny. He had the hood of his sweatshirt up, and his face was hidden in shadows, but there was no mistaking him. He caught Hannah looking and pulled his hood off, winking at her with one swollen eye, his teeth exposed in an unsettling grin. She turned away just as Kenny's second ball clanged into the gutter.

He kept his head down when he picked up another ball from the rack. This time he made the shot, scoring a ten.

"All right, buddy," Marcus said. "This is it. Eight to tie, nine to win."

"Hold up," Hannah said. She stood and went over to Kenny. "Listen, I saw him staring at us, but just ignore him, okay. He won't do anything here, and my dad will come get us when we're done. Don't let him ruin your night. Or Dawn's," she said, and winked.

Kenny's eyes widened a bit and his lips curled into a grin. "Do you think—" He shot a glance at where Dawn was sitting. "Do you think she likes me?"

Hannah smiled and leaned close. "I know she does. Forget about Campbell and win the game."

"Thanks, Hannah," Kenny said. Then, louder, "You can't psyche me out, Green. Take a seat and watch the magic." He rolled, getting six pins, leaving two on either side of the lane. With his second ball, he got only one of the pins on the left.

"Oh, the drama," Ashley yelled. "It all comes down to this!"

Kenny ignored her, strode to the line, and rolled. He nailed the two pins on the right, and one of them kicked all the way across, taking out the lone pin on the left. He turned and bowed, paying no attention to Derek Campbell.

Hannah and the others stood and clapped. When she finally turned to see what Derek was doing, he was gone.

They played three more strings, but none had the same excitement as the first. Dawn had picked up the game rather quickly and won the last string. They decided they would walk over to May's diner soon and see what they were serving for late-night dessert.

Hannah kicked off her bowling shoes and reached for her sneakers. Meanwhile, Ashley was talking excitedly to Marcus, replaying one of her shots, including reenactments of her moves. Kenny was huddled close to Dawn, his face a portrait of concentration as he fought to untangle a knot in one of her laces. Dawn's expression made Hannah smile. *That's probably how I look at Marcus.*

After they'd returned their shoes to the front desk, they headed toward the exit. She glanced at the clock above the desk, surprised to see it was after ten-thirty. "Hey, what time does May's close?"

Marcus looked at his phone. "I think they're open until eleven on Saturdays, we should have time."

"Cool," she replied as they walked out into the brisk night, and he slid an arm around her. She smiled and leaned her head on his shoulder for a second as they walked. They turned the corner onto Maple Street, heading toward Champlain Park. The lights were off, and the park was deserted. It looked so forlorn in the dim light, the trees starting to lose their leaves, knowing there wouldn't be any more baseball games or concerts until the spring. Even the gazebo— She froze. The tip of a cigarette glowed orange then disappeared. Someone was watching them.

chapter
twenty

"HANNAH?" Marcus's voice was tinged with concern.

She blinked, looking at the others. *It's happened again.* They were three steps ahead of her; she'd apparently stopped walking. She glanced back at the gazebo but there was nobody there.

"Hannah, are you okay?" Marcus had a hand on her shoulder and was leaning in close to look into her eyes.

"I'm okay, I just thought ..."

Ashley moved next to her and gave her a side-hug. "What, Hannah? What is it?"

She took a deep breath and let it out slowly. "I thought I saw someone in the gazebo."

"Wait here," Marcus said. We'll go check it out. Come on, Kenny."

Kenny grabbed his arm. "Was it Derek?"

Hannah tried to make sense of it but just shook her head. "No, I'm sure it wasn't."

"Okay," Kenny said, sounding relieved. "Let's go, Marcus."

Ashley and Dawn huddled protectively around Hannah while the boys jogged over to the gazebo.

"Hannah," Ashley said, "who *do* you think it was?"

Hannah swallowed back the lump that had formed in her throat. "I don't know, I couldn't really—" She stopped as Marcus and Kenny jogged back.

"Nobody there now," Marcus said, "but somebody *was* there."

"There was a cigarette on the floor of the gazebo, still smoldering," Kenny added, a little out of breath.

"I bet it was Derek," Dawn said.

"No," Hannah said. "I think it was a girl, or a woman. Wearing a trench coat and, like, a floppy rain hat."

"So, you found Carmen Sandiego?" Ashley quipped.

They all shared a laugh, then Hannah said, "Let's hurry before May's closes, I need a piece of pie or something." They resumed walking, although Marcus's arm around her felt more protective than romantic, and she felt his eyes on her.

"Hey," Kenny said suddenly, slapping a palm on his forehead, "I can't believe I forgot to tell you."

"You found out your real father is an alien?" Marcus joked.

Kenny turned to him. "Really? After all my expert tutelage, that's the best you can do? I'm a failure."

"What is it, Kenny?" Dawn was looking at him with puppy-dog eyes that made Hannah forget about the woman in the gazebo for a second.

"Well," Kenny said, a new bluster to his voice, "due to my upstanding status in the community and my keen leadership skills, I'm in charge of the wagon this year."

Marcus stopped. "Are you serious?"

"Would I joke about something like that?"

Ashley jumped in front of him, falling to her knees, hands clasped in prayer. "You're gonna let us help, right?"

"Wait," Dawn said, "what's the wagon?"

Hannah pulled Ashley to her feet. She'd forgotten Dawn

didn't know about the Hopedale Halloween tradition. "Every year, someone builds a wagon, fills it with wood and brush, lights it on fire, and sends it down Black Hill Road."

They renewed their trek toward May's.

Dawn laughed, then stopped, seeing the others *weren't* laughing. "You're not kidding? It sounds dangerous."

"Danger is my middle name, young lady." Kenny pulled his shoulders back.

Marcus punched him on the arm. "Herbert is your middle name, young man."

"So," Dawn said, "what does a burning wagon have to do with Halloween?"

They reached the diner just as the front door swung open. All thoughts of the wagon fizzled when Derek Campbell stepped onto the sidewalk in front of them, scowling. He raised a hand and pointed at Marcus. "You first, Diaz."

chapter
twenty-one

DEREK PULLED HIS HOOD OFF.

Hannah gasped. Up close, Derek's face was a mask of bruises. Both eyes were black, and his nose was horribly swollen. Still, his eyes burned with a palpable rage. His jaw was set hard as he took a step toward Marcus.

Kenny stepped in front of him, putting a cautionary hand on Derek's chest. "You don't have to do this."

Derek looked down at the hand on his chest, then at Kenny. His hands closed into fists that seemed almost as big as the bowling balls the friends had just used.

"Your beef isn't with Marcus, so just leave him alone. You have a problem with me, so why don't you be a man and deal with it?" Hannah was shocked not only at the words that came out, but how strong and confident she sounded.

Dawn stepped up next to Hannah. "And you don't have any beef with Kenny, either. I'm the one that hit you with the football."

Derek looked at her and laughed. "No stupid *girl* did this, new kid." He batted Kenny's hand away and shoved him to the ground. Then he moved in on Marcus. Marcus took a fighter's stance—knees bent and fists up.

"Derek," Ashley said quietly, "did it hurt when the football hit your nose?" He turned his head to glare at her. "It must have. I heard you cried like a little baby." Derek made a noise that was somewhere between a snarl and a growl. "Listen carefully," Ashley went on, "We all know you can kick Marcus's butt, right? However, if your nose hurt before, consider what it's going to feel like if Marcus gets just *one* lucky punch in." She made a pained face and shook her head. "You'll probably need surgery. If shards of bone don't puncture your brain ... then you might not feel anything. *Ever*."

Derek's scowl dropped.

"Yeah," Hannah added. "Remember when it happened to that boxer? What's his name?"

"Sugar Bear Williamson," Dawn said. "He ended up in a wheelchair, I think."

"Come on, Derek," Marcus said, putting his hands down. "I don't want to be the one to put you in a wheelchair. I'll probably end up in juvie."

Derek's lips pulled into a tight line, but his eyes still held that lunatic fire. "I'll take my chances," he growled, moving on Marcus. The door to May's opened with the jangling of a bell, reminiscent of a prizefight. Officer Ramirez stepped out, focusing immediately on Derek.

"Nice night, isn't it, kids?" His tone was jovial, but his face was hard. He grinned at Derek. "Campbell, isn't it?"

Derek grunted.

Ramirez frowned. "You look like you ended up on the wrong side of Mike Tyson's rage." He didn't wait for an answer. "Well, I think it's about time you kids all head home, isn't it?"

"Derek was just leaving," Kenny said with a sly grin. "He was helping us with some homework, but I think we've got it all straightened out." He gave Derek a salute. "Cheerio, old boy," he said, using a bad English accent.

Hannah was relieved that the fight had been averted — saved by the bell — but started feeling bad for Derek again. Out alone on Saturday night, looking for someone to beat up. How lonely must that be?

"Come on, Mr. Campbell," Officer Ramirez said. "I'll walk part of the way with you. Stay safe, kids," he called, pulling Derek with him.

～

Hannah and her friends huddled in the gazebo, laughing about how much fun they'd had. Thanks to Derek, they'd missed their chance to grab a late-night snack, but it didn't matter. She looked around at her friends, promising to commit this night to her memory. She smiled when she noticed how close Dawn and Kenny were sitting. Marcus's hand was warm in her own. Ashley was having as much fun as anyone and seemed to like Dawn.

"Kenny," Marcus said, "you are going to get yourself killed with that mouth of yours. "Oh," he went on, "Dawn, can you tell us more about the tragic career of Sugar Bear Williamson?"

They all cracked up.

"I could tell you all about him, but I'd probably get all misty. Besides, I don't like to show up boys with my in-depth knowledge of all things sports-ball related."

"Yeah," Kenny said, "that was a regular sports-ball mash-up. Sugar Ray Leonard, Sugar Bear Hamilton, and ..." he thought for a minute, "John Williamson, ABA star from the seventies."

Hannah shook her head. She knew who Sugar Ray Leonard was, but had never heard of the other two. Kenny really was a historian when it came to sports.

Dawn shrugged, then leaned into Kenny, nudging him

playfully with her shoulder. He took the opportunity to sneak an arm around her. He caught Hannah smiling at him, and grinned back.

"So, what are we going to do about Soup?" Ashley looked between Kenny and Marcus. "He's not going to leave you guys alone."

"By the way," Kenny said, looking at Ashley with a sort of reverence, "thanks. You really freaked him out."

Ashley just shrugged.

Hannah felt Marcus's grip tighten on her hand and she squeezed back. Ashley was right. Derek was really gunning for them, and he did have a scary background. Something Dawn had said during the confrontation bothered her. She decided since Ashley had dampened the mood, it was as good a time as any to bring it up. "Dawn, why did you tell Derek it was you who threw the football?"

"I was just trying to distract him, that's all," she said softly. Her eyes dropped to the ground and her voice went low.

She's lying, Hannah decided.

"I wish you'd have distracted him by laying some Krav Maga moves on him or something," Kenny joked. "You do know some martial arts, right? Something to keep me from getting killed?"

"Now that you mention it," Dawn said, looking intently at him, "I do know a few spells I could cast that might do the trick."

"Do you really know some kind of witchcraft?" His tone was as close to awestruck as Hannah had ever heard. Dawn stared into his eyes, unblinking, then burst into giggles. Everyone else joined in, Kenny more hesitant than the rest. "Sure," he said, pretending to be dejected. "Pick on the kid with a terminal case of Soup."

Hannah laughed along with the others but couldn't help from letting her gaze drift back to Dawn. She seemed to cringe at Kenny's joke before starting to laugh. She decided she would confront Dawn when they were alone. Something was up.

"I think we just have to make sure we use the buddy system," Hannah said. "Strength in numbers. Nobody goes anywhere alone until we figure out how to get him off our backs."

"Makes sense," Dawn agreed, then she threw her hands up in exasperation. "Why is he so creepy?"

Hannah realized they hadn't brought Dawn up to speed on his history. It didn't seem like the time or place to do it.

"Who knows what makes people act like that. Ashley suggested I dump Marcus and go out with him, but I think she's more his type. Maybe having someone on the inside would help and we wouldn't have to worry about him anymore."

Ashley stuck her tongue out at Hannah. "As appealing as the idea is, I've made the bold decision to hold out for a better offer."

Hannah's phone buzzed and she pulled it out of her hoodie. She stared at the screen for a minute, unable to believe what she was looking at. The others continued talking and joking around but she was only focused on her phone.

Ashley mouthed "What's wrong?"

Hannah shook her head and put her phone away.

She feigned a yawn and said, "Between the excitement of bowling and the prospect of Ashley dating Derek Campbell, I am all tuckered out. You guys wanna call it a night?"

Ashley nodded, catching on. *Mind meld.* "Yeah, I'm pretty beat, too."

Kenny stood and stretched. "Now that you mention it, dominating at a physical sport like bowling is taking its toll on me. Call for the limo, Master Diaz."

Marcus laughed, pulling out his phone. "Right away, sir."

MARCUS'S FATHER had picked them all up, dropping Dawn off first, then Kenny. Marcus had walked her to the door while Ashley went in, to give them privacy. Their kisses were becoming more intense, having an effect on Hannah she didn't know how to handle. She'd been the one to break the kiss off, saying a hurried goodnight and scuttling into the house, flushed and feeling warm all over.

She'd joined Ashley in the living room, giving her dad and Rick an abbreviated, red-faced account of the night, before dragging Ashley into her bedroom. Now, she lay on her stomach on the bed facing Ashley, who was sprawled on the beanbag.

"What happened?"

Hannah blew out a breath through puffed cheeks. Ashley was looking intently at her, probably knowing full well the news was not going to be good.

"It's easier to just show you," Hannah said, waiting for Ashley to crawl up on the bed next to her. She pulled out her phone and opened a text message with a video attached. She tapped "play" and set the video to full screen.

Ashley watched. It was the day of the football game where

Derek had gotten hurt, taken from behind where Dawn and Hannah had stood. When it came to the part where Derek was hit with the football, Ashley's eyes widened. "What the ..."

"Exactly," Hannah said.

The video wasn't crystal clear, but it looked like Kenny hadn't been the one to throw the ball. Dawn had grabbed it from him. The video ended as she ran off.

"Why did she say she *didn't* throw it?" Ashley said, then, "Who took the video?"

"That's the weird thing; it came in a text from an unknown number. She closed the video and went back to her texts, holding the phone so Ashley could see.

"Do you remember anyone else there that day? They would have had to have been behind us in the gazebo, which they weren't, or—"

"Hiding in the trees," Hannah finished. "That's what I was thinking." She thought of the figure standing in the gazebo after they'd left the bowling alley. "We could figure out exactly where they were," she said. "We can recreate this. I remember where we were standing, and we can film from different places until we get a match."

Ashley scrunched her nose. "What's the point?"

"Maybe there's something in the trees where they were hiding, like a cigarette butt or a candy wrapper—"

"Great," Ashley said, rolling her eyes. "Then we can send it to the lab for DNA testing and look it up in the database to find a match, just like on *Dexter*." Sarcasm dripped from her words.

Hannah smirked. "Got any better ideas?"

"At the moment, no," Ashley replied, grinning. "But I feel one coming."

chapter
twenty-three

DEREK STORMED INTO HIS HOUSE, slamming the door behind him. The names of his enemies pounded in his head. *Kenny Driscoll, Marcus Diaz, Hannah Green.* Dawn Holman was now definitely added to the list. And Ashley Wallace, too.

"Derek!" His mother's voice, shrill and angry, yanked him from his vengeful fantasies. "What did I tell you about slamming the door?"

He ground his teeth, clenching his fists as he tried to prepare an acceptable response. "Sorry, Mom," he called, hoping that would be the end of it. But it never was. His mother's angry footsteps echoed down the hall and he closed his eyes, summoning the message the fireflies had brought him. The usual fear his mother's anger instilled in him was absent. In its place, an eerie calm settled over him. He opened his eyes.

Alice Campbell glared at Derek, her eyes narrowed, her visage pure anger. Derek noted his mother's stringy mess of hair and the puffiness around her eyes. He'd woken her, probably from an alcohol-induced slumber. Normally, that was sure grounds for a beating. *Not tonight.* His mother was a formidable figure, tall and thick and strong. Years of working at a lumber mill, the only woman on the crew, had made her hard. That was before the mill had shut down and the heavy drinking started. Tonight, somehow, Derek did not find her threatening. Instead of the overpowering enforcer, Derek thought his mother looked kind of pathetic in her filthy t-shirt and sweatpants.

"Oh," he said flatly. "Were you asleep?"

His mother took a step forward, shoulders hunched and teeth showing. "Are you mouthing off to me? First you come in slamming the door, then you smart-mouth me?"

"Go back to bed, Mom," he said, keeping his eyes on her. Something in his voice, that unflustered tranquility, gave his mother pause. But Alice Campbell wasn't one to let the egregious crime of being woken up go unpunished. Not when it was compounded with wisecracks.

"I think you might need a little instruction," she growled.

Derek barely contained a sarcastic laugh. His mother's "instruction" consisted of hard slaps to the ear. Sometimes she used her fists. "Not tonight," he said, drawing another look of bewildered anger from his mother. "Go back to bed or *you* might get some instruction."

His mother's face flushed scarlet. She advanced on Derek, who stood his ground. "You think you're big enough that I won't take you over my knee if I need to?" Her lips pulled away from her teeth, giving her the look of a predator. "You're just a scared little boy in a flabby big-boy body."

Derek stared flatly, unbothered by her cruelty. Making fun of his weight was one of her go-to insults. Next, she would call him a baby. It was the same playbook she always used.

"You don't have your daddy to go crying to anymore, so what are you gonna do?"

Derek glowered, a guttural snarl rumbling in his throat. This stopped Alice, another look of uncertainty crossing her face. Derek juked like he was going to hit her and laughed when she flinched. "You look a little scared, Ma. Sure you don't want to have a few more drinks and go back to bed? You know, before something bad happens?"

Alice's nostrils flared, her face going a dangerous shade of red. She raised a powerful arm that once would have sent Derek to the floor, begging her not to hurt him. Instead, he moved quickly, slapping her hard across the face. It had the power of years of torment and ridicule behind it, years of fear and self-loathing. It left four white finger-shaped imprints on her shocked face. She took a step backward, raising a hand to her face.

Derek relished his mother's expression of confusion and took a step forward, wondering what it would feel like to hit her with his fist—

The blurry flash of a hand and pain exploded in his face, blinding him and unhinging his knees. He curled into a ball on the floor, clutching his nose as hot blood poured through his hands. He groaned as his mother kicked him in the back, screaming incoherently. He squeezed his eyes shut and drifted away.

Derek lay on his bed seething. I had her, he thought, trying to ignore the fresh and immense pain in his face. He'd come to on the floor, sticky with blood from his nose, his back already a mess of bruises. His mother had been sitting on the couch watching television and smoking. When she'd noticed him stir, she'd said, *"Want to try me again?"* and had laughed herself into a two-pack-a-day coughing fit. Derek had said nothing and staggered to his room. When he'd gotten up to pee later, his urine had been tinged red with blood. His mother's kicks must have bruised a kidney.

Maybe the direct approach wasn't the best way to deal with her. He knew he might not be the smartest person in the world, but he *was* smart. Surely, he could figure out a way to take care of his no-good mother without getting caught. It wasn't as if she had any friends, and she didn't work. Who would miss her if she disappeared? How to make it happen was what he needed to work on.

He heard her coughing up a lung in the living room and hoped it was cancer. It would be slow, he knew that, but he wouldn't mind watching her wither away. No, he realized, she was one of those people that was too nasty to get cancer. Too mean to simply die. It was up to him. His father used to say, *"If you want a job done, get off your butt and do it."* And that's just what his father had done. He didn't wait for the booze or the smokes to kill him, or for his wife to do it. No sir, old Walter Campbell had gotten off his butt and done the job. He'd hanged himself with a belt in the toolshed.

That was before. When they'd had a nice house in Manchester and Derek still had friends and his mother wasn't such an evil witch. Or maybe she was, but he wasn't her main target back then. He wasn't going out the way his old man had. *I am going to rectify the problem.* He giggled. Rectify sounded like 'rectum' and that meant butt. He was going to get off his rectum and get the job done.

Derek squeezed his eyes shut and thought of all the different ways he could get the job done. He didn't have a gun, so that was out. A knife would work, but it would make an awful mess. And what if he botched it? What if he only wounded her and she called the cops? No, that was no good. He'd seen movies where people held a pillow over someone's face while they were sleeping. No, she was too strong. What if she smacked him in the nose again?

He opened his eyes. Wide. The thought about the movies with the pillow suffocation had led him to think about other films in the same genre, which made him think about poison. He sat up and swung his feet to the floor, ignoring the waves of pain that emanated from his nose, spreading across his face and up into his head. He closed his eyes again, picturing the medicine cabinet in the bathroom and the brown bottle full of pills.

His father had hurt his back, supposedly pulling an engine out of an old Mustang. Derek's mother had screamed at him for being out of work, accusing him of getting the injury helping Ned Bankshaw get his boat in the water so they could waste their time fishing. He'd gone to the doctor and gotten the prescription filled. But after one pill, he refused to take any more. He'd said they were too strong and had knocked him for a loop. What would a few of those pills do if he snuck them into his mother's food?

He stood and headed for the bathroom to make sure the pills were there.

chapter
twenty-four

"I AM LORD OF THE FIREFLIES." Derek stood in front of the bathroom mirror, watching his reflection carefully as he said the words. He frowned, creating creases on his forehead. He had been sure reciting those words in front of the mirror would have resulted in...something. He did *feel* an odd sort of power, but he wanted to *see* a change. He licked his lips, not liking the way his tongue looked, like a fat, pink worm trying to escape his mouth. "I am Lord of the Fireflies," he repeated, louder. He shivered as a chill ran through him. Power. His mouth curled into a grin.

Satisfied his transformation was complete, he read the label on the bottle of pills he'd found in the back of the medicine cabinet. "Hydrocodone," he read slowly, sounding the name out carefully, enjoying the way it came out. Like him, it, too, had a certain power, he thought. He skimmed the label until he found the dosage. *One tablet every 6-8 hours. Do not exceed 8 tablets in a 24-hour period.*

He popped the cap off and shook the contents. There looked to be about 20 tablets, maybe more. They were pills, not capsules. Easy enough to grind up into a fine powder to mix in with one of his mother's meals. He replaced the cap and returned to the label.

He felt his lips curl into a smile as he read the warnings. Then Derek read the last line again. "Coma or death," he muttered, giving the plastic container another shake. He buried the bottle under a pile of rolled-up socks in his dresser, then flopped onto the bed. It would be easy enough to give her the overdose, but then what? He couldn't have a body lying around, decomposing. The house smelled bad enough from his mother leaving half-eaten frozen dinners and Chinese food in the kitchen. A rotting body wouldn't do.

Derek had watched enough television to know that most murderers dumped lime on their victims' corpses to speed up decomposition. He decided he would visit the local garden store and see what they had to offer. But where to dispose of the body? He couldn't risk driving anywhere since he didn't have a license. Being caught would be bad enough, but being caught with his dead mother's body and a bag of lime? "Like *Driving Miss Daisy* meets *Weekend at Bernie's*," he said, and laughed at the absurdity of it.

He could bury her in the backyard, but it would be risky. The neighbors on either side could see right into the yard. Especially old Mrs. Dowling: she watched the neighborhood like a hawk, seeming to never sleep. No, he couldn't plant her back there.

Derek's mother—and his teachers—had pounded into his head mercilessly that he wasn't smart. They were wrong. He knew he possessed a certain slyness and he used it to his advantage. Sometimes, as he was doing now, he was able to work through fairly complex issues. Other times, things just came to him, like in the cartoons he watched, where a lightbulb would appear over the character's head. *Enlightenment,* he thought the word was.

That's how the idea of the basement came to him. First

there was nothing, then the answer was just ... there. It was an old house, and the basement had a dirt floor. He knew that because he used to go down to there to play. In this case 'play' meant catching various bugs: flies, ants, the occasional centipede, and dropping them into the spider webs that festooned the nooks and crannies. He loved watching the spider approach its prey at the shaking of the web, then pounce, administering its venom and wrapping its victim in its silky bindings.

Sometimes, the victims would put up a pretty good fight, but the spider almost always won. One particular instance stuck in his head. The cicada killer was a large, wasp-like insect, named for its favorite prey. The female's weapon was a long stinger for paralyzing its victims. It would then drag the cicada into its nest and lay eggs in its carcass. The spider also had the ability to paralyze its victims.

The fight had been epic. Derek had watched them battle fiercely for almost two hours, ignoring the calls of his mother, who thought he was outside. He'd missed dinner and gotten a fresh cigarette burn on his back for the trouble. But it was worth it. The spider had eventually won out, mainly due to its dexterity in maneuvering about the web. The best part was after the duel, when it had wound its prey in a cocoon-like web.

He'd been fascinated as the spider entombed the wasp, wrapping it like a mummy. He laughed. *Mummy, like mommy.* He wished there was a web big enough to throw her into so he could and watch her become paralyzed by the spider's venom and—

He blinked, looking around, unsure how much time he'd lost fantasizing about spiders and what they could do to his mother. But he had his answer. He could bury her in the basement, covered in lime instead of silk webs.

chapter
twenty-five

BRIAN LOOKED up from the grill when he heard the front door. "Hannah, is that you?" Scout remained seated at his heels, waiting for an errant burger or hotdog to fall into his clutches. If it was Hannah, Scout would have bounded into the house to greet her even if Brian had been cooking filet mignon. "Rick? Out here," he called.

Rick joined him on the deck and gave him a grim smile.

Brian's gut churned as Rick knelt to pat Scout. "What's wrong?" Rick had been looking into Hannah's claim that one of the women in the clearing that night had been her mother. He wasn't sure he wanted to know what Rick had found.

"Mostly dead ends," Rick replied, but Brian could tell there was more. "I went through all the statements of the followers that were arrested, then tried to interview them. Most declined, of course."

"Most?" Brian prodded, as he expertly flipped the burgers and rolled the hotdogs on the grill.

Rick paused, then said, "One of the younger members, Julie Dionne, agreed to a phone call."

Brian waited, getting frustrated with Rick's reluctance.

"Come on, what did she say?" His tone was clipped, bordering on angry.

"She said she might remember a woman matching your wife's description."

Sensing Rick had doubts about Julie's story, he said, "But?"

"She's been very cooperative all along. She had only been a member for a short time and that night was going to be her first sacrifice. She's been adamant that she didn't know what the cult was all about, and that Mama Bayole had tricked her. Either drugged or brainwashed her. Maybe both."

Brian scooped all the food off the grill onto a plate and shut the gas off. His movements were stiff, deliberate. He spun on Rick. "What are you doing?" His muscles were tight as he struggled to control his temper. "Just say it."

Rick's shoulders slumped, as if Brian's words had taken the air out of him. "I don't believe her, and I'm trying not to get your hopes up. And especially not to get *Hannah's* hopes up."

Brian grabbed the plate of food and brushed past Rick into the house. He was embarrassed by his outburst and needed a minute to compose himself. He put the food on the table and busied himself getting condiments and drinks from the fridge, then setting the table. He needed to know what else the woman—Julie—had said. And he needed to end the conversation before Hannah got home, which would be any second. "Rick, I'm sorry," he said. "I just—"

Rick placed a hand on the back of Brian's neck. "I understand. I'm sorry I'm dragging this out, I just don't want you to jump to any conclusions." Brian nodded and Rick continued, "I think she's lying to me, trying to earn points toward a reduced sentence if she cooperates. It feels like she's trying too hard, you know?"

Brian nodded. But was that really it? He took a deep breath. "Okay. Did she ever see Faye without the hood? Could she identify her?"

Rick shook his head. "She claims to have seen a woman take her hood off in the confusion after the fire started. I was very careful not to lead her on, but the description she gave loosely fits your wife."

Brian's legs went rubbery, but he covered it up by taking a seat at the table. "What's next?"

"She agreed to a meeting. Only if her lawyer is present, which is no big deal. The plan is to run it like a line-up. I'll have a dozen or so photos of different women. We'll see if Miss Dionne can pick Faye out."

Brian was still. He stared at the pile of meat on the plate, the salad he'd made earlier, and realized he'd lost his appetite. Something was still off with Rick. But he knew Rick was only trying to spare his feelings. To protect him.

"What's the catch?"

Rick smiled, but it was humorless. "She's local," he finally said. Brian only stared, confused. "There's a good chance she saw the pictures on the news or in the papers when Faye disappeared. Even if she picked her out, I'm not certain we can trust her."

Brian opened his mouth but remained silent when he heard the front door open, and Scout launched himself up to greet Hannah.

"Just in time for dinner," Rick called.

Hannah walked in to find her dad and Rick seated in the kitchen. The table was set, a pile of burgers and hotdogs sat steaming on a platter, and Scout was circling her legs, begging for attention. A perfectly normal, all-American scene. Except something was wrong. The tension was palpable, like a physical presence in the room. She searched the faces of both men but got no answers.

"What's going on?"

Her father gestured toward her chair. "Sit down, honey. Rick and I just want to talk to you. Nothing's wrong."

Hannah swallowed, ignoring the lump that had magically appeared in her throat. Thoughts clamored in her head, one crazier than the next. *Something's happened to Ashley. They found Mom. They think I'm having sex with Marcus.* She sat in the chair, deciding on the best irrational idea. "You found Mom," she said flatly.

Dad's eyes flicked toward Rick then right back to Hannah. It was quick, but she didn't miss it. "No, it's not that. Please, just listen for a minute, okay?"

She nodded, dazed.

Rick cleared his throat, giving Dad a look. "Hannah, your father and I are concerned about you." She opened her mouth to tell them she was fine. To ask them why they were concerned. But Rick silenced her with a raised hand. "We think you're still reacting in a way to the events with Mama Bayole and the cult. We think you should talk to someone about it. A professional."

Hannah's eyes moved back and forth, looking for any hint of a smile on either man's face to indicate they were pulling her leg.

Rick added, gently, "What you went through last summer can have long-term impacts. Your best friend kidnapped, the rescue in the clearing, the finale at Champlain Park ... any one of those things could cause damage, and you survived all three."

Hannah scoffed. "I'm fine." *Why are they ganging up on me like I'm crazy?* Her dad exchanged another look with

Rick. "What? Why do you keep looking at each other like that?"

"Hannah," her dad began, "we're just concerned. There's been some changes in your behavior since—"

"Since Scout found a human foot practically in our back yard? Or since my best friend was kidnapped and almost sacrificed?" She got to her feet, face burning with irrational anger. "Or maybe my behavior changed when *I* was kidnapped and had to shoot that old witch!"

She stormed out to the yard and stalked toward the woods. She ignored the cries of her father and Rick to come back and was relieved when they didn't try to follow. She got to the edge of the forest and heard Scout jogging behind her.

"Good boy," she said, kneeling to pat him. "They're just being mean, aren't they?" Unexpected tears spilled from her eyes. She sniffed and wiped them away, wondering what behavior changes they were talking about, what they were *imagining*. But she knew. The instances she'd seemed to have lost a few minutes. Just spaced out with no memory of the time passing. And her angry outbursts at Kenny. *What if they're right?*

Her stomach growled, earning another one of Scout's curious stares. She realized she'd left without eating dinner and she was hungry. While the idea of going back in with her tail between her legs didn't exactly thrill her, she knew she was being immature. Causing a scene then storming off like some petulant child who didn't get their way. With a heavy sigh, she stood and started the walk of shame back to the house, knowing her dad was watching her.

She got to the deck as the screen door opened. Her father stepped out and approached her. Hesitantly.

Then he took another step and wrapped her in a hug. "I'm sorry we upset you," he said softly.

Hannah shook her head, pulling away and swatting fresh

tears from her face. "It's not your fault, I just overreacted." Her stomach announced its presence, and Dad gave her a knowing smile.

"Come back in and have some dinner, then we'll talk about it, okay?"

She nodded, following him into the house.

chapter
twenty-six

THEY DIDN'T TALK about therapy during dinner, but the subject hung there, looming everywhere Hannah turned. They each tried to make small talk but none of the subjects caught, and there were long stretches of silence that left Hannah to her own thoughts. It would explain a lot if her odd time-lapses were the result of trauma.

"So, I have to go see a shrink?" she asked, jumping in with both feet.

Her father and Rick stared at her for a second, then Dad laughed. "What year is this?"

Hannah couldn't resist a smile. She realized her expression was something she'd probably picked up from some old sitcom. "I'm sorry," she said. "I mean a *professionally trained* head shrink."

"All kidding aside," Rick said, bringing back the seriousness. "Trauma-focused psychotherapy can be very beneficial to people who have been involved in or even witnessed violent crimes. It uses techniques like visualization and talking about the traumatic memory. It's designed to change unhelpful beliefs about the trauma."

125

"How do you know so much about it?"

Hannah watched Rick carefully. His face had tensed when she'd asked the question. Her father answered because Rick had waited a beat too long. "Rick's taken training on the subject."

"You've been through it, haven't you?" Hannah said.

Rick tried to smile but it looked more like a grimace. "Yes, I have." He spoke slowly, as though he had considered carefully even those three simple words.

She was about to ask what happened when she caught her father's eye. A barely perceptible shake of his head told her the question was off limits. Instead, she said, "If you both think I need it, I won't argue. But if I try it and it feels like a waste of time, I'm out. Okay?" She held her father's gaze until he nodded.

"That's fair," he said. Then, "I'm just worried about you, you know?"

Hannah reached for his hand. "I know. Things have been a little crazy lately, I guess."

Rick coughed. Hannah turned to him and realized it was more of a laugh. "A little," he said with a grin. "By the way, I can recommend a very good therapist." His expression grew serious again. "I only brought this up to your dad because I care about you, too. *Both* of you."

Her father blushed, and Hannah was filled with an odd happiness that made her want to cry for some reason. Seeing her father so happy after everything he'd been through filled her with joy.

"Okay," she said. "Let's not turn this into a Lifetime movie. I'm going to call Ashley and see if she'll still be friends with a crazy girl." When her dad started to protest, she held up her hands in surrender. "Just kidding. Too soon?"

Rick laughed, shaking his head, but her father just looked

flustered. Then, regaining his composure, he said, "Maybe I can get a two-for-one deal on therapy. A shrink would have a field day trying to figure that girl out."

Hannah stuck her tongue out at him and bounded for the phone.

≈

"Whoa," Ashley said. "I never had a crazy friend before."

Hannah laughed. Leave it to her best friend to say the most irreverent thing she could think of.

"I'm here for you, Ash. Check 'crazy friend' off your bucket list." Hannah's attempt at humor was met with silence. "What's wrong?"

"It's just—" Ashley paused, then blurted out, "What's wrong with *me*? I went through a bunch of stuff, too. And I'm fine." She made a noise. "At least I'm the same as I was. So, does that mean there's something whacked with me because it *didn't* affect me?"

"Let me get this straight: you want to have whatever I have?" Hannah was annoyed with her friend for making this about her.

"No," Ashley replied. "It's not like that."

Hannah heard real pain in her friend's voice and felt bad. "Different things impact people in different ways," she said. "You've always been tougher than me. Stronger."

"I don't know about that," Ashley said, "but thanks. So, are they making you go to a shrink?"

"Yeah, I agreed to go. But I made them promise to let me stop going if I didn't think it was helping." Hannah immediately realized they had both used "them" when referring to Dad and Rick. *Does that mean I have two dads?* Not wanting to analyze that right now, she said, "Did you notice anything different about me? You know, since the whole Mama Bayole thing?"

"Only that you're all gaga over Marcus-boy," Ashley replied.

Hannah could almost hear her friend's smile through the phone. "Well, Ash," she said, trying for a serious tone. "Thanks for talking me through this crisis." That got a laugh. "Hey, are you going over Kenny's to help with the wagon?"

Ashley oozed with enthusiasm. "Are you kidding? I wouldn't miss it! I've wanted to help with the wagon since I was like five."

"Yeah, same," Hannah replied. "I think it'll be fun."

"It's a weird tradition, but it's cool," Ashley said, "I don't know why we just don't have corn mazes like every other New England town."

"Hopedale is not your ordinary New England town," Hannah said, in her best creepy narrator voice.

"Haha! You got that right. If the past few months haven't taught us that, we weren't paying attention."

As always, the mention of the recent events made Hannah feel strange. Armed with the knowledge that she might be suffering from the trauma, she analyzed how she felt. She didn't feel anxious or even nervous, just strangely disconnected. The worst part was, she didn't really feel like talking to Ashley anymore. Didn't feel like talking to anyone.

"Hannah?"

Ashley's voice pulled her from her reflection. "Yeah, sorry. Just thinking."

"You okay?" Ashley's voice was filled with concern. Their mind-meld thing was in perfect working order. "Because you really don't sound okay."

"I don't know," Hannah said. "I'm just feeling weird about the whole therapy thing, I guess."

"It's going to be fine, you'll see. Maybe they'll have a 'bring a friend to therapy' day and I can go with."

"It's funny you say that. Rick was wondering if he could get a two-for-one discount and bring you along."

Ashley laughed. "Great minds, Hannah, great minds."

chapter
twenty-seven

HANNAH STOPPED HAMMERING when she felt someone watching her. She turned, and there was Marcus, wearing that goofy grin. "What?" She couldn't help grinning herself. Marcus's face immediately turned red. She wondered if he'd ever stop blushing over her.

"You just look..."—he paused, the flush growing deeper—"...you look cute, that's all."

Hannah blinked, her cheeks growing warm despite the crispness of the day. Marcus was the epitome of shyness, and for him to blurt out something like that—with their friends potentially within earshot—made her all tingly. *He really likes me.* It's not like she didn't already know, but still ...

She dropped the hammer and made her way over to him, her eyes never leaving his. She put her hands on either side of his face and kissed him. His burning face warmed her hands, and his lips warmed her heart. He put a tentative hand on her waist—the other still holding a saw—and returned the kiss. She heard the others making comments, but it all sounded far away. In that moment, there was only Marcus and the kiss.

Hannah pulled away with a gasp. She didn't want to, but ... the tingling sensation that spread to every nerve in her body scared her a little. She smiled, feeling sort of dazed. Marcus looked exactly like she felt.

"Back to work," she said, her voice too thick, and turned away to retrieve her hammer. *What was that?* She was still shaky. All over.

"Hey," Kenny said. "Anybody want a drink? Things just heated up."

Hannah grinned to herself. *They sure did.*

"Seriously, let's take a break. I'll grab some stuff from inside." He trotted across the yard and disappeared into the house.

Ashley bounced over, smiling as brightly as Hannah had ever seen. It made her glad to have a friend who was happy because *she* was happy.

Ashley nudged her with her shoulder. "What's up, hot lips?"

Hannah's mouth opened in surprise. Thankfully—maybe for the first time in her life—Ashley had managed to whisper. Hannah snuck a peek at Marcus, but he was busy sawing another plank for the wagon. Dawn was painting the side of the wagon they'd already finished. It seemed like a lot of work for something they were going to light on fire, but Dawn was enjoying herself. And, Hannah noticed, she was very talented. She'd finished painting the gazebo and was working on the rest of Champlain Park.

"I can't believe I did that," Hannah said. "It just ..." She shook her head, heat rising again in her cheeks.

"I don't think Marcus can believe it either. Let's get some beverages."

They went over to the picnic table as Kenny came out with a six-pack of bottled water, a two-liter bottle of Coke, plastic cups, and a bag of chips. They passed the bag around, eating and drinking in silence. The sun was dipping toward the treetops, turning the autumn leaves into a burning array of reds, yellows, and oranges.

"Dawn, that mural is amazing," Kenny said, looking over at her artwork. "Where'd you learn to paint like that?"

Dawn shrugged. "I don't know, it's just something I always liked to do. I used to get bored staying in the lines when Mom—" She paused, her face clouding, but only for a beat. "When my *parents* would give me coloring books. I always thought I could make the pictures better. So, I asked them to get me drawing pads and colored pencils. At some point, when I got a little older, I started using watercolors." She *humphed*. "It's just one of those things."

"Well," Ashley said, "you better keep at it. It's a gift."

"Yeah," Kenny added. "A gift."

Hannah loved the way Kenny looked at Dawn. He was crushing hard. Dawn busied herself opening a bottle of water, clearly uncomfortable with being the center of attention.

"Hey," she said, "how did this whole wagon thing start, anyway?"

Hannah looked over at Kenny. He was the talker in the group, and if Dawn's gift was painting, his was storytelling. She gave him a nod.

"The legend of the burning wagon," he began with a dramatic flair...

chapter
twenty-eight

"THE LEGEND of the burning wagon started back in the late 1800s. Hopedale was a rough town back then. It was mostly a logging settlement, hardworking, hard drinking lumberjacks sent in to clear cut the trees up past Black Hill Road. Eventually, sawmills started popping up, which meant instead of having to transport the raw lumber to Manchester or Concord, it was processed right here. That meant faster turnaround, drawing more lumberjacks in to work. Besides the sawmills, the other booming business was saloons.

"Now, this wasn't Tombstone or Deadwood, but it wasn't that far off, either. Along with the saloons, the gambling and prostitution came. The competition was fierce among the saloons to draw the logging crews in on weekends. To increase profits, some saloons helped usher in Hopedale's next big business: moonshining."

Kenny paused to fill a cup with Coke and take a drink.

Hannah smiled, thinking of her father saying, *"Storytelling is thirsty work."* Kenny was no Brian Green, but he was good.

"Saloon owners could get corn mash whiskey at half the cost from moonshiners compared to what they paid to have it sent up from Manchester. The loggers didn't seem to care what they drank as long as it got them drunk. As Hopedale tried to establish some sort of law and order, the stills were deemed illegal. This forced the moonshiners out of Hopedale town limits and up into the foothills. The problem was, they were setting up their operations in the same woods the loggers were trying to clear. Eventually, tensions between the lumberjacks and the moonshiners became violent. Turf wars were fought in the shadows.

"Logging camps were torched while the lumberjacks were working or while they were in town drinking on weekends. Stills were destroyed in retaliation. Hopedale lawmen turned a blind eye to whatever was going on up in the woods. If the violence didn't touch the townspeople, Sheriff Mason Abernathy told his men to stay out of it. Naturally, lines were drawn between the townspeople. Sawmill owners and workers sided with the loggers. The more nefarious saloon owners and gamblers sided with the moonshiners.

"It all came to a head in October of 1885. Kirby Vancleave owned the Black Bear Tavern, arguably the most successful saloon in town, certainly the most notorious. The loggers had dynamited one of Vancleave's biggest suppliers' still, killing several of the moonshiners in the blast. Vancleave called in markers from as far away as Boston and Hartford, filling Hopedale's boarding houses with some of the East Coast's most infamous criminals. Hired guns, enforcers, bounty hunters, pretty much anyone that was good with a gun or their fists and didn't mind using either to make a buck."

Hannah snuck a glance at the others. They were rapt. Ashley and Marcus knew the story, of course, but Kenny had them mesmerized anyway. Dawn was transfixed as well, but there was something else, too. Kenny definitely had a shot with her.

Kenny wiped his mouth after finishing his Coke. "Okay, where was I?"

"Hopefully getting to the burning wagon one of these days," Marcus quipped.

Kenny grinned. "Almost there, wise guy. So, Fridays were busy in the taverns but most of the loggers worked too hard to go crazy on Fridays. Saturday nights were the big drinking night. Vancleave kept his hired guns out of sight all week. Saturday night, they started making their way to the saloons. Not just the Black Bear, either. *All* the saloons. Vancleave planned to have his men follow the loggers to their camps and find out who had used the dynamite. See, one of the moonshiners killed was Vancleave's cousin.

"What Vancleave *didn't* know was that old Mason Abernathy had gotten wind of the plan. Or, part of the plan, anyway. Abernathy expected the showdown to happen in town when he saw Vancleave's men arriving, so he called in some backup of his own. When Abernathy saw Vancleave's thugs showing up in the saloons, he sent his men as well to be ready. Well, nothing happened. Vancleave's guys were yucking it up with the loggers and buying them drinks. Eventually, Abernathy's men were buying drinks for Vancleave's men. One big happy party."

Kenny was into it now. His face was flushed with excitement.

Dawn was leaning forward, her elbows on the table and her chin cupped in her hands, completely hooked.

"Finally," Kenny continued, gearing up for the big finish, "the loggers began heading back up to their camps. Vancleave's guys started toward the boarding houses. Abernathy, thinking it was over, told his own men to call it a night. And Vancleave's plan worked. As soon as the hired lawmen were tucked in, Vancleave's guys reconvened behind the Black Bear. It turns out they hadn't been drinking nearly as much as the loggers or the lawmen. Most of the night they'd dumped their drinks—

sacrilege back then—to stay sober while keeping the others drinking fast.

"Vancleave's gang marched straight up the logging road, figuring the lumberjacks were zonked out for the night, same as the lawmen. So, they went right into the camp, but instead of looking for the one who blew up the still, they started killing them all. They were all loaded for bear, but the massacre started quietly, the gang wanting to kill as many as they could before firing guns and waking the rest. They used the lumberjacks' own tools on them: saws, axes, cane hooks, misery whips, tongs, even the smaller logs.

"At some point, the lumberjacks woke up. That's when the shooting began. See, the lumberjacks all kept guns— mostly rifles—to scare off the wildlife in the woods, sometimes to hunt. Even with all the loggers Vancleave's gang had already killed, his men were still outnumbered. It turned into a blood-bath for both sides. Vancleave's guys had started burning the tents and bunkhouses as soon as the shooting started, turning the scene into total chaos. Vancleave's guys started to even the score and eventually pinned down the remaining lumberjacks in the lumber house."

"Here we go," Marcus said, grinning. He looked at the others. "You ready to hear about the wagon?"

Kenny was too caught up in his own story to realize how he had the others hanging on his every word. "The lumber-jacks knew it was only a matter of time before Vancleave's guys picked them off or burned them out. It was a standoff, but one the loggers couldn't wait out.

"The thing about logging in the foothills and low moun-tains, getting the raw lumber to the sawmills is difficult. They weren't cutting near a river, the most common way to trans-port logs, and they'd worn out teams of horses and mules the year before hauling wagons up and down the steep road. So, they laid down some mining tracks and bought some old mining cars from a played-out Feldspar mine in Cheshire. They customized the cars to maximize the number of logs they could hold and developed a pulley system to haul the cars back up the tracks.

"There was a driver's car with a rudimentary braking system and the tracks were fairly centralized to the sawmills in town. Gravity took the cars down and the loggers took turns on pulley duty, hauling them back up to reload. It was an older logger named Whispering John who came up with the idea of sending the wagon down."

Dawn sat up. "Why'd they call him Whispering John?"

Kenny grinned. It was as if she was an audience plant, asking the question people would wonder about. "The story was, he'd caught the kickback of a branch in the throat while logging in Wisconsin. Damaged his larynx so all he could do was kind of croak out his words."

Dawn smiled and nodded, urging him on.

"So, a bunch of the loggers created a diversion from the back of the lumber house, while Whispering John and a few others loaded one of the cars with lumber, dowsed it with kerosene, lit it, and sent the wagon down the tracks. No driver, brakes be damned.

"The car screamed down the tracks, blazing like a hellfire. It derailed in town with a crash that woke even the drunkest sleepers. Abernathy figured it out right away and roused his hired guns. They formed a line and started up the road.

"Well, Vancleave's gang knew once the wagon went down that the law would be headed their way, so they had started down the road to hole up in the Black Bear and try to get out of town at first light. They walked right into the approaching posse, and the lumberjacks were following them down. They were surrounded and outnumbered. People say Vancleave's guys dropped their weapons and surrendered, but the lawmen and the loggers executed them. Others say it was a gunfight to the end. Of course, that story doesn't hold up, as not a single lawman was wounded in the battle.

"It was Hopedale's defining moment, the claim to fame, though it isn't widely publicized because of how it ended. Anyway, it became a tradition for kids in town to secretly build a wagon and run it down Black Hill Road on Halloween night. The police know it's coming every year, but they let it go. The fire department is always at the bottom of the hill, ready to—"

"Hey," Dawn said, "Black Hill Road isn't far from my house, it's some sort of cut-through street, my dad said." She turned to Kenny and smiled. "Sorry, I didn't mean to interrupt."

Kenny just shrugged, still grinning.

"That's right," Marcus added. "Your neighborhood is the 'old' downtown Hopedale. When logging started to die out and Hopedale turned into a mill and factory town, they used some of their newfound prosperity to revitalize and basically rebuild the center of town in a new location. Black Hill Road used to be the old logging road. Supposedly, the old tracks are still under the asphalt."

Kenny started to say something else, and Hannah was pretty sure it was the other story about Black Hill Road, but Dawn cut him off.

"That's pretty crazy, like, why isn't that in all the history books?" She looked over at the under-construction wagon. Her face held an expression of pride now that she knew what she was a part of.

"History is written by the winners, right," Ashley said. "Hopedale decided it didn't want to be the little town with the dark past, so they downplayed the whole thing as best they could. Most of the locals know through word of mouth. I'm not sure if it's ever really been written about."

"Maybe I'll write about it someday," Hannah said.

"Hey," Kenny said defensively, "do you think I just happen to know all these gory details? I already wrote about it!"

"Yeah!" Marcus laughed. "How'd that work out?"

Kenny had indeed written about it, with even more graphic detail than the story he'd just told. He'd been sent home with a 'D' on his paper and a note for his parents to come meet with the principal.

"Crap," Marcus said, looking at his phone, "I have to get going, I'm already late for dinner."

Hannah looked around, surprised at how much of the day had slipped away. It was after 6:00. "Whoa. I have to go, too. I'll call my dad. Anyone else need a ride?"

"I'm good," Kenny said.

"Funny," Marcus said, rolling his eyes.

"You're the only one that lives out in the sticks, Hannah. The rest of us can walk." Ashley stuck out her tongue.

Hannah turned to Dawn. "You have a bit of a hike, do you want my dad to drop you off?"

Dawn considered it, then shook her head. "I'm going to walk. It's a nice night and I need to know my way around."

"What about Derek?" Kenny asked, looking around at the others.

"I'll be fine," said Dawn. "I have my phone if I see him lurking around."

Hannah wanted to insist, always on alert after the events of the summer, but Dawn seemed pretty sure of herself. "Okay, suit yourself, walkers." She tapped her dad's contact and waited for the ring.

chapter
twenty-nine

DAWN STOPPED ON THE CORNER, glancing up and down the street, then looking west where the sun now hung below the treetops. It would be full dark soon, and she wasn't sure about her plan anymore. She'd wanted to take what would be the long way home to check out Black Hill Road. Kenny's story had gotten to her. She wanted to walk the same road that had been such a big part of her new hometown's history.

Her thoughts derailed, turning to Kenny.

She liked him. There was something about him that she couldn't put her finger on. He was cute and funny, but it had been his story that had cemented it for her. Well, not the story itself, but the way he'd told it. She smiled at the memory.

"Black Hill Road," she whispered, the decision made, and began walking. The scenery quickly changed from a residential neighborhood with side streets bisecting Black Hill Road to more of an old country road with houses every quarter mile or so. Then, the houses stopped, and she was surrounded on both sides by dark, shadowy forest. The sun was no longer visible through the trees to the west. Dusk had arrived.

Dawn quickened her pace. She wasn't afraid but also

didn't want to be stumbling along the rough shoulder of the road in pitch black night. The air had cooled as soon as the sun went fully behind the tree line, and she was thankful for her heavy sweater. Luckily, there was no breeze to add to the chill. Late-season crickets and peepers woke, and she smiled again. She breathed in the heady aroma of pine trees and something else, a sweet smell she couldn't identify. She loved being out in nature, especially when she was alone. The walk through the ancient Hopedale woods was an adventure.

She was glad to be heading downhill, as the road was steep.

The road curved slightly, and lights blinked in the distance. The old downtown, she thought, remembering Kenny's story. She knew people called it Cabbagetown, the poor section of Hopedale, but she liked the sound of 'old downtown' better. She judged the distance to the lights and figured it was only about a mile. She'd be home in less than a half hour, and close enough to town before the last light faded to not have to worry about face-planting on the side of the road.

She stopped suddenly, squinting down the hill. Her eyes had to be playing tricks on her, there was no way a little kid could be out on the road. Alone in the dark. No way. She started walking, keeping her gaze fixed on the small figure in white on the other side of the road. She realized no cars had passed her in either direction, and the thought sent a violent chill through her. The sense of adventure and being content surrounded by nature was gone. Something was wrong, every bone and nerve in her body told her so.

"Hello?" The sound of her voice scared her. It was shaky, querulous, the voice of an old lady. Worse, it was drawing attention to her. The figure didn't move, didn't respond. She slowed her pace as she drew even with the child—now she could see it was a girl—and only a couple dozen feet of asphalt separated them now.

"Do you need help?" The girl just stared, motionless. The woods had gone deathly quiet. No critters rustling the leaves or underbrush, no insects buzzing or chirping. There was only the sound of her breathing.

She took a tentative step toward the girl, then stopped. Goosebumps raised on her arms and her whole body had gone cold. Not just chilled, *freezing* cold. She watched in amazement as her breath plumed in front of her in a white fog. When the mist of her breath cleared, the figure was still there. The girl's face wasn't visible in the darkness, so Dawn's brain superimposed another face on the specter's body. And it *was* a specter, she knew that now. There was no little girl wandering alone on the dark road.

"Eden?" Saying her sister's name out loud did nothing to allay the icy panic that had gripped her. A tiny voice in her head tried to tell her this girl, this *apparition*, was too old to be her dead sister, but the shrill, irrational voice of hysteria shouted it down. *Maybe this is what she would have looked like*, the voice whispered, *if—* "No!" Dawn screamed, pressing her palms to her ears as if that could silence the voice. She squeezed her eyes shut, falling to her knees as the strength in her legs betrayed her.

Blocking her ears and eyes couldn't protect her. The fresh scent of the pine trees and the pleasantly pungent scent of the dying leaves disappeared. Something bitter, something acrid replaced it. Something impossible. "Is that smoke?" She opened her eyes and the final glimpse of the girl threatened to shut her mind down completely. An angry wind tore down the road, she could almost see it. It surged around the girl, drawing last season's dead leaves with it, forming a funnel around her, a cyclone of leaves and pine needles. In its vortex the girl remained, her hair and clothes swirling but her body still. Then, her nightgown—Dawn somehow knew that was what it was—began to burn. Flames licked hungrily up the cloth, turning it black. The flames reached her face. Only then did the girl move. She threw her head back and opened her mouth in a horrible silent scream as her face blackened. Just before the darkness mercifully took her, a single word—a name—echoed in Dawn's head. *Amie.*

chapter
thirty

"HANNAH, PHONE'S FOR YOU!"

Hannah looked up, dazed. She glanced at the clock and was shocked to see it was almost nine o'clock. After her dad had fetched her from Kenny's, they had eaten a quick dinner, then she had retreated to her room and dug out one of her unused notebooks. She'd sat staring at the empty page for a long time before putting pen to paper. But once she'd started writing, the words had poured out of her.

"Hannah?"

"Coming, Dad," she called back, giving the notebook a final glance. How many pages had she written?

She waved at Rick—when had he gotten there? —and picked up the phone. "Hello?"

"Hannah ..."

The voice on the other end of the phone dissolved into a puddle of sobs. She knew it wasn't Ashley, but it took her a second to place the voice. "Dawn?" The crying went on for a few minutes. Hannah glanced at her father and Rick, but they were watching something on television. When the sounds quieted to hiccupping gasps, she said, "Dawn, are you okay? What's wrong?"

"Hannah, I'm so scared." The weeping resumed.

"Do you need the police? My dad's boyfriend is here."

"No," Dawn managed to say. "I'm okay, it's just ... something happened ..."

Hannah heard muffled voices and the phone being passed.

"Hannah, this is Ned Holman. Dawn had a bit of a scare on her way home tonight."

Derek, Hannah thought. She *knew*. Her hand shook as she switched the phone to her other ear, once again checking to make sure her father and Rick hadn't caught on that something was wrong. "What happened?"

"I guess she decided to take the scenic route home. She thought she saw—"

"I did see her!" said Dawn, in the background.

Hannah tightened her grip on the phone. Her heart thumped a staccato rhythm. *Her*. She knew what was coming.

"Fine," Mr. Holman said, placating his daughter. "She saw a little girl on the road and then ..."

"Lonesome Amie," Hannah whispered.

"What did you say?" His voice had gone up a few octaves. "Did you say 'Amie'?"

"Yes. She's kind of a local legend." There was more noise on the other end of the phone before Mr. Holman passed the phone back to his daughter.

"Hannah?" she said frantically. "You know about this?"

"I mean, everyone has heard the stories ..." Hannah paused. "What did you see?"

Hannah listened with a cold, creeping dread as Dawn recounted her walk home from Kenny's.

"Then, I don't know, I guess I fainted. I woke up on the side of the road and ... she was gone. Is that ... is that the same as the stories?"

Hannah considered it. "Not exactly. I don't remember the

part about the smell of smoke or seeing her on fire. Or even the swirling leaves. Usually, it's just a little girl in white, seen walking on Black Hill Road." She laughed nervously. "There's a silly rhyme that goes along with the stories, you'll probably hear it as we get closer to Halloween."

"How does it go?"

Hannah sighed.

"*Stay at home, stay at home,*
Lonesome Amie will find you alone.
Stay off the road, stay off the road,
Lonesome Amie will take your soul."

"Lonesome Amie," Dawn breathed. "That name—Amie —that's the last thing I remember before I blacked out."

Hannah chose her next words carefully. "Is there any way you could have heard about it before? Could Kenny's story, I don't know, have freaked you out?"

"I know what I saw," Dawn said, her words clipped. "And I have never heard any ghost stories about Hopedale before."

"Okay," Hannah said. "I'm sorry, I just don't know anybody that's actually seen her, that's all. It's always a friend of a friend kind of thing."

"But you believe me, right?"

Even though the story had been something floating around town for as long as she could remember, Hannah had never actually thought about it in terms of it being true. Could Dawn have really seen a ghost? As soon as the thought entered her head, she was ashamed of herself. After her experience with Mama Bayole, she knew she had to keep an open mind about all sorts of supernatural phenomena.

"Of course I believe you," she replied.

"Thank you," Dawn said softly, obviously relieved. "I thought you'd think I was crazy."

"Well," Hannah said, "just because I believe you saw a

ghost doesn't mean I *don't* think you're crazy." The awkward silence told her she'd said something wrong. "Wait, it was a joke." Silence. "Dawn, I was kidding, I'm sorry if—"

"It's okay."

But she didn't *sound* okay. "Honest, I really didn't mean anything, it's how Ashley and I joke around all the time, and ..."

"No, I get it," Dawn said. "It's just ... there's a lot of stuff you don't know about me."

Hannah remembered the rumors about Dawn's sister— could there be some truth behind them?

"We're friends, right?"

Dawn sniffed. "I think so."

"Well, I *know* so," Hannah said emphatically. "And I know Ash, Marcus and Kenny all like you, too." She couldn't keep the smile out of her voice. "Kenny a little more than the rest of us, I think."

"Wait," Dawn said, her tone completely changed. "Do you think he *likes* me, likes me?"

Hannah laughed. "I think if he *liked* you, liked you more, his feet wouldn't touch the ground when he walked near you."

Dawn laughed, and it was a wonderful sound. Between her terror and confusion at the beginning of the call, then her despair at an ill-timed bad joke, it was music to Hannah's ears.

"Haven't you noticed the little hearts floating out of his head, like in the cartoons?"

"Hannah!" Dawn said with a laugh. "Stop. Actually, don't stop. Tell me more. I think I like him, too. *Should* I like him?"

"If you mean is Kenny a good kid, the answer is yes. He can be a little over the top ... okay, a *lot* over the top, to the point of being inappropriate. Sometimes he doesn't know when to stop, you know? But he's got a good heart." She remembered the fight they'd had the first day of school and was embarrassed by the memory.

"Thanks, Hannah. You're a good friend. I'm sorry I'm such a mess."

Hannah bit her tongue before responding with another wisecrack, like she would to Ashley. "We're all kind of a mess. That's why we're friends, I guess."

chapter
thirty-one

HANNAH HUNG up the phone and joined her father and Rick in the living room. Scout padded over, abandoning his spot on the couch.

"Wanna watch some television with us? It's a little late to start a movie but we could find some *Seinfeld* reruns or something." Rick patted the couch. "Still nice and warm, courtesy of Scout."

Hannah smiled and took the seat on the couch. Scout sat in front of her with a disapproving look.

"Honey, what's wrong?"

She could never get anything past her dad. "Have you heard the stories about Lonesome Amie?"

"Who hasn't? Those stories have been around since I was a kid."

"Did you ever know anyone that saw her?"

Rick leaned forward. "We get reports all the time, usually out on Black Hill Road. I've talked to a few of the people who claim they've seen her. Most of them are either looking for their fifteen minutes of fame or they're—" he twirled a finger next to his head. "But I have to say, I've talked to a few who I really think saw something."

Brian looked at him for a minute before speaking. "You're serious?"

"Sure. I've questioned a lot of people in my time as a cop. Suspects and witnesses alike. You get a feel for who's telling the truth, who's lying, who's afraid, you know?"

Hannah pulled a loose thread on her t-shirt. "So, you think there's something out there on Black Hill Road?"

"I didn't say that," Rick said carefully. "I said I've talked to people who believe they've seen something out there."

"But," Hannah said, "if they're not lying and they're not crazy, doesn't that mean they actually did see something?"

"Yes, Officer," Brian said, smiling. "Please continue."

Rick gave Brian a sideways look, then went on, "It's like when you interview people who witnessed an accident. Five people watch the same two cars collide, but you get two, maybe three different descriptions of what happened. Two people saw the red car run a red light. Two others saw the white car turn right on red without stopping. The fifth saw the white car stop abruptly for no reason and its brake lights were out and *that's* why the red car hit it. None of them are lying. It just happened so fast, and they think they saw what they saw. The mind can play funny tricks with your memory, even for something that happened a few minutes earlier."

Hannah considered this, feeling her father's eyes on her the whole time. "So, what do you believe, Rick? Did they see a ghost, or was it just their mind playing tricks on them?" She finally risked a glance at her father and saw worry lines on his forehead. She looked quickly back to Rick.

"I think it's probably a combination. Look, people have been hearing these stories for years, then they're out on a dark road and ... I don't know, maybe it's something as easily explained as the flash of a deer's tail, or the way headlights reflect off the undersides of the leaves." He paused; his eyes focused on something far away. "But to give you my honest answer, Hannah, I think some of them saw a ghost."

Dad scoffed. "Rick—"

Rick cut him off with a raised hand. "Brian, come on. After everything that happened over the summer, is it so hard to believe ghosts are at least *possible*?"

Brian opened his mouth, then closed it. His befuddled expression was comical. "I guess I never thought about it, not after ..." He looked at Hannah, the concerned expression returning. "Did *you* see something out there?"

Hannah shook her head. "No. Dawn—you remember the new girl? She did. That's who just called." Her dad and Rick exchanged a quick glance, but Hannah didn't miss it. "What?"

"That girl's had it rough, from what I hear," said Brian.

Hannah jumped to her feet, blood rising in her cheeks. "See? You're doing the very thing you just criticized Dad for. You've never met her, didn't interview her, but you're all ready to judge her because of whatever happened to her in the past. Do you even know the real story?"

Rick shook his head. "No, I don't. And you're right, I should know better than to jump to conclusions. I'm sorry. Do you *want* me to talk to her?"

Hannah's eyes widened a bit. "No, that would only make things worse, there's enough rumors going around school already. Wait... do either of you know who Lonesome Amie is ... or was?" She took her seat on the couch. "Like, was she a real person?"

"It's funny you mention that," her dad said. "There are a few stories I've heard but nothing concrete. Rick?"

"Probably the same stories you've heard. She was walking on the road at night—of course, nobody ever knows *why*— and was hit by a car. Another one I heard was that she was mentally ill, and her parents didn't want her, so they dropped her off in the woods and she died there." He shrugged. "I'm pretty sure those are unsubstantiated and just made up to make the story scarier."

Brian cleared his throat. "You know what, honey? I'll bet Ashley would love a trip to the library to do some investigative work with Mrs. Cheevers."

Hannah laughed, remembering how Ashley had cringed at the thought of visiting the library last summer, but had only agreed to it because the alternative was talking to Mama Bayole. "You know, she's not as opposed to the library as she used to be ... or as she probably should be after ..." The library —the one in West Meadow, not Hopedale—was where Ashley had been kidnapped. "Anyway, I think it's a great idea."

Brian frowned, crossing his arms across his chest. "Hannah, you're not going to—"

"Dad, stop," she said with a smile. "This is nothing like the Mama Bayole thing. Dawn saw something out there, and you both think it's possible, so what's the harm in learning a little more of Hopedale's glorious past? It can't be any worse than the Burning Wagon."

Rick laughed. "She's got a point there, Brian."

Hannah glanced at the time on the cable box. "I'm going to give her a quick call now, make a plan."

chapter
thirty-two

ASHLEY PICKED up on the first ring. "What's up?"

"Wow, it's like you were waiting for my call," Hannah replied.

"How do you know I wasn't waiting for someone else to call?" Hannah could hear the smile in her voice.

"Touché, but enough about you. Do you want the good news or the bad news?"

"Here we go," Ashley said.

"In the words of Frank Costanza, 'they're both the same' ... We have a date at the library this week."

"Huh?"

"Listen," Hannah said. "Are you sitting down?" Ashley started to say something, but she cut her off. "Dawn saw Lonesome Amie." Hannah had asked Dawn if she was okay with her telling the others. Dawn had agreed, as long as it went no further than their small group.

Hannah waited out Ashley's long silence on the other end of the phone.

"Are you joking? Is Dawn on the line and this is some kind of play to punk me?"

Hannah heard the concern in her friend's voice, and

maybe a little bit of hope that she was being punked. "Sorry, dude," she said, trying to keep it light. "This is all legit. She decided to take the scenic route home after Kenny's, that's where she saw her, on Black Hill Road."

"Holy crap, and you believe her?"

Hannah winced, hoping her best friend was going to start calling Dawn crazy. "I do, and if you'd heard her after it happened, you would, too. She was hysterical, Ash. She passed out on the road. She was terrified."

"I don't know, Hannah ..."

"Does it help knowing Dawn's never heard about the legend before?" Hannah asked.

Silence answered.

"Come on, Ash. After Mama Bayole? Really?"

Ashley sighed loudly. "That's different—"

"Is it?" Hannah snapped. "Or is it because of the rumors about Dawn and her sister?"

"Hey, hey, you're not going to go all Kenny-in-the-lunch-room Hannah on me, are you?"

Hannah laughed; the anger that had started creeping up had gone, just like that. It was one of Ashley's best qualities. "No, it's just ... I believe her, that's all."

"Fine, Nancy," Ashley said with a laugh. "What's the plan?"

"You can either go interview Lonesome Amie or come with me to the library to see if we can figure out who she was."

"Hmmmm," Ashley said. "While that is a real Sophie's choice, I think I need a little Mrs. Cheevers time. Do you think we'll be able to find any info? I can't remember anybody *ever* saying anything about who she was."

"I don't know. It's a place to start." She paused, another thought hitting her. "If we can't find anything, maybe I'll call Big Jake."

"Good idea! How's he doing?"

"Large and in charge," Hannah said.

"So ..." Ashley began, "what happened? With Dawn, I mean."

Hannah retold the story as best she could, hoping she conveyed it accurately. "She came to on the side of the road and ran the rest of the way home. Her father calmed her down after a while. She was such a mess, and her clothes were all covered with leaves, she said her father thought she'd been mugged or worse."

"Hannah, I hate to break this to you, but nobody has used the word 'mugged' since 1993."

"Well, excuse me for not being on the cutting edge of violent crime slang."

"Hey, is she gonna hook up with Kenny, or what?"

There it is. She'd been wondering if Ashley was going to feel like a fifth wheel if Dawn and Kenny did get together. Based on how much fun they'd all had bowling; she wasn't too worried about it. Ashley was just fine on her own. "Good to know romance isn't completely dead," she said, hoping to keep the mood light.

"I don't picture Kenny anywhere in the same universe as romance," Ashley said with a laugh. "I mean, he's kinda cute and he's funny, but I don't know if he's boyfriend material."

"He's no Marcus Diaz."

"That's what I'm talking about," Ashley agreed.

Hannah slid down the wall until she was seated on the carpet. Scout crept over and sniffed her, trying to figure out what she was doing. She reached out and patted him. She didn't like the way Ashley sounded. "Ash, are you okay?"

"Fine as frog's hair, as the cool people like my dad would say."

Her response was fast. Too fast, in Hannah's opinion. A thought struck her. The only time Ashley had ever really been down was when her parents had been going through a rough patch. "Are your mom and dad fighting?"

Ashley didn't answer for a long moment. When she finally did, she sounded defeated.

"Not really. They're just acting weird. I can't explain it, but I know something's up."

"Maybe your mom is pregnant." The words were out before Hannah knew they were coming. She raised a hand as if she could pluck them out of the air and put them back in her mouth before Ashley heard them.

"I'd thought of that," Ashley replied. "It's in the top three."

Hannah was relieved that Ashley sounded okay about the comment, but also concerned that Ashley had put so much thought into it. *How long has she been worried? And why haven't I noticed?* Hot shame filled her. She knew the answer was that she'd been spending all her time being Marcus's girl-friend instead of Ashley's best friend. "Um, what are the other two?"

"They're getting a divorce, or one of them is dying."

Hannah gasped at the last one. She pictured Ashley's parents. Craig was a big, burly man but Jill was very thin. Could she be sick? Ashley's tone was casual, matter of fact, but she knew that was her tough-girl act.

"I've kind of ruled out the divorce, though. They're acting weird, squirrelly, not fighting or anything. So, obviously I'm pulling for pregnant, given the choice."

"It kind of makes sense," Hannah said. "They would probably keep it a secret until after the first trimester, right? And..."—she chose her words carefully— "... they were away on that couples' retreat when I was busy saving your life, so maybe..."

Ashley snorted a laugh. "As disgusting as the whole

concept is, I've already done the math, too. The timing works... But what am I supposed to do with a baby sister?"

Hannah laughed. "I hate to be the one to break it to you—"

"Don't even say it—"

"A baby brother! Can we help pick out names?" Hannah was cracking up, barely able to get the words out. Ashley screamed on the other end of the phone.

"Can we please talk about something cheerier, like Lonesome Amie?"

"Listen," Hannah said, "this might be something they want for themselves, you know? They see you growing up, off to college in a few years ..."

"Yeah, I get it," Ashley sighed. "But I don't have to like it. Crying babies, dirty diapers ..."

"Ashley," Hannah said in her most serious voice, "you *love* kids, and you'll love your little sibling. Even if it's a boy."

"Yeah, I know. I really hope that's what it is, Hannah, I'm a little freaked out."

"You know, I had this crazy idea ... maybe you could ask them?" Hannah gasped as if it really *was* a crazy thing to suggest. Ashley said something but she didn't hear. "What? I didn't catch that?"

"I'm scared."

Hannah did not have an answer for that.

chapter
thirty-three

HANNAH CLOSED the door softly behind her and fast-walked down the hall. Instead of waiting for the elevator, she crashed through the steel fire door to the stairs. She sat on the top step, ignoring the stale-smelling humid air, put her head in her hands and began to sob. The tears came relentlessly. Every time she thought she couldn't possibly have anything left, more tears came. After some time—it could have been five minutes, it could have been half an hour—she wiped her face, took a deep breath, and started down the steps.

Her first therapy session had gutted her. She'd gone into the office tense and unsure what to expect. She'd told herself she'd only answer the questions she was asked. She wouldn't elaborate, and she sure as hell wouldn't spill her guts to a complete stranger. Her plans had failed. Once the lid had been pried off her bottled-up feelings about her mother's disappearance and the events with Mama Bayole, there was no putting it back on until the container was empty. Which is exactly how she felt: empty.

She glanced at her phone. Her father was waiting for her outside and her session had ended twenty minutes ago. He was probably frantic, and she was surprised he hadn't tried to call or text already.

He's giving me space.

She reached the bottom of the steps and entered the lobby. The sudden brightness of the autumn sun streaming in through the all-glass frontage made her squint. It also made her feel better. Dr. Moore's office had been cool and dimly lit, the north-facing windows preventing direct sunshine from reaching the small room. The stairwell had been worse, hot and dirty and somehow sad, as if others before her had come and shed their tears there. Stepping into the relative fresh air and welcoming brilliance of the lobby was like being reborn.

She pushed open the heavy glass doors and took a deep breath. Spotting her dad's car, she gave a wave and started walking toward it, preparing herself for the interrogation. Once in the car, she powered down the window, letting in the crisp, cool October air.

"What a day," she said, closing her eyes and letting the sun warm her. She waited, but her dad said nothing, just fiddled with the radio until he settled on his go-to classic rock station. Bob Seger crooned *Shame on the Moon*. It was perfect. Her grueling therapy session and the breakdown that had followed were already drifting into the past, like the remnants of a bad dream. Above it all, Hannah's heart was filled with love for her father.

He must be dying to ask about therapy, but he's letting me be.

"Everything went great, Dad," she said, grasping his free hand. "I'll tell you all about it later, okay?"

Dad smiled as Bob Seger gave way to Toto singing *Africa*. "Whenever you're ready," he said.

Hannah leaned back and closed her eyes.

～

"Is Rick coming over for dinner?" Hannah tried to sound casual, but she was on edge after therapy. She knew her father was waiting to hear about the session, but she still wasn't in the right frame of mind to talk about it.

Dad looked up from the batch of chili he was stirring. "I don't think so, just the two of us tonight."

"Oh, I just thought since you were making a cauldron of that..."—she gestured toward the oversized pot— "...you were expecting company."

Dad laughed. "You know chili just keeps getting better when you reheat it."

Hannah forced a laugh. "Is Rick busy?"

Dad gave her a long look before answering. "Honey, you don't have to tell me about therapy." She started to speak but he held up a hand. "Yes, of course I want to know, but I also understand how hard it is to unpack all those feelings." He looked down at his masterpiece. "I've been there, you know."

She knew he'd gone to therapy following her mother's disappearance, but they'd never really talked about it. It hit her again how hard this all must be for him. His wife had left him. He'd carried the guilt around for a long time before finally admitting his real feelings. Then, Hannah had gone and almost gotten herself killed. And now she was acting strange to the point where *she* needed therapy. Circle of life, she thought, but this is no Disney story.

"I know, Dad," she finally said, drawing a look from him. "I want to tell you all about it, but—"

"But you're not ready. I get it." He smiled one of his now patented sad smiles. "I love you and I'm here for you. Whenever you *are* ready. Now, why don't you call Rick and Ashley to help us eat all this chili?"

"Can we invite Dawn, too? I think she really needs a friend."

He glanced down at the huge pot. "I think we can accommodate that."

~

After dinner, Rick drove Ashley and Dawn home, then came back to the Greens'house. The chili-fest had been a success, leaving them all too full. Rick claimed he returned for dessert and coffee, but Hannah thought his reasons might have more to do with finding out about therapy. Sure enough, through half a mouthful of brownies, he said, "Hey, didn't you meet with Dr. Moore today?"

Hannah eyeballed her dad and Rick to see who looked guiltier. She landed on Rick. "Why, yes, I did meet with Dr. Moore today. Thank you for asking." She paused, examining the rest of her brownie, knowing her dad and Rick were losing their minds. When she could feel their curiosity turning to frustration, she snorted a laugh. "Sorry, sorry. But you guys are a little ridiculous."

Scout moved from his spot under the table, ever alert for the dropped crumb.

Rick said, "Whatever happened between you and Dr. Moore is none of my business. I'm just concerned. Same as your dad." He stuffed another hunk of brownie in his mouth and sipped his coffee.

Brian was swishing his coffee around in his cup, not looking up. "Dad?" Finally, he raised his eyes and gave her a small smile. "I'm fine," Hannah said pointedly. "I agreed to go to therapy. I went to therapy. Now, you both need to let me sort it out. Okay?" She caught the sheepish look that passed between them.

"Hannah—"

"I know, Dad, you're worried," she said, curter than she'd intended. She sighed. "I'm okay. I think therapy was a good idea, and I think it's going to help. But it was hard. And I just don't want to relive it right away. Do you understand?" Both men nodded and mumbled more apologies. "Thank you," she said, standing to clear the plates and load them in the dishwasher. She kissed her father on the cheek and gave Rick a quick hug. "Thank you for caring, both of you. I'm really okay, and I'm very tired. Goodnight."

She went to her bedroom, leaving the two men to talk among themselves. Scout followed, choosing her company over the slim possibility of a dropped brownie

chapter
thirty-four

"SAY MY NAME," Derek said to his reflection in the mirror.

"Lord of the Fireflies," he answered, watching in fascination as his lips curled into what he considered an evil grin. A *powerful* grin.

Earlier that day, he'd ground up the entire bottle of Hydrocodone. Just before going into the bathroom, he'd poured a can of chili into a bowl and put it in the microwave. In three minutes, it would be hot. He would add some shredded cheese and a generous lump of sour cream. And enough Hydrocodone to kill a horse.

The microwave beeped.

Derek's grin widened.

He went to the kitchen and prepared his mother's final meal. She'd fallen asleep on the couch watching a rerun of some old game show. It was all she ever watched, because she'd lost the remote to the cable box and didn't know how to change the channel. He added the cheese and sour cream along with his special ingredient and put the bowl of chili on the table. He went to the couch where his mother was sleeping. A string of drool connected her lip to the pillow. *Like a spider web.* He shook her gently by the shoulder. "Mom, have some dinner, okay?"

It wasn't unusual for him to heat up a frozen dinner for her, or a can of soup. Sometimes he even cooked hamburgers and beans. Keeping her fed seemed to stave off her bouts of anger. Something he'd never have to worry about again.

She opened her bloodshot eyes and stared at him for a second. Derek stared back; suddenly afraid she knew. Then she mumbled, "What'd you make?"

"Chili," he said, trying to smile, "just the way you like it: with cheese and sour cream."

She reached up, putting a hand to his cheek. "You're a good boy," she said, then got to her feet and shuffled to the table, sitting down heavily.

Derek's stomach tightened, the same way it had done the first time his father walked him to school, leaving him alone with all those other kids and Mrs. Vincente. He'd wet his pants that day, too afraid to raise his hand and ask to use the bathroom. The other kids had laughed and called him a baby. His mother had come and taken him home, telling him not to listen to those kids. She'd bathed him and given him clean clothes, telling him it was okay and that he was just nervous. Telling him it would be better the next day. She'd talk to his teacher and made sure Mrs. Vincente allowed him to use the restroom if he needed it.

This led to another memory. Derek bringing home a "Happy Thanksgiving" card with a drawing of a turkey that he'd made by tracing his hand. His mother had been so proud, hugging him and telling him what a beautiful picture it was. She'd fixed it to the refrigerator with magnets, then called *her* mother to gush over her son's artistic talent.

He realized the knot in his stomach wasn't the same as that first day of school. This was different, an unsettling sort of fear that it took him a minute to recognize. *Regret.* His mother had been nice, had taken care of him, *loved* him. It was only when his father had done his final dance in the toolshed that she'd gotten mean. Maybe she could be nice again. Maybe he could draw her a picture and she'd love him again. It wasn't her fault. No, it was his father's fault. Yes, he could draw her pictures—

"How did you manage to screw up canned chili?" His mother's voice pulled him from his fantasies. "It tasted like chalk."

Derek turned, seeing the empty bowl in front of his mother. He'd been daydreaming. "What?" He went and sat at the table, across from her.

"I said it tasted like chalk," she repeated. Except it came out *I thed it tathted like talk*. She dropped the spoon and it bounced off the table onto the floor.

She was breathing funny, and her eyes looked weird. Her pupils had shrunk to pinpoints and were moving crazily, independent of one another, like the googly eyes on a stuffed animal. Her lips were blue. Her face began to twitch, then her shoulders. He sat back quickly when slimy, red vomit burst from her mouth. Derek couldn't tell if it was chili or blood. Her whole body started to tremble, then she stiffened, sending her chair tipping backward with her still in it. The tremors, or the seizure ... whatever it was, continued for another minute. He watched in fascination as she jerked violently about the floor, occasionally spewing more blood-red vomit. Then she was still. The stench of piss and shit reached him, and he wrinkled his nose in disgust.

After some time had passed and his mother remained motionless, Derek stood and approached her body, careful not to step in any of her ejected bodily fluids. He knelt by her, reaching out to feel for a pulse. He let his hand hover there, inches from her throat. *What does it feel like to touch a dead body?* He realized the Lord of the Fireflies *needed* to know.

This wouldn't be the last dead body he touched. Oh, no. Not by a long shot. He put his fingers to his mother's throat, surprised at how normal it felt. Other than the lack of a pulse, of course. He moved his fingers around in case he was in the wrong spot, but the result was the same. She was dead.

He stood, considering the mess he had to clean up. "At least it's on the linoleum floor and not the rug," he said, then plodded toward the cellar door to find a shovel.

chapter
thirty-five

DEREK SAT on the couch watching reruns of Gene Rayburn hosting *The Match Game*. Every time someone gave the answer 'Making whoopee,' Derek giggled. He knew it really meant sex, and sometimes when Lee Meriwether or Mary Ann Mobley gave it as an answer, he would get a weird feeling. This episode wasn't one of those times. The celebrity guests were all guys and old ladies. He was sitting in the spot his mother always sat when she watched television. When she used to watch television, he thought, and giggled again.

The mess in the kitchen was all cleaned up and he'd dragged his mother's body to the basement. He'd started digging a hole, a grave, but after a few minutes he'd gotten tired. He'd decided to take a break and watch television. "It's not like she's going anywhere," he whispered, and had himself a good laugh.

The phone rang, putting an end to his laughter. He stood and went to the kitchen to answer it. "Hello?" He wasn't sure what to expect: his mother always answered the phone, and it was never for him. Usually, she would slam the receiver down and yell incoherently after.

"Hello," the smooth voice on the other end of the phone said. "Is Alice Campbell available?"

Derek almost hung up, but instead said, "She can't come to the phone right now," and burst into another fit of laughter.

"Well, I'm calling to offer her a great deal on a satellite dish. We at Jupiter Dish know how unreliable cable television is in your area. Imagine over two hundred digital channels including news, sports, and, of course, movies."

"What do I have to do?" Derek was picturing television beyond seventies game shows. Movies, maybe with shootouts and fires.

"Just say the word and we'll have a crew out there to install the dish on your house," the now giddy-sounding voice said. "Easy as that."

Derek stared at the television. *The Match Game* was over and now it was *Family Feud*. Richard Dawson was kissing all the female contestants and making stupid jokes. He'd heard kids at school talking about what they watched on television or on their computers, and it sounded a lot better than this.

"Okay," he said. "When can you come?" Derek half-listened to the man, grunting answers when he thought the man was waiting for him.

"All right, sir," the man said, starting to sound hungry to Derek. "We'll just need a credit card to take your deposit. Visa or Mastercard?"

Derek frowned. "What do you mean?"

"There's a non-refundable deposit and a monthly rental for the dish, as well as the fees for the premium package. We just need your credit card number."

Derek knew what credit cards were, but he didn't know if his mother had one. Or where it would be even if she did. He couldn't remember ever seeing one around the house. On the rare times they had pizza delivered, his mother always paid with a handful of rumpled bills. Money, he thought. He would need money to buy food.

"Are you still there? Visa or Master—" Derek slammed the phone down and sat heavily on the couch. Where did his mother keep her money?

He ran upstairs to her bedroom and found her pocket-book. He pulled out used tissues, a roll of butter rum life-savers, a hairbrush, a rolled-up issue of People magazine, and a keyring with more keys than his mother could ever possibly use. No wallet. No money. Next, he pulled open her night-stand drawer and rummaged through it. Old greeting cards, a bible, take-out menus, and a journal. Out of curiosity, he flipped through the journal; it had never been written in.

He looked around the bedroom for other places she could have squirreled away money or credit cards. Her dresser, maybe? He crossed the room and started rifling through the drawers, finding nothing but clothes. When he pulled open the last drawer, he paused. It was his mother's underwear drawer. Another weird feeling ran through him; a chill of sorts, but different. It reminded him of the night of the fire-flies. And of the day he'd talked to Emma outside the girls' bathroom, told her all the things he wanted to do to her.

Derek licked his lips, then put his hand in. The underwear was smooth, not like his own. Silky. Then his hand touched something hard, and the thoughts of his mother's underwear vanished. He pulled out her wallet and took it over to her bed, emptying the contents and marveling at his fortune. There was a wad of cash: tens and twenties, and two credit cards. One was for Walmart but the other was a Visa.

We'll just need a credit card to take your deposit. Visa or Mastercard?

"Visa," he whispered, and began to giggle.

chapter
thirty-six

HANNAH AND ASHLEY walked into the library, and Hannah's thoughts immediately returned to the last time they'd been there. She shook the memory off as Ashley nudged her, pointing at Mrs. Cheevers on the other side of the library, shelving books. They headed her way just as she turned to bring her empty cart to the front desk.

Hello, girls," she said in a hoarse whisper. "What brings you here today?" She raised an eyebrow, her smile turning into a mischievous grin. "On another case?"

Hannah and Ashley snickered. "Not quite, just looking for some information."

Mrs. Cheevers nodded, but her expression made it clear she wasn't buying it. "Anything I can help you with?"

"Maybe," Ashley said. "Have you always lived in Hopedale?"

Mrs. Cheevers motioned for them to follow her and started back toward the front desk. "I went to college in California and lived there for a while after, but I was born and raised here, and came back to stay over thirty years ago. So, I haven't *always* lived here, but pretty close."

"So, you've heard of Lonesome Amie?" Ashley asked.

"My goodness, of course. Who hasn't?" She looked at the expressions on the girls' faces and frowned. "Why the sudden interest? Spill it. I'm not going to help you if it's something that's going to put you girls in danger." Then she added sternly, "Again."

"It's nothing like that, Mrs. Cheevers, we promise. The thing is..."—Hannah paused to make sure nobody was within earshot— "...one of our friends saw her."

Mrs. Cheevers shifted her gaze between the girls for a long moment before speaking, as if making sure they weren't playing a joke on her. When neither girl cracked a smile, she sighed. "Okay, why don't you start researching on the computers. I get my lunch break at eleven-thirty." She glanced at the clock. "I'll tell you what I know over lunch at May's. My treat."

Hannah shot a glare at Ashley. "Hey, don't look at me," Ashley said, holding her hands up. "This is your circus."

Hannah smiled. "It's a date. Thank you, Mrs. Cheevers."

"Okay, girls. Eleven-thirty."

"Come on, Ash," Hannah said. "Let's see what we can find on our own." They crossed the room to the row of computers available for public use and took seats next to each other. After a few quick Google searches, Hannah was engrossed in the reading. There was a lot of information on Lonesome Amie, but she quickly realized it was mostly the same stories regurgitated over and over. Just about every reported sighting had taken place on or near Black Hill Road. The people who had seen her ranged from teenagers to the elderly and everything in between. Unfortunately, they were just reports of sightings, nothing on who Lonesome Amie might have been. If she had ever been a real person at all.

"Hey," Ashley whispered. "You find anything?"

Hannah shook her head. "Nothing new, same old ghost stories."

"Same," Ashley said. "I even tried googling obituaries of children named Amie, A-M-Y and A-M-I-E, that died around here but didn't come up with anything that fits."

"That was a great idea," Hannah said, impressed. A few minutes later, Mrs. Cheevers waved at them from the front desk. Hannah was surprised to see that it was already eleven-thirty. "Let's go," she said, gesturing toward Mrs. Cheevers.

Once they were seated in May's waiting for their lunch, Mrs. Cheevers asked how they had done with their research.

"Not great," Hannah said. "Same old, same old. Young girl all dressed in white on Black Hill Road."

The waitress came over, gave Hannah a curious look after overhearing her, then took their order. Mrs. Cheevers and Ashley had both ordered Caesar Salads while Hannah had gone with a grilled cheese and tomato.

"So, Mrs. C," Ashley said when the waitress walked away. "You've heard the stories about Lonesome Amie, but do you know if there's any truth behind it? Like, was Amie a real person?" Mrs. Cheevers smiled, and her eyes went far away, as if she was searching the past for a memory.

"I've always been the curious sort, just like you two. Naturally, I'd heard the stories when I was a kid." She gave the girls a conspiratorial look. "I used to walk Black Hill Road at night, hoping to see her."

Ashley gasped. "You did not?"

"Indeed, I did. It wasn't paved back then, and there weren't any houses there yet. It was just an old dirt road that dead-ended up in the woods. I wanted to see her so badly."

"Why?" Ashley blurted out.

Mrs. Cheevers stared at her. "Why *not*?" She laughed. "If you think Hopedale is boring now, you should have been around back then. Seeing a ghost would have been the most exciting thing around here since the Main Street Savings Bank robbery back in nineteen sixty-three."

"Whoa," Hannah said. "There was a bank robbery in Hopedale when you were a kid?"

"Oh, yes!" Mrs. Cheevers' face lit up with excitement. "I was at the A&P ... that's a supermarket that used to be in town. I think it's a gym now. The bank is still there, of course. Anyway, my mom had dragged me to help out with the shopping and to carry the groceries home. We didn't have a car, you see. We were going through the checkout—they were at the front of the store, so we were facing the windows—when the robbers ran out of the bank. They had hit the security guard over the head, but he came to as they were trying to escape. He chased them out of the bank and started shooting at the car, hitting one of the tires."

"Holy crap," Ashley said. "That's some serious Bonnie and Clyde stuff. Did he capture the robbers?"

Mrs. Cheevers shook her head. "They drove that car on three tires out to old Concord Road and made their getaway on foot through the woods. Police searched for weeks—"

The waitress arrived with their food, and they waited until she was gone before resuming. Mrs. Cheevers continued between bites of salad, "As I was saying, there was a manhunt that went on for weeks, but not a trace of the robbers was found."

Ashley asked, "Did anybody identify them?"

"That's the strange thing. Nobody did. They got good descriptions of the two men, but nobody could recall seeing them around town. They must have driven in specifically to rob the bank. They found the car, of course, but the men had burned it. Forensics back then weren't what they are today, so ..." She spread her hands out. "Clean getaway."

Hannah was enthralled. "How much did they get?"

"That's the *other* weird thing," Mrs. Cheevers said. "The Brinks truck was supposed to make a pick-up the day before the robbery but never showed up. So, the entire week's deposits were on hand. Rumor has it they got over fifty-thousand dollars. A pretty tidy sum back in those days."

"Wow," Ashley said. "I can't believe so much happened in Hopedale in the old days."

"Watch that," Mrs. Cheevers said with a laugh.

"That is crazy," Hannah said. "I wonder why my dad never told me about that."

"Wait," Ashley said. "You were at the store when they ran out, did you see them?"

Mrs. Cheevers nodded. "My mother was busy paying the cashier, but I was looking out the window and saw the whole thing. I was just a kid, though."

"But you saw them," Ashley prodded.

Mrs. Cheevers' expression darkened. She still had that faraway look, but it was different than before.

"Oh, yes. I saw them, and I told the police what I had seen, but I was quite a distance away ..."

Hannah shot a glance at Ashley and realized her friend wasn't buying the story any more than she was. "Wow," she said. "Did we get off track. We're supposed to be asking you about the ghost of Lonesome Amie." Mrs. Cheevers' face relaxed, her relief on changing the subject obvious. Hannah filed the information about the bank robbery to revisit later.

"Yes, yes, of course," Mrs. Cheevers replied. "My mind does take some twists and turns."

"You were telling us about walking Black Hill Road at night, hoping to see Lonesome Amie," Ashley reminded her. "Did you ever see her?"

"No," Mrs. Cheevers said sadly, "never. I had a friend who did, though."

"Yeah?" Ashley said, leaning forward. "Tell us what she saw."

Mrs. Cheevers smiled, a sudden twinkle in her eye, "Actually, it was a *he,* and I'm afraid his story is going to have to wait. I have to get back to work. I'm so sorry I spent all that time blathering on about the bank robbery."

Hannah glanced up at the clock and saw it was almost 12:15. "That's okay, it was a great story. When could we meet again and talk about Lonesome Amie?" Mrs. Cheevers paid the bill and left a generous tip. She looked truly distraught over not telling the girls everything she knew.

"My assistant, Jeremy, comes in at two o'clock. If you want to come back, I can take a few minutes to tell you then. Does that work?"

Hannah looked at Ashley. "We could take a walk over to Dawn's house and come back after two?"

Ashley shrugged. "That's fine. Maybe she'll want to come back and hear what Mrs. C had to say." She turned to Mrs. Cheevers. "If that's okay with you? She's our friend who saw Lonesome Amie."

"That would be fine," said Mrs. Cheevers. "Besides," she added, "I'd like to hear about her encounter."

chapter
thirty-seven

"SO ..." Ashley said as they walked toward Dawn's house.

Hannah looked at her questioningly. "So ... what?"

"Are you kidding me?" Ashley said, jumping in front of Hannah and walking backward so she could face her. "What is Mrs. C hiding about the bank robbery?"

"Yes!" Hannah said, grabbing Ashley by the shoulders and spinning her back so she was facing the right way. "She totally saw the robbers, and I think she knew who they were."

"That's what I was thinking," Ashley said. "It's so weird how much stuff there is about Hopedale that we don't know."

"Yeah," Hannah said, already thinking about making the bank robbery her next mission after they figured out who Lonesome Amie was. Ashley laughed, and Hannah turned to see what she was laughing at.

"It's like I can see a little billboard in your head," she said, then stopped. "No, it's more like a book cover. 'Hannah and the case of the Hopedale Heist,' am I right?"

Hannah giggled. "Close enough," she said. "But not until we're done with The Ghost of Lonesome Amie."

"Great," Ashley said, her voice dripping with sarcasm. "That gives me something to look forward to." She stopped walking and looked around. "Are you sure we're going the right way?"

Hannah scanned their surroundings, unsure. "It kind of all looks the same. All these old factories." Her eyes widened. "There's the pizza place we went to," she said. "Dawn's house is just up the next street, I think."

They walked in silence for a few minutes. Hannah was still trying to get her bearings. She stopped at the next corner and looked up the street, recognizing one of the more derelict houses from her first visit. "It's right up here," she said, pointing.

"I hope it isn't the gray one," Ashley said. "It looks like Lonesome Amie might live there when she isn't galivanting around Black Hill Road."

"Don't worry, her house is a lot nicer than that one. Come on." She started running up the street toward Dawn's house. When they got there, she rang the doorbell and stepped back.

The door opened, revealing Dawn's father. Hannah heard Ashley's gasp but managed to keep her composure. Dawn's father was still in his pajamas, unshaven, eyes hidden by the deep hollows that encircled them. He looked awful.

"Hi, Mr. Holman, is Dawn home?" He turned without a word, leaving the door open, disappearing into the shadows of the house. A moment later Dawn came out, closing the door behind her.

"I'm sorry, my dad is having a bad day." She tried on a smile. "What's up?" They quickly explained their plan. "Sounds good," Dawn said. "Just let me grab a jacket and tell my father I'll be home later."

When she was gone, Ashley nudged Hannah. "What was that?"

Hannah licked her lips, remembering her first meeting with Mr. Holman. "I don't know, but—"

Dawn opened the door and joined them on the porch. "Ready?"

They started walking back toward the library. Hannah couldn't help herself. "Dawn, is your dad okay?"

They walked in silence for a bit before Dawn answered. "He has good days and bad days. The stuff we went through in Hartford took a toll on him." She swiped the back of her hand across her eyes. "He can't seem to pull himself completely out of it sometimes."

Ashley put a hand on her shoulder. "Hey, if you ever need someone to talk to, Hannah and I have both been through some parental challenges."

A tear slipped out of Dawn's eye and rolled down her cheek. "That means a lot, you guys. Thanks."

They walked the rest of the way talking about Mrs. Cheevers and the story she'd told about the bank robbery.

"Wow," Dawn said. "Between that, the logging camp, and the cult, Hopedale really isn't your average small town, is it?"

"You know," Hannah replied, "I was thinking about that. I wonder if this type of thing really isn't that uncommon, but just stays under the radar? Ash and I have lived here our whole lives and had never heard about the bank robbery."

"Or the cult," Ashley added. "Until Hannah's dog changed that." They all laughed. "Maybe Hannah's right and this stuff happens more than we think. Before social media and the internet, these stories wouldn't go much farther than local papers, right? And then they get passed down by word of mouth over the years."

"You're probably right, I guess I never thought about it before," Dawn said.

Hannah looked at her phone as they arrived at the library. "We're a few minutes early but we might as well go in." Hannah pulled the heavy wooden door open and held it for the others. As she turned to follow them in, she saw something

185

from the corner of her eye that caused her to turn. A lone figure ducked into the alley between a pair of shops on the other side of the street. Hannah only had time to see an overcoat and a wide-brimmed hat before they disappeared. A plume of cigarette smoke faded into the air behind the figure.

"Hannah?"

Hannah turned to see Ashley looking at her questioningly. "Yeah, coming," she said, entering the library with a final glance over her shoulder.

chapter
thirty-eight

"SO," Mrs. Cheevers said after Hannah had introduced her to Dawn. They were seated in a small conference/study room. "Where did I leave off?"

"I think you were parking with some guy on Black Hill Road," Ashley teased.

Mrs. Cheevers smiled, a flush coloring her cheeks. "You're not far off, Miss Smartypants. I was with a young man, but I assure you it was all completely respectable." She got that faraway look in her eyes, as though she were watching the memory unfold on a movie screen only she could see. "His name was Michael Gaines. I was a sophomore in high school when this happened. I'd been telling Michael about my trips to Black Hill Road, and he was intrigued. He was a senior and had his driver's license. He agreed to take me up there one Friday night in October." She turned to Ashley with a mischievous twinkle in her eyes. "Don't get me wrong, I was *hoping* for more than just a ghost hunt. He was a cutie."

The three girls giggled.

"Anyway, he picked me up and went through the parental inquisition. We told them we were going to a movie and then for ice cream, so I didn't have to be home until eleven o'clock.

If I had been out walking, they would never let me stay out that late. I was sure it would be the night I would finally see Lonesome Amie.

"We didn't completely lie to my folks," she continued. "We got ice cream and ate it as we drove up and down Black Hill. The later it got, the more I began to think it was a fool's errand. Luckily, Michael was a wonderful partner in crime. We had been friends before, but we spent those hours in his car really getting to know each other. We talked about everything from school to friends to college and our dreams for the future."

"After you finish telling us about Black Hill Road," Dawn said, wide-eyed, "you have to tell us if you and Michael got together."

Mrs. Cheevers' eyes glistened with tears, but she blinked them back.

"Well, it was after ten o'clock and we only had time for a couple more trips up and down the road before I had to get home. That's when Michael's car died."

Hannah gasped. Even in the bright fluorescent light of the library, she could picture the scene all too well.

"I'm not talking about the engine conking out or running out of gas. I mean it died. Engine stopped, all the lights and the radio off. Suddenly, we were in the most complete darkness I can remember. Michael steered over to the side of the road until we heard the underbrush scraping the side of the car. Let me tell you, girls, I was scared. The *last* thing I wanted to see right then was Lonesome Amie."

"Oh, my gosh, Mrs. C, what did you do?" Ashley was all in on the story, leaning forward in her seat as if the words would reach her sooner that way.

"Do?" Mrs. Cheevers said. "I didn't do anything, except try not to completely fall apart. Michael, though, he was cool as a cucumber. He asked me if I was all right, then pulled a flashlight out of the glove box and got out of the car. He popped the hood and began fiddling around with whatever it is that men fiddle around with under there.

"After a few minutes, I stepped out of the car to get some fresh air and stretch my legs. Where he'd pulled over, strangely enough, was next to a cornfield. Right there in the middle of nowhere. I remember the stalks were all dead, the corn long gone. There was a little bit of a breeze, just enough to get the old brittle stalks waving. It sounded like bones rattling together." She shuddered, her eyes coming back into focus. "I leaned against the car looking out over the cornfield. Not that I could see anything, it was pitch black. I remember crossing my arms, feeling a bit chilled. Isn't that odd? So many years ago, but so clear in my mind." She shook her head, then continued, "I was just gazing out over the cornfield while Michael futzed with the car. I heard him muttering to himself and tried not to giggle. Then, he called to me. Or I *thought* he did."

This time, her pause lasted a beat too long. Hannah glanced at Dawn and Ashley and saw her own concern— no, *fear*, mirrored on their faces.

Hannah finally whispered, "What happened?" Mrs. Cheevers turned to her, wearing an expression of surprise, as if she'd forgotten the girls were there.

"Well, I called back to him, 'Do you need help?' but didn't move from where I stood. There was something almost mesmerizing about the rustling sounds the wind made blowing through the corn. When it didn't sound like bones, it sounded like voices. He said something else I couldn't hear. I ignored him, figuring he was just swearing at some thingamajig or another under the hood."

Hannah waited as Mrs. Cheevers composed herself to finish the story. Her throat was sandpaper, palms clammy. Still, she wanted to hear the rest.

"After another minute or so, he yelled my name. I

remember stiffening at the sound of his voice. He sounded ... I don't know, hurt, but something else ... scared. I thought he'd injured himself badly and was bleeding. I turned, but the open hood blocked my view, so I rushed to the front of the car, prepared for the worst. He was just standing there, staring down the road. I ran to him, looking him over, looking for an injury or blood. Then I looked at his face." She took a deep breath, letting it out slowly. "I'd never seen terror etched on a person's face like that, and I haven't since. I think he might have been in mild shock. I asked him what was wrong, if he'd hurt himself. But I knew." She smiled a bitter smile. "I knew he'd seen Lonesome Amie. The funny thing is, the first thing I felt wasn't fear, or concern, it was jealousy. *I'd* been the one wandering the road all that summer. *I'd* been the one that talked him into going. *I* should have been the one to see her. It only lasted a few seconds, like a wave of irrational anger, but I'll never forget it. And I'll never forget the shame I felt in its wake."

Ashley put a hand on Mrs. Cheevers' shoulder. "It's okay, you can't control your feelings all the time. I mean, you knew he wasn't hurt. I get it."

Hannah and Dawn nodded.

Mrs. Cheevers sighed, waving a hand in the air. "I'm just being a silly old woman; it was so long ago."

"What happened next?" Dawn prompted.

Mrs. Cheevers nodded, glanced at her watch, and continued, "I asked Michael a couple more times what was wrong. He just kept staring. I remember starting to shake, thinking he might really be in shock. I tried to move him back toward the car, thinking I could drive far enough to get help. It was like trying to move a statue. He was frozen there. I closed the hood and ran to the driver's side and got in. I turned the key before remembering the engine had stalled." She paused again, an unreadable look on her face. "But the car started right up. I jumped out and went back to Michael. The sound of the engine starting seemed to bring him back a little. He was still dazed but at least he was moving and talking. I asked him if he could drive, and he said he thought he could. It was good enough for me. We got in the car, and I asked him to take me home and that we didn't have to talk about what happened right then."

"You must have been dying to know," Ashley said.

"Oh, you have no idea," Mrs. Cheevers replied, "but I was terrified, too. We were on that dark road in the middle of the woods ... suddenly seeing Lonesome Amie didn't sound like fun anymore. And seeing the impact it had on Michael shook me. I was wondering if she was the reason the car died in the first place." Mrs. Cheevers shivered. "That was what scared me most. We drove in silence back to my house, but he kept looking in the rearview mirror, and his hands were so tight on the wheel, it looked like the bones of his knuckles were going to pop through the skin.

"We got to my house, and I made him come in. My parents were up watching television." Her face lit up with another mischievous smile. "Or pretending to watch television while they waited for me to get home. I told them something had happened, and Michael was a little shaken up and I was going to get him a drink and make sure he was okay before he drove home alone. Of course, they wanted to know what had happened. By that time, he was doing better. He said it was fine, he didn't mind telling them what he'd seen. So, we all went into the kitchen and sat at the table while Mom made tea for all of us. Then, he told us what he saw."

chapter
thirty-nine

"DAWN, are you okay? I mean, are you sure you want to hear this?" Her eyes were somehow desperate, like she *didn't* want to hear any more, but also knowing she had to. "I'm okay," she said hoarsely. She turned to Mrs. Cheevers with a weak, sickly smile. "Go on, this is the good part."

Mrs. Cheevers seemed torn, reluctant to speak for fear of upsetting her.

"It's okay, honest. Go on, I'll be fine."

"All right, if you're sure. Well, Michael told my parents everything, including that we'd never gone to the movies and had been cruising Black Hill Road for most of the evening. You should've seen the look my parents gave me. It was scarier than Lonesome Amie!" She laughed. The girls chuckled nervously with her, but Hannah knew they were dying to hear the rest. "He got to the part about the car breaking down, and that he'd gone to check under the hood. Then he told us about Lonesome Amie."

Their faces were glowing with anticipation, as if Mrs. Cheevers was about to announce the winning lottery numbers and they were holding tickets. Hannah knew how they felt. It was one thing to hear kids at school talking about somebody's friend's cousin seeing Lonesome Amie, but to hear an adult that you trusted talking about it was different. Hannah was glad they were in a brightly lit room in the middle of the day. If they'd been around a campfire out in the woods, she'd have been terrified.

"Michael was checking to make sure the battery cables and spark plugs were all secure when he felt the hair on the back of his neck stand up. I remember when he said that part he blushed and said he'd always heard that expression but had never actually had it happen to him. He felt like someone was watching him, so he whirled around, shining the flashlight down the road. That's when the flashlight went out."

Hannah jumped and uttered a squeal when Ashley grabbed her arm, then they both giggled. Dawn glared at them, clearly anxious to hear the rest of the story.

"Sorry," Hannah mumbled.

"Michael started banging on the flashlight and making sure the cap was tight, but it was dead. When he looked up, he saw her. At first, he thought it was a person walking along the road, maybe doing what I'd told him I'd done, looking for Lonesome Amie. Then it registered that she was wearing what looked like a dress or a nightgown." As Mrs. Cheevers smiled wistfully, Hannah was able to see the teenage girl that had gone ghost-hunting on Black Hill Road. The gleam of wonder and curiosity in her eyes.

"At that point," Mrs. Cheevers continued, "he said he figured I was playing a prank on him. That I'd lured him up there, did something to the car, and had a friend dress up like Amie."

"No offense, Mrs. C," Ashley said, "but I could totally see you doing that."

They all laughed, then Hannah prodded her. "Go on, Mrs. Cheevers, what happened next?"

"Like I said, Michael thought I was playing a joke. He took

a sip of his tea, then his face went pale. I remember his hand started shaking so badly the tea slopped out of the cup. He put it down, then told us that the figure had raised a hand and pointed at him. He said it felt like she was marking him. Then she was gone. He said she didn't wander off down the road or into the woods, just disappeared. That's when he called my name."

Mrs. Cheevers' youthful expression from earlier was gone, replaced with something else. Something dark and ominous, like an errant storm cloud obliterating the sun on a warm summer day.

Ashley must have seen it, too. "Mrs. C, are you okay?"

Mrs. Cheevers blinked. "Oh, my. Yes, just got lost in my memories."

"So," Hannah said, "you believe in the ghost?"

She paused for a beat too long before answering. When she finally spoke, her words were careful. "I believe there are a lot of things that can't be explained by science. Just because there's no evidence, no fancy machine to prove they exist, doesn't mean there's not *something* to it." She tilted her head and looked at Dawn. "You saw her, what do *you* think?"

"What I saw was a little bit different," she said softly, "but I know what I saw."

"How was it different?" Mrs. Cheevers asked excitedly.

Dawn quickly recounted her experience on Black Hill Road. Hannah watched Mrs. Cheevers, again able to see the young girl who liked to ghost hunt.

"Well," Mrs. Cheevers said when Dawn had finished, "that is the first time I've heard anyone mention fire."

"I know what I saw," Dawn said, tight-lipped.

Hannah was about to say something, but Mrs. Cheevers beat her to it. "I believe you," but it's given me something to think about. Let me do some research. Can you girls come back tomorrow?"

chapter
forty

HANNAH REGARDED THE FINISHED PRODUCT. "I think this is the best wagon Hopedale has ever seen," she said proudly.

"Yeah," Ashley agreed. "It's almost a shame we have to burn it."

"You guys really killed it," Kenny added. "Dawn's artwork is perfect, too." His face flushed as he kept his gaze on the wagon.

"Thanks," Dawn said, "but it really was a team effort."

Marcus stood and started taking pictures with his phone.

"Hey," Kenny said, also getting to his feet. "Let me get my mom to take a picture of all of us with the wagon."

"Great idea," Hannah said as he bounded toward the house.

"You really are an amazing artist," Ashley said, moving closer to examine Dawn's work.

One side of the wagon depicted downtown Hopedale: May's diner, the movie theater, and the bowling alley, all with the backdrop of Champlain Park. The other side featured Black Hill Road as it might have been back when the logging camp was there. Men in flannel worked cutting down trees while the rail car trundled down the tracks fully loaded with giant pine trunks. A small town sat at the bottom of the hill.

Hannah moved next to Ashley, peering at the Black Hill Road mural. She nearly gasped when she noticed the faint smudge of white. From a distance it was indistinguishable, but up close, it was clearly the figure of a girl walking down the hill.

"Lonesome Amie," Hannah said softly.

"Whoa," Ashley said, her voice full of wonder. "I didn't see that before."

Hannah pulled out her phone and started taking pictures. Then she switched to video and walked around the wagon, getting every detail in the shots.

"All right," Kenny's mom called. "Let's get a group—"

She stopped mid-stride when she saw the wagon. "My god," she breathed. "It's incredible. Who painted that?"

"Dawn painted the murals," Kenny said proudly.

Dawn blushed. "Everyone helped," she murmured.

"It's absolutely breathtaking," Mrs. Driscoll said in awe. "You have such a talent."

"Thank you," Dawn said, clearly uncomfortable being in the limelight.

"Here," Mrs. Driscoll said, gesturing. "Line up there and I can get you all in the shot with the wagon." She had a nice digital camera and took several photographs of the gang as well as several shots of the wagon by itself. "I'm going to call Jason Fredricks at the paper. He does a story on the wagon every year but I'm willing to bet he's never seen anything like this."

"Whoa," Marcus said. "That would be cool. Dawn, you'll be famous!"

Hannah watched Dawn's face go from a light blush to a deep crimson. She was glad her new friend was getting the attention. Even if Dawn didn't like it outwardly, it had to make her feel good.

"Come on, you guys," she said. "I'm sure the wagon is great every year."

Kenny shook his head. "I'm telling you; this makes every other wagon look like amateur hour. This..." he walked around it again, as if soaking in the detail. "This is like, next level."

He stopped and turned to Dawn. His expression didn't change. Hannah saw the same admiration and affection in his eyes for the artist as he held for her creation. Dawn smiled at him. Hannah saw real joy on her face.

"You really have outdone yourselves," Mrs. Driscoll said. "I think I have some ice cream in the freezer, anyone interested?"

chapter
forty-one

HANNAH STARED at the computer screen, waiting for the host to enter the meeting. After countless attempts to set up a face-to-face with Emma Gould, the best they could get her to agree to was a Zoom call. It had taken Ashley spilling her guts in an email to Emma, talking about her encounter with Mama Bayole and what it meant to be a trauma survivor. Then she had dropped the bomb about being harassed by Derek Campbell. Still unwilling to meet in person, Emma had reluctantly decided a Zoom call would be okay.

The monitor flashed and a choppy image of a blonde girl came on the screen. The second thing Hannah noticed about her was how pretty she was. The first was the wide-eyed, deer-in-headlights expression etched on her face. Hannah turned to Ashley to take the lead.

"Emma," Ashley started, then paused.

Hannah's eyes pivoted between Ashley and the monitor. What she saw hit her like a gut punch. She was overcome with sadness and confusion. She was looking at two people in pain. Ashley had seemed okay following the events of the past summer, but now she recognized a deep-seated anguish that her best friend had somehow managed to conceal under her brash humor and unbridled enthusiasm.

Have I been so wrapped up in myself that I couldn't see Ash was suffering? The possibility, no —*probability*—filled her with shame.

"Hi, Emma," she said, her voice thick and shaky. "I'm Hannah Green. Thanks for meeting with us. I know it can't be easy."

"I'm not sure I'm doing the right thing," Emma said.

"If you can help us protect ourselves from Derek Campbell," Ashley said, seeming to have recovered, "then you're doing the right thing."

Emma winced at the mention of Derek's name. For a second, she was sure the other girl was going to end the call. Her hand moved toward the keyboard, but then stopped.

"I don't know how to do that," Emma said tightly, and a tear snuck down her face. She didn't wipe it away.

"We're afraid, Emma, but we don't know *how* afraid we should be." Ashley's words were coming fast now, and she was gesturing with her hands out of frustration.

"We know he can be violent," Hannah said, putting a hand on Ashley's forearm to settle her down. "But ..." Hannah bit her lip, unsure how to ask the tough question. She and Ashley had to know.

Ashley's face hardened with what Hannah took to be resolve. "When you left, there were stories about what happened that day, but nobody knew for sure. Or, at least, nobody that did know would tell."

Emma's tears were coming steadily, and she reached off-camera to grab a tissue. She wiped her face, took a deep breath, and let it out slowly. "What did you hear?" Her voice was low but steady.

Ashley looked at Hannah, who nodded, urging her to go on. Ashley recounted the two rumors in the gentlest terms she could. Emma remained stoic, though the tears continued to spill faster than she could wipe them away. When Ashley had finished, there was a long silence. Finally, Emma sniffed, then began to speak.

"He had been creepy from the first time I met him in class. First, it was nothing, just catching him staring at me, you know? He'd turn away, trying to pretend he wasn't staring, but his face would go beet red every time. After a while, he stopped looking away and would just keep staring, even after he knew I'd caught him. It was..." Emma sobbed, her breath catching, and covered her face. "I'll be right back," she said, and moved out of sight.

Muffled voices came from the computer, but Hannah couldn't make out the words. She put an arm around Ashley and squeezed her shoulder. Ashley nodded but her eyes never left the monitor.

Emma returned, eyes puffy from crying and red-faced. "My mom wanted me to end this but ... I can't." She looked away then back at the camera. "She's listening in. I hope that's okay."

"Of course," Ashley said gently. "We don't want to upset you, or, you know, rip the scabs off old wounds. We're just scared."

"Derek has been ... escalating." It was a word Hannah had heard Rick Benson use about some of the criminals in cases he'd worked on. It seemed to fit. "We think he's been following us. And that he's going to do something really bad."

"Do you think he could?" Ashley asked. "Do something really bad, I mean?"

Hannah hated how afraid Ashley sounded. It wasn't like her to be scared of anything or anyone. Ashley was fierce. Fearless.

Emma's eyes darted to her mother then back to the camera. The fear Hannah had seen in them earlier was still there. Maybe it was always there, she thought, but there was something else. A strength, she realized. A determination. When Emma spoke, her voice was even. The tears had stopped.

"I don't think there's any limit to how bad he can get," she said. "*Escalating.* That's the word you used, Hannah, and it's exactly what was happening before. I told you he'd gotten bolder, stopped looking away when I caught him starting. That was only the beginning." She took a deep breath, and with a quick glance at her mom, went on. "He started talking to me. Or talking at me, I guess. It wasn't like he said anything I could ... anything I knew how to respond to. At first it was stuff like 'your hair is long' or 'your skin is really white' ... Creepy, you know? I mean, what do you say to that? Then it got worse. *Escalated.*" She laughed. "He asked me if I ever cut myself. How red my blood was. Then he asked if he could have some of my hair. I never answered him, never said a word to him. Then, that day in the hall—"

A muffled voice cut her off. Emma's mother, no doubt protesting, begging her to end the call. "I have to do this!" she said with determination. "I let him get away with it once and I won't do it again." She turned back to the camera, grim-faced, and went on. "Derek's class was next to mine. I think he must have been watching for me, waiting until I needed to use the bathroom during class." She shivered. "I came out of the bathroom, and he was there. Right outside the door, waiting. He had this look on his face, like he was a little kid about to open the best Christmas present. He said, 'I am going to see what you look like on the inside. Just like the flies in the spiderweb.'"

"Oh, God," Ashley whispered.

Hannah realized she'd been squeezing Ashley's shoulder and forced herself to loosen her grip. "Emma, if this is too much ..."

Emma shook her head. "He told me he was ready for me. He said, 'Your blood must be the perfect crimson, I can tell by your skin, you know.' I tried to just w-walk away, but he grabbed me. He told he'd been p-practicing on animals. Mice at first, then cats and dogs. He said he knew just where to c-c-cut—" Emma moaned, unable to go on, and a woman appeared—her mother—looking scared and angry.

"I knew this was a bad idea," she said, frantically tapping on the keyboard, trying to end the call. Emma screamed, a feral cry of rage, and grabbed her mother's hands.

"I have to finish," she said, her expression so primal that her mother stepped back. "I'm sorry," Emma said, her voice once again level. "After he said that, he tried to push me back into the girls' bathroom. I screamed and fought and managed to pull away ..." She shivered again, staring off at something the others couldn't see. "I can't help thinking what would have happened if he hadn't been waiting outside the bathroom, but came in. If he'd ... escalated just that much more." She gritted her teeth and took another deep breath. "I ran straight to the nurse. I was afraid to go to the principal."

"You wanted to talk to a woman," Ashley said softly.

Emma nodded. "Yeah. I didn't want to have to tell a man what Derek had said. It was just too ..." She shuddered. "Anyway, after all the meetings and talking to lawyers, there was nothing we could do. Derek said he'd seen me trying to hide something in the trash can outside the bathroom. He said it looked like drugs, so he confronted me, and I made up the rest to throw the spotlight on him. The police found a baggie with some marijuana in it. I'm sure Derek planted it there while he was waiting for me to come out of the bathroom. They investigated missing pets—and there were a few in his neighborhood —but there was nothing to prove he had anything to do with it. In the end, his family attorney negotiated just a suspension and Derek recanted that he saw me put the drugs in the trash as part of the deal. The kicker was the gag order that prevented me from telling anyone about my accusations. Rumors started anyway, but they didn't come from me." She gave a humorless laugh. "I guess I'm breaking that order now."

"We're not going to spread any of this around," Hannah said. "We promise. This is just so we know what we're dealing with."

Emma gave another one of those grim laughs. "At this point, I don't care. Let his lawyers come after me. What are they going to do?" She leaned forward, as if trying to get closer to Hannah and Ashley. "Just be careful, okay? I've been doing a lot of reading ... *research.*" Emma's eyes darted again to her mother. "He's not going to stop. And he will keep escalating. He may be stupid when it comes to school, but he's ... *sly* when it comes to what he does. The whole thing was premeditated, including his alibi by planting the weed." Her face hardened, and Hannah saw rage and conviction burning in her eyes. "Don't underestimate him."

chapter
forty-two

THEY ENDED the call a few minutes later, after Hannah and Ashley had thanked Emma profusely. They even made Emma bring her mother back on camera to thank *her*. Emma and her mom were both in tears as they disconnected, but Hannah thought they might be better off having had the call, too. Maybe it had helped them bond, or maybe letting Emma express herself had helped expel some of the rage. It made Hannah think about her conversation with Dr. Moore and wonder if Emma had the same opportunity. How could Emma not need professional help after something like that?

"Now what?" Ashley asked, pulling Hannah from her thoughts.

"I don't know," she said. "I do know we have to be careful. We know Derek has been following us around. But we're in the same boat Emma was; we have no proof."

"Everyone saw him at the bowling alley," Ashley argued.

"It's a public place on a Saturday night in a small town," Hannah said. "Who *wasn't* there?"

"We need a plan," Ashley said. "We can't *ever* be anywhere he can get one of us alone."

"That's definitely the first step, but we need more. We need to catch him doing something. We need witnesses, or ..."

Ashley smirked and tapped Hannah's head with her index finger. "What's going on up there, girl?"

Hannah smiled. "I think I have an idea."

"So, just how do you plan on getting this incriminating evidence, exactly?" Ashley was standing with a hand on her hip and her head cocked to one side. Hannah almost giggled at the incredulous look on her face. She looked like a teacher asking a scared student how that dirty word ended up on the whiteboard. "Do I have to ask you again?"

"Are you loath to repeat yourself?" Hannah managed between fits of laughter.

Ashley's attempt at a serious demeanor crumbled and she joined Hannah, snorting a laugh. "It's all fun and games until someone gets murdered by Hopedale's answer to Ed Gein," she said, again unable to keep a straight face.

"S-soup strikes again," Hannah said, doubling over.

"Unsolved murder at the brothel," Ashley said, howling, "Get it? *Broth*-el?"

Hannah knew they were using gallows humor to deflect the terrifying news they'd gotten from Emma, but it was cathartic. The laughter was just what they needed to ground themselves. "Damn, if all this crazy stuff wasn't going on in Hopedale, we'd have the makings of a career in comedy. Brothel, that's pretty good."

"Okay, okay," Ashley said, finally able to control herself. "Let's hear the plan."

"Technology," Hannah said.

Ashley leaned forward in anticipation. "And?"

"Think about it,' Hannah said, holding up her phone. "We have everything we need right here to get him. Just like you did with the fake blogger."

"You mean, like I would have done if one of us hadn't lost the phone."

Hannah felt the burn in her face. Ashley was just making a joke, but Hannah held a deep guilt about the impact that mistake had, what it cost. More than guilt, she felt shame.

"Hey, I'm sorry," Ashley said, reading the hurt on her friend's face.

Hannah shook her head, blinking back tears. "No, it's true," she said. "If I hadn't lost the phone, things might have played out a lot differently."

"Everything turned out fine in the end. Did you ever think if you didn't lose the phone, maybe you would have let the police do their job instead of tracking down Susan?" She paused, waiting for Hannah to figure out the rest. "Hannah, they never would have found the guy in time to stop the ritual."

Hannah opened her mouth to argue, then snapped it shut. Ashley was right. Even if they had figured out who the guy was right away and picked him up, there's no guarantee he would have said anything. Hannah shook her head. All this time she'd been beating herself up about losing the phone and it might have been a blessing in disguise. She lunged at Ashley and pulled her into a bear hug. Tears ran down her face and her sobs released weeks of pent-up grief and self-loathing. She finally let Ashley go and swiped the tear from her cheeks. "All this time, I didn't need therapy," she said, sniffling. "I just needed a dose of Ashley." She smiled, and another tear snuck out. "Thanks, Ash."

"At your service, fool," she said. "Now, let's nail down this plan. And maybe this time I'll hang on to the phone?"

Hannah stuck out her tongue. "Actually, I was thinking this might need to be a group effort." She waited for Ashley's response, hoping her friend would agree.

Ashley stared at the ceiling for a minute, then began to nod. "Team effort," she said. "If Dawn, Marcus, and Kenny are all in, we could pull a serious sting operation on Derek."

"It has to be foolproof," Hannah said, mustering her sternest voice. "No way can he get out of it, and no risk to any of us. *None*."

"It can be done," Ashley said, her face bright with excitement. "And I know the perfect time and place. The night of the burning wagon. Halloween."

Hannah thought about it. It would definitely be a night when most of Hopedale was out and about. Looking at it from Derek's perspective, everyone's focus—including the Hopedale Police—would be on the wagon and the trick-or-treaters. Halloween was notorious in Hopedale for teenagers partying in the woods and other shenanigans. Derek would see this as the perfect night to exact his revenge. "Ashley, you're a genius. An *evil* genius, but still. Derek will think he's in the clear to get us that night."

"And he'll conveniently know *where* to get us if a little birdie slips him the intel that we're in charge of the wagon this year."

Hannah gave her friend a look. "Everything about that is diabolical and perfect. Except for one thing."

"What's that?"

"Use of the word 'intel' eliminates you from spy of the year contention. Very bush-league." She waited for a laugh from Ashley but didn't get one. Instead, Ashley wore the same frightened look she'd had during the call with Emma.

"What aren't you saying, Ash?"

Ashley blinked and Hannah saw cold terror in her eyes. "Did you notice anything about Emma?"

Hannah thought back. Other than the fear and apprehension, she hadn't noticed anything. She shook her head.

"Emma looks just like you. You could be sisters."

Something twisted in Hannah's gut. She pictured Emma and realized with dread that Ashley was right. "These people," Ashley went on, "they usually have a type, right?"

"And I fit Derek's," Hannah said.

chapter
forty-three

HANNAH FIDGETED IN HER SEAT, eyes flicking to the clock for the millionth time. Mr. French gave her a curious look but kept going with his lecture. The plan that had sounded so simple before just felt foolish, now that the time had come to execute it.

She glanced at Marcus, who seemed to sense her looking and turned to her, giving her a slight nod. She reached into her notebook and slid out the folded sheet of paper with one word visible: *Marcus*. It was written in the girliest script she could muster—with purple ink, no less—and she'd even drawn a heart in place of the 'a' in his name.

When the bell finally rang, she gathered her books and stood, giving Derek Campbell a close-up of her butt when she did. Then, she dropped the note on the floor at her feet and rushed out of the room, feeling somehow slutty and clever at the same time. Once in the hall, she darted to her locker and waited for Marcus, as planned. A moment later, he strode toward her, wearing a goofy grin and giving her a thumbs-up.

"He jumped on the note like a football player on a fumble," he said, still grinning. "I thought he was going to pull a muscle getting to it."

"I'm surprised he even saw it," Hannah replied. "I could feel his eyes on my—" She stopped and felt heat rise in her cheeks. She'd almost mentioned her butt to Marcus. His red face told her she didn't catch her mistake in time, and she felt the needle move closer to *slutty*.

It's all for the best, she thought, Derek will get what he deserves.

"Well, that part of the plan was flawless," Marcus said, clearly trying to steer the subject away from her backside. "Now we just need everything to go smoothly on Halloween."

"Yeah," she replied softly. Marcus must have picked up on the doubt in her voice.

"Hey, what's wrong?"

"I just feel weird about the things I said in the note." She ground her teeth. "I don't like writing stuff like that, even if it's not true."

"Yeah, I know what you mean. But think of the alternative. What if we don't do anything, and he goes on to really hurt someone or ... you know."

Hannah did know. The conversation with Emma haunted her. And Ashley's observation about her resemblance to Emma was terrifying. Marcus was right: next time, Derek might not get interrupted. She shuddered just thinking about some poor girl — maybe even herself — being cornered by him. "You're right," she said, with renewed conviction. "Let's get him."

chapter
forty-four

DEREK TRUDGED up the cellar stairs, tired and angry from his second attempt at burying his mother's body. His second *failed* attempt. He'd only gone down to try it because he'd noticed a strange new smell in the house. Not the usual bad smells of his mother's cigarettes or rotting food from the dirty dishes in the sink or even his own body odor. This was worse than all those combined. And it didn't take him long to figure out where it was coming from.

As soon as he'd opened the door to the cellar, the stench had slapped him in the face, provoking a gagging cough that almost made him puke. The feeling had passed, and he'd become used to the smell. He'd stared at his mother for a long time, trying to see if she'd changed. She did look a little squishier, but otherwise the same.

He'd started digging again and had gotten almost two feet down when he'd hit a bed of crushed stones. They were a pain to try to dig out, so he'd dropped the shovel and gone back to staring at his mother. The lighting in the basement consisted of two bare bulbs hanging from wires, so when he'd seen something move on her face, he'd assumed it was a shadow. When he had looked closer, he had seen it was a fly creeping across her cheek. He'd waved it away, but it came back, followed by a second, then a third. When they began to find their way into her nose and eyes, he'd had enough.

The other reason he'd gone down there in the first place was to avoid dealing with the note that Hannah had dropped. He pulled it out of his pocket and unfolded it, feeling his anger rising just seeing the flowery, girly handwriting.

Marcus,

I want to talk to you about Halloween. I'm so glad we got to work on the wagon (and it came out AMAZING) but I'm a little worried about Derek finding out. If he knows we built the wagon, that means he knows EXACTLY where we'll be Halloween night. And you know how crazy it is in Hopedale, the entire police force will be busy breaking up parties and watching out for the trick-or-treaters. If he wanted to get back at us ... that would be the perfect time.

I know I'm being silly, sorry. We've made him look like a real clown a couple times already. Even if he had the guts to show up, which I doubt, we'll just handle it like we did at Champlain Park and that night outside May's. The more I think about it, I don't even know why I was worried. Part of me wants that jerk to show up just so we can beat him again!

Looking forward to the best Halloween ever! Tricks for Soup, treats for you!

Hannah

Derek snarled, squashing the paper in his meaty fist. He wanted to rip the note to shreds, wanted to rip Hannah and her stupid boyfriend to shreds as well. But he restrained himself. The letter also stirred strange feelings in him. Not the letter itself, but the circumstances of how he'd obtained it.

The way Hannah had stood in front of him, her butt close enough to touch. The way her yoga pants had looked. He'd almost been able to feel the heat coming off her body. Maybe there were other ways to get back at her, he realized.

A fly landed on him, and he swatted it away, thinking not of buzzing houseflies but blinking fireflies. The strange thoughts he'd been having about Hannah faded. No, he needed the anger the letter provoked in him. He wanted to hold on to that feeling of rage, that thirst for revenge, the desire to inflict pain and suffering. Yes, the letter would do that for him.

He opened his fist and smoothed out the letter as best he could on the table. He reread just the first paragraph again. Derek, like every kid his age, knew how the burning wagon worked. The group of kids who'd built the wagon would "sneak" it to the top of Black Hill Road. Of course, the cops knew it was happening, and simply looked the other way while this allegedly covert operation was taking place. A member of the Hopedale Fire Department—usually the youngest member, or youngest *looking*—would be there in street clothes to help them light it safely. Other members of the HFD were strategically placed along Black Hill Road, prepared to extinguish a runaway wagon or other fires caused by stray sparks. This was all done to maintain the illusion that the Hopedale Police were unaware of the event and the kids had miraculously pulled off the prank again.

Derek clenched his fists, thinking about Hannah and Marcus and the others all right there at the top of Black Hill Road. His for the taking. And what better night to wreak such havoc than Halloween? Maybe he would take care of the others and save Hannah for later. Yes, maybe Hannah would join his mother in the basement.

chapter
forty-five

DEREK STARED at the group of kids at the corner table. He knew he shouldn't be watching them but knowing it and doing something about it were two different things. The Diaz kid looked up, catching his gaze. Derek grinned and Diaz quickly turned away. *Maybe he felt me watching him. Maybe it's one of the powers I gained from the fireflies.* He longed for the summer when he could see them again. He should have captured some in a jar. He could have learned so much more from them.

"Mr. Campbell!"

Derek turned to see Mr. French, face red, eyes blazing. "What?" He realized French must have been talking to him while he was thinking about ... What had he been thinking about? Yes, the fireflies.

"What, exactly, are you doing, Campbell?"

Derek shrugged, paying no attention to the irritation in French's voice. "Just standing here," he replied. He wasn't in the mood for French hassling him. He saw Diaz and the rest of them watching eagerly. He grinned. Maybe he'd give them a show. He turned to Mr. French, and said in a raised voice, "Is there some rule against me standing here, minding my own business?"

French gave Derek a humorless smile. "The thing is, Campbell, I don't think you were minding your own business." He stepped closer. "I think you were feeding your obsession with Marcus Diaz and Hannah Green."

Derek narrowed his eyes. When he spoke, his voice was just below a shout. "No crime looking at people, is there? *Frenchie*." He smiled at French's reaction. The guy's face looked like a giant blood blister with eyes.

"Crime?" Mr. French replied. He grinned, and Derek questioned how far he wanted to push the guy. "No, not a crime at all. But given your history, it's enough to concern me. You see, stalking *is* a crime, and what you're doing is starting to fit the definition. Unfortunately, I can't really do anything about it. *Yet*."

Derek scoffed and turned away, wanting to see Diaz's reaction. Before he could, French grabbed his upper arm in a surprisingly strong grip. "But," he continued, "speaking to a teacher with disrespect is something I *can* address. Immediately." He turned toward the door. "Let's take a walk, shall we? I think you know the way to the office?" He dragged Derek along.

Derek managed a look back at the corner table and wished he hadn't. They were all staring at him. Staring and laughing. He tried to pull away from Mr. French, but the teacher's grip was like iron. Once they were in the hall, out of view of Diaz and his friends, Derek hissed, "You're not supposed to put your hands on a student. I could sue you."

French didn't break stride and kept pulling him toward the principal's office. "Sue away, Mr. Campbell. I'll even discuss the lawsuit with your mother when I call her."

Derek opened his mouth to reply, but no words came. His jaw hung open as he stumbled to keep up with Mr. French's pace. Something about French calling his mother had stopped Derek's response cold. Why should he care? He'd been in trouble plenty. Then the vision of his mother's half-buried corpse in the basement hit him. He stopped walking, but French didn't. Derek was almost pulled off his feet, but the teacher steadied him.

"You c-can't call my mother," he said.

"That horse, as they say, has already left the barn, Campbell."

French's words were like clubs, bludgeoning Derek with their power. With their *potential*. After a few unsuccessful tries to reach his mother, someone would eventually check on her. Maybe someone from the school, but probably they'd just have the Hopedale Police do a wellness check. At some point they'd get a search warrant, or some other legal means to enter the Campbell home. All the times he'd been told he was stupid echoed in his head, but he knew how this would end. He knew enough about probabilities. Maybe they wouldn't notice the smell, but *probably* would. Maybe they wouldn't find the body, but *probably* would. Maybe Derek wouldn't be arrested, but—

He closed his eyes and saw the message the fireflies were sending. *Play it, cool, man.* "Please, Mr. French," Derek said, his voice several octaves higher than normal. He was looking around wildly, as if help might be nearby. Part of it was acting, but most of it was real fear. The kind that hunkered down in your gut and grew from there. Gnawing its way into your chest. "Please, give me detention, but don't call Mom. I can't ... she can't take any more ..."

French stared at him, sizing him up. "Give me one good reason why I shouldn't call her."

Derek bit his lip. To French it probably looked like remorse, but Derek was doing his best to suppress a grin. Maybe even a giggle. He knew he had him. "It's just ... since my dad ... she's been really sad, depressed. I'm afraid if I ..." Derek swallowed hard and rubbed his eye with a knuckle. "I'm afraid if I ... disappoint her again ..." He stared at his shoes for a long beat before risking a glance at French. The man was not just staring at him, he was examining him, as if searching for anything that would give away his lie. Finally, French sighed.

"Very well, Campbell," he said, "no phone call. You will report to detention, and you will toe the line. I'll be watching you, and so will the rest of the faculty. I'll be alerting them to what's going on. All eyes will be on you." He stepped closer to Derek. "There's something more than a grudge here. If you so much as look at any of those kids the wrong way, I won't be calling your mother, I'll be driving over there to talk to her myself." He leaned in closer still, and it was all Derek could do not to head butt him. "And I won't be alone, I'll have one of Hopedale's finest with me. Then we'll see what's what. Do you *feel me*, Campbell?"

Derek choked back a laugh and hoped it sounded like a sob. He somehow managed to squeeze out a tear, not wiping it away as it etched a wet snail track down his cheek. He nodded, then when French started toward the office, he followed.

chapter
forty-six

DEREK STEPPED INTO THE HOUSE, about to call out to his mother that he was home when the smell hit him, reminding him that she wouldn't be answering. Strangely, the smell didn't really bother him anymore. It served as a reminder of who he was. Who he had *become*. How powerful he was. Still, he thought, if anyone comes to the door ... A sudden idea struck him, sending a knife of fear into his gut. What if people can smell it outside? It occurred to him that he might just be desensitized to the smell. As quickly as it came, the fear dissipated. This phase of his plan—of his *transformation*—was nearing the end. Come November first, he would be dust in the wind. When he reemerged, he would no longer be Derek Campbell. He would truly be Lord of the Fireflies.

He realized he was still standing in the open doorway and swung the door shut behind him. Like so many of his ideas, the plan to deal with Marcus Diaz and the others had come from nowhere. He'd come to start thinking of them as "those meddling kids," always in the voice of a Scooby Doo villain. One minute he was reminiscing about the time he'd captured a cicada killer and dropped it into the complex and somehow mesmerizing web of a huge spider in his basement. The next minute, the answer was there.

Not a nugget or an idea to build upon, the entire plan laid out in his head, beginning to end. To the bloody end. He had a lot of preparations to attend to and a short time to do it. Everything would be so much easier if he didn't have school eating up most of his day. The thought to simply stop going was a pleasant one, but with French on his back already it would only draw unwanted attention. And that meant unwanted visitors to the house. No, he had to keep up appearances. He had to keep on keeping on. Keep the faith. Keep on loving you. He began to giggle.

chapter
forty-seven

HANNAH SAT across from Dr. Moore, waiting for him to start. All the emotion of their first session had come flooding back once she'd entered the waiting room. Now, sitting on the same chair where she'd opened Pandora's box, she wanted to get up and run. She risked a glance at Dr. Moore. He was reviewing his notes from the last session but must have felt her gaze. He raised his eyes, offered a small smile, then went back to reading. *Is this a trick? Is he waiting for me to start talking?*

Dr. Moore flipped the page of the notebook and clicked his pen. Hannah watched him write the date on the top of the fresh page. "Okay," he said, adjusting his position. "How are you doing, Hannah?"

Hannah stared. *That's it? After baring my soul to him a week ago, that's all he has for questions?*

Dr. Moore somehow perceived her frustration. "It's okay, Hannah. We don't have to pick up where we left off last time." He crossed his legs, leaning back. "Sometimes it helps just to have a normal conversation where you don't have to feel like a patient." He waited, then repeated, "How are you doing?"

"I ... Okay, I guess."

"Can you elaborate?" Dr. Moore wore a bemused expression. "Is okay good or not so good?"

Hannah tried to think of an answer that was noncommittal until she got her bearings. Dr. Moore had her off kilter and she felt trapped. "Both, I guess," she said, avoiding his eyes.

"Well then, where should we start? With the good okay or the bad okay?"

"I guess the good okay," Hannah said slowly. Dr. Moore gave her a nod, encouraging her to continue. "Everything at home is good, you know, with my dad. And I have a boyfriend, Marcus, and a lot of really good friends."

"That is good, Hannah," Dr. Moore said with a warm smile. "Now, why don't we talk a little about the things that aren't so good?"

Hannah clenched her jaw, then nodded. "There's a kid at school, Derek, who's sort of terrorizing me and my friends."

Dr. Moore frowned, then jotted something down in his notebook and said, "You mean he's bullying you and your friends?"

Hannah hesitated. *Is he bullying them?* "It sort of started out that way, but ..." She pictured Derek at Champlain Park, at the window of the pizza place, and at the bowling alley. "Now it's more like he just shows up wherever we go. He doesn't always say anything ... he's just *there*." Deep lines appeared on Dr. Moore's forehead. He straightened up in his chair.

"Hannah, is this boy stalking you and your friends?"

Hannah considered this for a beat before answering. "I'm not sure. I mean, he definitely has it out for us. He's holding a grudge because I laughed at him in class one day." She pictured Derek's bushy eyebrows waggling but now it didn't seem so funny. "Since then, he's threatened my friends, and like I said, he's been showing up everywhere we go. The thing is ..."

Dr. Moore made another note, then said, "Hannah, this is a very serious matter and a situation that could become dangerous."

"There are rumors," Hannah said softly, "about things he's done in the past. Scary stories. And we talked to one of the girls that was involved." She sighed. "So, I guess they're not rumors. Derek caught this girl in the hall at school when nobody else was around and said some things to her. Sick, disturbing things." The doctor's jaw flexed, and his eyes narrowed slightly.

"Have you told your father about this? Or the school authorities?" Dr. Moore's voice was tight, far from his usual gentle tone.

"This happened a while ago," Hannah said carefully. "I think he was disciplined for it."

"I think it would be prudent to inform your father. This boy ... Derek?"

"Yes, Derek Campbell," Hannah said. She watched color rise in Dr. Moore's cheeks.

"He sounds like he's escalating. The way he's following you and your friends could be indicative of a growing obsession. It's something he may act on, and not necessarily verbally."

Shaken, Hannah stared at Dr. Moore. She hadn't expected this strong a reaction to her story. The fact that it was coming from a professional had her rattled. "Okay," she said, "I'll tell Dad."

"I want to you promise you'll take this seriously." Dr. Moore's tone had gone from one of professional concern to that of a stern parent.

"Of course," she replied. "That's why I brought it up."

Still, she had neglected to tell him about her resemblance to Emma.

Something occurred to her, triggered by Moore's reaction. Before she could stop herself, she blurted it out: "You *know* him. Did you treat him after the incident with Emma?"

Moore's head jerked up from his notes. "Hannah, I can't discuss any people I may or may not have treated. Just as I would never reveal your name to anyone." He went back to his notes, but she had seen him stiffen at the question. It was all the answer she needed.

chapter
forty-eight

HANNAH JOGGED across the parking lot where her father sat waiting. She smiled at Scout, his head hanging out the back window, tongue wagging. She stopped to give him a pat then jumped into the passenger seat. Her dad had the usual classic rock station playing and he turned up the volume as he pulled out of the parking lot. It was becoming a sort of tradition. He knew she didn't want to talk right after therapy, so he let them both tune out to his oldies. Bob Dylan was telling the story of Hurricane Carter, a song that always made Hannah sad for the world.

She closed her eyes thinking about the session with Dr. Moore. It had gone well, she thought. After the short discussion about Derek, she'd focused on the growing complexity of her friendship with Ashley as her time was spread thinner between Marcus and Dawn. That had led to a lengthy conversation, specifically about Dawn. She'd told Dr. Moore about her growing concerns for her new friend, about the mood swings.

For the rest of the session, they'd talked about Hannah's mom. Looking back, she wished she'd started with that topic. Time had run out before they were even close to examining her conflicting emotions. She told Dr. Moore about her anger and confusion about her mother being there in the clearing that night. Knowing it was Ashley on the stone slab and apparently still willing to go ahead with the ritual.

She stared out the window as they drove through town, listening now to some old Chicago song, heavy on the horns, before they'd gone soft, according to her dad. The day was warm and overcast, not quite an Indian summer day, but pretty nice for October in New Hampshire. Chicago ended and J. Geils started, reminding Hannah of a story her dad had told about the night he and his friends had gone to the Boston Garden to see Geils in concert. It was something about them drinking beer while riding the train to North Station. She smiled to herself, her mood lifting despite the gloomy day and the therapy hangover.

"Dad, is Rick coming over tonight?" The question was out before she'd realized she'd come to a decision.

"Not until after dinner," her father said. "He's meeting with the woman who recognized your mother." He paused, worry lines creasing his face. "The assistant DA and the woman's lawyer are going to be there. Rick expects her lawyer to lay out the plea bargain demands for cooperating."

Hannah contemplated this and decided it didn't matter. Tonight, she was going to finally open up to both of them about therapy. She thought she was making good progress and hadn't had one of those "lost time" episodes in a while. She wanted to put it all behind her and enjoy high school. She also wanted to tell her dad and Rick that she approved of their rela-tionship. It sounded silly to her to put it that way, but Dr. Moore had said it was important to make sure communication lines were open, and honesty was the best way to accomplish that. They had discussed how Hannah felt about her dad's relationship, and it became clear to her that she was truly happy about it. She wanted her father to be happy—and to her, it seemed like a long time since he had been, until Rick came around.

She realized her father had said something, but she was too deep in thought to catch it. "Sorry, Dad, I was just thinking about something Dr. Moore said. What were you saying?"

"I was just wondering why you were asking about Rick."

Hannah could read his expression like a billboard. He was worried that something had been revealed at therapy. "Because I'm ready," she said. "Ready to talk to you and Rick about therapy. About everything Dr. Moore and I have been talking about. Mama Bayole, the cult, Mom, you and Rick … everything." He didn't respond right away. She glanced at him and for once couldn't read his expression. "Is that okay?"

He smiled, but his eyes were shiny with tears. "That's great, honey." When the song changed to Bruce reminiscing about Glory Days, he turned the radio up and sang along with it. Hannah couldn't help but join in.

chapter
forty-nine

"YOU KNOW THIS IS INSANE, RIGHT?" Ashley said.

Hannah peered at her friend through the darkness, considering the question. They were on Black Hill Road in the pitch black at ten o'clock at night. After Hannah had had her heart-to-heart with Dad and Rick about therapy— though for some reason she had not told them about Derek— she was wiped out. She cajoled her father into letting her hang with Ashley, claiming she needed to clear her head. Hannah had told her dad they were walking to Dawn's house and would be home by eleven. They'd walked up and down the road twice already. Hannah was hoping to see Lonesome Amie. All things considered; Ashley's question was a fair one. "Dispute not with her: she is lunatic," she replied with a giggle.

"No shit," Ashley muttered.

"That was Shakespeare, for your information," Hannah said, smacking Ashley on the shoulder.

"You don't say? I thought it was a quote from your dad." She paused. "Or, literally, anyone else who knows you."

Hannah laughed. "That's the spirit, Ash." She barked out another laugh. "Get it? *Spirit*?"

"Seriously, Hannah, how about we call it a night?" Ashley

had reluctantly agreed to the plan, but Hannah could tell she was bored. The spookiest thing they'd seen was a deer. True, it had scared the crap out of them when it bounded across the street, but still, maybe Ashley was right.

"Okay," she sighed. "We'll go to the top of the hill, then turn around and head home."

Ashley recognized the disappointment in her voice. "Maybe we can try again another night?"

"I don't know," Hannah said. "Maybe this whole thing is just ..." She didn't want to say 'stupid' because it would mean she didn't believe Dawn and Mrs. Cheevers, and she *did* believe them.

"Maybe she only shows herself, like, when people aren't expecting it?"

Hannah knew Ashley was trying to cheer her up, one of the countless reasons they were best friends. "Maybe—"

A branch snapped in the woods behind her.

"Did you hear that?" Hannah whirled around.

Ashley grabbed Hannah's arm. "I'm not deaf," she said, but her tone lacked its usual brashness. "Probably just another deer."

Hannah peered into the darkness beyond the tree line. "Why didn't we bring a flashlight?" she muttered, pulling out her phone. The flashlight app's beam did little to penetrate the murky shadows beyond the road.

"Ghosts are supposed to, like, *glow*," Ashley said. "Why would we need a flashlight?"

"Excellent point," she said, then went quiet when something rustled in the undergrowth very close to where they stood. Ashley's grip on Hannah's arm tightened.

"Hannah? I don't think ghosts snap branches and make the leaves rustle."

Hannah grasped her friend's hand and hissed, "Run!" She took off, not letting go of Ashley's hand. They didn't stop until they reached the streetlight at the bottom of the hill. Hannah put her hands on her knees and tried to catch her breath.

Ashley gasped. "What was that?"

Hannah shook her head, forcing a laugh. "Probably a deer, like you said."

"No way," Ashley said, staring up the hill. "I heard footsteps. Like, *people* footsteps."

Hannah followed Ashley's gaze up Black Hill Road. "Come on, Ash," she said, "You can't be sure—"

"No." Ashley's voice rose. "Don't do this. I heard someone walking in the woods practically right next to us. A deer doesn't make that kind of sound walking, and it would have run away, not gotten closer."

Hannah shivered. Ashley was right. A deer wouldn't have snapped a branch either, not one big enough to make that loud a noise. "Could it be a bear?"

"Why are you being like this?" Ashley said, her voice tinted with anger. "Someone was in the woods. Following us. Not a deer. Not a bear. And not the ghost of Lonesome Amie. A real person."

Hannah froze. A thought so chilling hit her that she was unable to speak. She couldn't get air. She reached for Ashley, but she was suddenly too far away. It was as though she was looking at her through the wrong end of a telescope. She heard Ashley calling her name from miles away. Then someone was shaking her. She blinked, gulping at the air, finally able to breathe.

"Hannah? Are you okay?" Ashley's voice was shrill. Panicky.

Hannah nodded, trying to regulate her breathing. Then, she burst into tears. Ashley wrapped her in a tight hug and held her until she was able to get control of herself. "We have to get out of here. What if it's the cult?"

Ashley pulled away and stared at her, eyes wide. "Oh, crap. I didn't even think of that." She stared up the road again, her face creased with tension. "Can you run?"

Hannah was still crying, but she nodded. "Let's go, Ash. I'm scared."

Ashley took her hand, and they began running toward Hannah's house.

Hannah thought she heard laughter echoing in the woods behind them.

chapter
fifty

"YOU KNOW that was no ghost, right?" Ashley said quietly.

Hannah considered the question. Actually, she was just stalling for time. They were in Hannah's bedroom, after putting on convincing smiles for her dad about the walk to and from Dawn's house. The truth was, she'd thought about it the entire walk home and didn't know what to make of it.

"I don't think it was a ghost," she said. "Remember I saw someone in the gazebo that night after bowling?"

Ashley nodded.

"I was wondering if it might be ..."

"The same person?" Ashley finished, then her eyes widened as she said, "Your mother?"

"Maybe. I don't know. The thing is, nobody else saw anyone that night—"

"But Marcus found the cigarette butt. And tonight, I heard someone just like you did."

"I know," Hannah said, unable to keep the frustration out of her voice. "It just doesn't make sense. Like, why would she watch me from a distance and creep around in the woods following me, scaring the crap out of me?"

"Maybe she thinks you hate her because she left," Ashley

said, then winced, probably realizing how harsh it sounded. "Or maybe she's got amnesia or something and isn't sure who you are."

Hannah knew her friend was trying to help, trying to cheer her up, but that wasn't really what was bothering her. It was something that had occurred to her after the panic of thinking it might be a cult member had subsided. What if her mother was leading the cult now? Then she had another thought, so obvious it should have been her first. "What if it was Derek?"

Ashley's face tightened, then she said, "That actually makes more sense." She got up, drawing a cocked head from Scout, and paced the room. "Doesn't he live not far from there?" She snapped her fingers. "Maybe he was trying to get up the courage to try something."

Scout gave an exaggerated sigh and put his head back down.

"Aaaash," Hannah said slowly, "how dangerous is he?"

Ashley's face seemed to darken. This time, Hannah could tell, Ashley was being selective with her words. "I think it depends on the situation. Like, in school or when there's a crowd of us, I think he'd start a fight and I could see him getting carried away and really hurting someone. You heard what Emma said."

Hannah wanted Ashley to confirm her suspicions. To say it out loud and make it real. She said, "But if there *wasn't* a crowd, if he followed two girls on a dark road at night?"

Ashley's eyes showed real fear. She licked her lips, then swallowed.

"I think he might ..." Ashley sat down hard on the bed, elbows on knees, head in hands. "I think he could do anything." She looked at Hannah. "I think I'm gonna be sick."

Hannah got to her feet. "I'll get you a drink. Don't move." She moved as fast as her unsteady legs would carry her to the kitchen for a can of Coke. Thankfully, her dad was asleep in the recliner. She grabbed two cans and slipped quietly back into the bedroom.

"He might have tried to rape us," Ashley said, and her face contorted into an ugly mix of rage and disgust. She closed her eyes, then opened them slowly. "He might have killed us."

"Here," Hannah said, holding out one of the sodas. They both opened their cans and took a drink.

Ashley let out a shaky sigh. "This is gonna sound weird, but I think I'm more afraid of Derek than I was of Mama Bayole."

chapter **fifty-one**

ASHLEY OPENED the door and stepped into her house, expecting dinner preparations to be in full swing. Instead, it was eerily silent. She peeked into the living room on her way by, stepping into the empty kitchen. Normally, she'd be bewildered at the lack of activity but with everything else going on, she was unsettled. She opened her mouth to call out, then thought better of it. The sound of a door closing followed by footsteps quickened her pulse. She swallowed hard but then recognized her mother's steps as she came down the stairs.

"Mom?" she called out.

"Oh," her mother replied, clearly startled. "I didn't hear you come in."

Ashley waited for her in the kitchen. When her mother entered, it did nothing to quell her uneasiness. Mrs. Wallace was always put together, as if she expected guests to arrive any moment. Ashley's dad joked that she rolled out of bed ready to host a party. He had once called her June Cleaver and Ashley had found a rerun of the old *Leave it to Beaver* sitcom to understand the reference. Her mother didn't run around vacuuming the house wearing pearls, but the point was valid.

Now, however, her mother looked distraught. Her blouse was untucked on one side and her ponytail was crooked. Ashley felt nauseated when it occurred to her she might have caught her parents fooling around. But one look at her mother's tense face told her that was not what was going on. "Mom, are you okay?"

Her mother smiled tightly. "Of course, why wouldn't I be?"

"You look … disheveled. And usually, you're cooking dinner at this time."

"Your father and I are going out to dinner," her mother replied, too quickly. "I thought I'd mentioned it. Do you mind just getting a pizza delivered?"

Ashley shook her head. "No, that's fine. What's the occasion?"

"Nothing special, it's just been a while since we've been out. Your father wants to try a new Italian place in Manchester."

Ashley nodded slowly. Something wasn't right. Her father's footsteps echoed in the hall as he made his way downstairs.

"Hi, honey," he said. "Did Mom tell you the plan?"

"Sure did," Ashley said, studying her father. He was stressed, his face set in hard lines, even his body held rigid. "Are you guys going to keep up this 'date night' story or tell me what's going on?"

Her father's eyes darted to her mother, then he tried to cover it up with a perplexed looking smile. "Ashley—"

She held up her hands, not having any more of it. "Never mind, just leave me money for the pizza guy, okay?" She shouldered past her father and ran up the stairs, tears stinging the back of her eyes. Her parents both called after her, but she silenced them with a slam of her door. She knew it was childish but at the same time she was furious that they treated her like she was too stupid to see that something was going on.

A few minutes later, a knock sounded at the door, followed by her father's voice: "Ashley, can I come in? We should talk—"

"Are you going to tell me what's up?" she called back. A long pause gave her the answer. "Just go to dinner, okay? I don't want to talk right now."

"Are you sure you're okay?"

Her father sounded so despondent she almost ran to the door and threw it open to give him a hug. She clenched her teeth and squeezed her eyes shut so tight it hurt. "I'm fine, really. We can talk when you get home." Another long pause.

"Okay," he said. "Money for pizza is on the counter."

She waited until she heard his footsteps retreating before she relaxed. Earlier that year, when her parents had been having trouble, she'd figured it out, and when she confronted them, they were very honest about it. What could be so bad—worse than the possibility of divorce—that they were keeping it from her? She thought back to the conversation with Hannah about her mom possibly being pregnant and now realized how silly it was. She choked back a sob when the thought hit her: which one of them is sick?

She grabbed her cell and called Hannah's home number.

"Hannah Green's answering service, how may I help you, Miss Wallace?"

Ashley couldn't help but smile at Mr. Green's lame dad joke. "Hey, Mr. G, did you guys finally get caller ID out in the sticks, or are you psychic?"

Mr. Green laughed. "Caller ID today, indoor plumbing tomorrow. Sorry, kid, Hannah just took Scout for a walk. You can try her cell ..."

Ashley laughed. "Maybe after indoor plumbing you'll get cell service. Thanks, Mr. G. Just tell her I called, please?"

"Sure thing."

Ashley ended the call and then scrolled through her contacts for Dawn's number. *Will Hannah be mad?* She shook her head. She had to talk to someone, or she was going to drive herself crazy coming up with horrible scenarios about her parents.

"Hello?"

Ashley smiled sadly. Dawn sounded so tentative. "Hey, Dawn, it's Ashley."

"Oh, hi!"

Ashley almost laughed out loud at the change in her tone. Who did she think was calling? "Hannah gave me your number; I hope that's okay?"

"Yeah, totally fine," she said. "What's up?"

Ashley gulped in a breath and let the tears flow. She held the phone too tightly as she sobbed.

"Ashley? Are you okay?" Dawn's voice sounded so far away, so concerned.

She took a couple of deep breaths and managed, "Sorry."

"Ashley, what's wrong? Are you hurt?" Concern had turned the corner to fear.

"I'm all right, really," she said, and took another long, slow breath. "I didn't mean to scare you ... I just needed somebody to talk to."

"It's fine, as long as I know you're not hurt. What is it? Did something happen to Hannah?"

Ashley choked back another sob. It made sense that Dawn would think that. A wave of guilt coursed through her. Was she using Dawn? Calling in the back-up friend because Hannah wasn't available immediately?

"No, no, it's nothing like that. Maybe I shouldn't have called."

"I'm glad you did. Really. It sounds like you needed to

hear another voice. You don't have to tell me what happened, we can just talk if it helps?"

The sincerity and kindness in Dawn's voice brought another round of sobs. "Gah, I'm really sorry," she finally sputtered. "I feel like a jerk calling you in this state." Her phone buzzed and she saw Hannah trying to call her back. She bit her lip, then declined the call. "It's just ... my parents have been acting really weird and they keep telling me nothing's wrong, but I know something's wrong and I'm afraid one of them is really sick or something ..." She stopped, realizing she'd been babbling.

"What do you mean when you say they've been acting weird?" Dawn asked.

Ashley paused, wanting to answer more coherently this time. She didn't want Dawn to think she was a raving lunatic. "It's hard to explain. Like, I walk into a room and they both stop talking and look at me. They've always been very open with me and are always relaxed when we're all together." She laughed. "Before tonight, I thought my mom might be pregnant and that was the big secret."

"What happened tonight? To change your mind, I mean."

"When I got back, at first, I didn't think anyone was home. That would have been really strange, because they never both go out without letting me know. And my mom is kind of anal about certain things, dinner being one of them. When I got home, she should have been in the kitchen, cooking. She came downstairs and told me they were going out for a meal. Dad came down a few minutes later and they both ... they just looked tense, on edge. I confronted them and they said nothing was wrong, but I know there is something. I got upset and stormed up to my room," she said, and barked out a bitter noise. "Like a five-year-old throwing a tantrum. They ended up going to dinner, and here I am freaking out."

"Wow," Dawn said. "I'm really sorry to hear this. I don't

know what to say ... maybe you should try talking to them again when they get home? I know it sounds lame—"

Ashley sighed. "No, it doesn't sound lame. It sounds mature. I'm really glad you were here for me, Dawn, but ..."

"What is it?"

"Part of me is afraid they'll tell me."

chapter
fifty-two

DAWN HUNG up the phone and turned to find her father staring at her.

"Dawn, what is it? Did something happen with your friends?" Her father's face was creased with worry.

She sighed. It was no use trying to fool him. He may not have been the same person he was before, but his dad-radar was in perfect working order. "I'm okay, really." She thought about it, then smiled. She really was okay. "I never had good friends back in Hartford, but Hannah and Ashley are good friends."

"I don't understand. Then why do you look so upset?"

Dawn laughed and wiped a sneaky tear from her eye. "I'm not upset," she said. "I think ... I think I'm happy. For the first time in a long time. And I'm not sure how to deal with it. I'm not sure I deserve it."

Her father wrapped her in a hug. "Dawn, of course you deserve to be happy. What happened back there, in Hartford ..."

She waited, trying not to let her body tense. They'd never really talked about that day. The day her little sister died. She wasn't sure how much her father blamed her.

"You know I love you," he whispered, holding her tight.

"Your mother ..."

Dawn's muscles turned to stone. All the warmth left her body. She didn't want to hear this.

"...Your mother didn't know how to deal with her grief. She lashed out, looking for someone to blame. Looking for a reason." He sighed, pulling away and putting a gentle hand under her chin, tilting her head to look at him. "She used you as a target for her own anger and confusion. And guilt," he added, shaking his head. "It was wrong. It's *still* wrong and it's not fair that you carry that weight around every day." He put his hands on her shoulders. "Listen: you did not have anything to do with what happened to Eden. You deserve to be happy."

Dawn's body went limp, and she fell into her father's arms. The tears poured out of her as her entire body trembled. It was as if she was trying to expel all the sadness and regret and confusion, squeezing it all out of her in the form of tears. Her father whispered over and over that she deserved happiness. Deserved the good friends she'd found. Deserved the new life they were starting. At some point—she wasn't sure how much time had passed—her tears ran out. She felt like a dried-up husk. She was exhausted, mentally and physically.

"Thank you," she managed, her scorched throat allowing just a croak. "I need to rest, okay?" Her father nodded, his own eyes red-rimmed and glistening. "I love you, Daddy," she said, and gave him another hug. She held on, suddenly so tired she thought she'd slip to the floor if she were to let go.

When she felt like she could walk again, she said goodnight and headed to her room. The memories of the day Eden died were somehow fresher since they'd moved. Like a scab had been ripped off the wound in her heart. She still didn't know who was right: her father for loving her, or her mother for blaming her. She closed her eyes and willed the dreams to stay away, but they never did.

chapter
fifty-three

DAWN WOKE from the clutches of her nightmare, sweaty and shaky and sad. She uttered a frustrated sigh. Would the dreams ever end? She knew sleep wouldn't be easy so she decided to focus on her present situation. The past was too painful. Her father was adjusting to life as a single parent, and despite his lapses into morose silence, seemed to be doing better in Hopedale. She had already made a group of new friends who all seemed nice. And then there was Kenny. When she'd met him during that painful first week of school, she thought he was going to be like the kids back in Hartford. Listening to rumors and judging her on her eclectic sense of style. But then something changed. She was pretty sure he liked her. And she *knew* she liked him.

Derek Campbell. The name popped up in her head like an evil Jack-in-the-box. That kid was beyond creepy. The way he stared at her and kept showing up everywhere she went. Was he following her? Stalking her? Or was it because of his grudge against Hannah and Marcus and the fact that she'd been with them? Or had he seen her throw the football?

Dawn paced about her room. The bone-tiredness she'd felt moments before was gone, replaced with a manic, nervous energy. If she couldn't solve the problems that plagued her past, she could work on the ones troubling her now. What was there to do about someone harassing her? The police would laugh it off, chalking it up to boys being boys. That was best case. If they looked into Dawn's past, maybe they'd set her in their crosshairs instead of Derek. She couldn't worry her father with it.

Friends, she thought, I have friends that can help. She flopped back on her bed and closed her eyes. "I'll call in five minutes," she said, again wondering why she was talking to herself so much.

Dawn woke up feeling like she'd never slept. A pain at the base of her skull signaled the approach of one of her killer migraines. She should take a Lasmiditan and stay in bed. If she caught it early enough, it would save her a lot of pain. School, however, couldn't be missed. She dragged herself out of bed slowly, trying to limit any sudden movements that would worsen her headache. She took a pill before getting in the shower.

Twenty minutes later, when she was dressed and ready for school, the pain had intensified and the lights in the house suddenly seemed too bright. Her common sense and experience told her it was a bad idea to try to push through it, but her instincts were overruling that part of her. She had learned over the years to trust her feelings, and right now, going to school to deal with Derek was what her gut was telling her to do. *Screaming* at her to do. She grabbed her backpack.

She made it as far as the kitchen before her father stopped her. "You've got one of your migraines," he said. "You need to go back to bed."

Dawn smiled and shook her head, sending tidal waves of

pain through her skull. "I took a Lasmiditan as soon as I felt it coming on. I'm already feeling better," she lied.

Her father squinted. "Dawn, I've seen you suffer through enough of these to know when it's just building and when it's receding. This one is still on its way."

"I'll be okay, Dad, I promise. It's not that bad and I really caught it early. If it starts getting worse, I'll go see the nurse." She knew he wasn't buying it, but she had to get to school. Whatever intuition she possessed was compelling her to go against what she knew was the smart thing to do. She doubled down on the lie. "I have an algebra test second period; I'll leave after that. I can't get further behind." Her father cringed, and she knew he was blaming himself for everything that had happened in Hartford. His guilt for moving at the beginning of her first year of high school would win and he'd let her go. At that moment, the victory did not feel worth the shame she felt. She vowed to sit down and have a real conversation with him when this was over. Get everything out in the open: what she was going through now and what had happened last year.

"Okay," he said, defeated. "Have the nurse call me and I'll come get you."

"Thanks, Dad," she said, forcing a smile. She gave him a hug, preventing her expression from revealing the jarring pain that small movement caused. Then she turned, and walked to the door, willing her legs not to buckle or her balance to fail. She made it out and slumped against the side of the house to let the dizziness pass before she headed for the bus stop.

chapter
fifty-four

DAWN SAT in second period math class trying to focus on what Mr. Kaplan was saying. In the rare moments where the tide of her migraine ebbed and she could think clearly, she agonized over the lies she'd told her father. *At least second period really is math.* One less lie.

"Miss Holman?" Dawn looked up, ignoring the auras that surrounded whatever she was trying to focus on. "Are you still with us?"

"Yes," she croaked. "I just have a bad headache."

"Do you need to see the nurse? You don't look well," Mr. Kaplan said.

She clenched her teeth and tried to nod, but it sent fresh waves of agony radiating from the base of her skull up to her temples. Instead, she said, "No, I'll be okay." Mr. Kaplan watched her for a moment longer, then continued with the lesson. Dawn closed her eyes, again trying to will away the pain. When she opened them, Mr. Kaplan was standing directly in front of her. He was leaning toward her, one hand extended. Dawn gasped, confused by the sudden time jump. Then she felt the eyes of the class and knew she'd either passed out or had a mild seizure.

She got to her feet, grabbing her books and bag, planning to go to the nurse and have the school call her father. She reached for her math book, but her hand remained empty. She stared, uncomprehending, as her hand seemed to float right through the book.

Mr. Kaplan said something, drawing her attention away from the spectacle of her semi-transparent, disembodied hand. She gasped. The teacher was surrounded by a shimmering, multi-colored aura. His mouth was moving but she heard no words. Then Mr. Kaplan began to waver, becoming transparent, too.

chapter
fifty-five

HANNAH PUT her lunch on the tray—allegedly meatloaf and mashed potatoes, but it could have been anything—and scanned the cafeteria for Dawn. She spied Marcus and Kenny at their usual table and went over to join them.

"Where's Dawn?" she asked, taking the seat next to Marcus. She saw the two exchange a furtive look and something started squeezing her guts. "What? Is she okay?" A thought struck her like a wrecking ball. "Did Derek do something?"

"We're not sure what happened," Marcus said calmly. "But Rhonda King said she sort of passed out in Kaplan's class and was sent home."

Hannah was suddenly afraid. Dawn hadn't looked well in first period, but Hannah had stayed to ask Mr. Costello a question about homework and hadn't had a chance to check in with Dawn. Her fear went beyond normal concern for a possibly sick friend. It was dread, a gnawing sense that something was *very* wrong. Buried beneath her unease about Dawn was a sickening feeling of jealousy. Rhonda King was a blonde-haired, blue-eyed cheerleader who somehow had a golden-brown tan all year long. Her athletic body and dazzling smile made her the prettiest freshman at Hopeland High School. She pushed the image away of a smiling Rhonda leaning in with her patented low-cut blouse to tell Marcus about Dawn.

"She passed out? Is she okay? I mean, did they call an ambulance or anything?" Hannah was blurting out questions without waiting for answers. "Did anyone try to call her?" The two boys looked at each other again, then shook their heads. Hannah sighed, resisting the urge to roll her eyes and make a derogatory comment about boys. "Never mind," she said. "I'll try her." She got up and went to the hallway where it was quieter, and pulled out her cell phone.

She tried Dawn's cell first, but it went straight to voicemail. She ended the call and tried the house number. It rang five times before Dawn's father's voice came on telling her to leave a message. Hannah smiled when she heard Dawn in the background telling him which button to press to end the message. She left him a quick voicemail with her cell number. She redialed Dawn's cell and this time blurted out a message. "Dawn, it's Hannah. Are you okay? Weird stories going around at school and we're all worried. Call me back."

She hurried back to the table. Her friends' faces were filled with apprehension. She noticed Kenny's usual half-smirk was missing, replaced by a heartbreaking sadness. "No answer at either number. I left her a message on her cell to call me."

Kenny stood. "I'm going to the nurse to find out what happened. If she's in the hospital—" Hannah sensed he was angry at himself for not acting sooner. "I never thought it might be anything serious ..." He didn't say anything more, just turned and stalked away.

Hannah watched, stunned, as Kenny left the cafeteria. He was always the one to make a joke and downplay stressful situations. Now, here he was, risking getting in trouble to find out what happened to Dawn. "Wow," she said after the door had slammed shut. "He *really* likes her, doesn't he?"

Marcus pulled his gaze away from the cafeteria door and turned to Hannah. "Yeah. I mean, I knew he liked her a lot, but I've never seen him like this. Did you see his face?"

Hannah nodded. Kenny had looked beyond troubled. He'd looked scared. "We should go with him—" Hannah was interrupted by the buzz of her cell phone vibrating. It was a local number, but one she didn't recognize. "Hello?"

"Hello, Hannah. This is Mr. Holman." She nudged Marcus, who had gone back to staring at the cafeteria door, and mouthed 'Dawn's father' to him, pointing at the phone. "I just got your message. I'm still at the hospital with Dawn." He paused, and Hannah heard him heave a deep sigh. "She's prone to migraines. She has been ever since …" Hannah looked at the phone to make sure the connection hadn't dropped, then Mr. Holman continued. "I knew she had one brewing but she insisted she had to go to school today. I should have made her stay home." Hannah cringed at the burning guilt that filled his voice. "Anyway, this one was bad, and she became disoriented in class. She may have gone unconscious very briefly. She's doing okay but we are still waiting for some test results. I wanted to thank you for calling. For being such a good friend to her."

Hannah swallowed, overcome with emotion. Mr. Holman was in pain. The anxiety for his daughter was clear, but so was the remorse he held for not following his instincts. "She's a good friend to us, Mr. Holman. We're all very worried. Can we see her?" She glanced at Marcus, who was now staring at her, eyes wide with worry.

"I'm not sure if they are going to admit her. I guess it depends on the test results." His words hung there, ominous in their possibilities. "If they do, I'm sure she'd love to see you. If they let her go home, of course you're all welcome to visit her. I'll let you know as soon as I hear anything."

Hannah said goodbye and ended the call, then brought Marcus up to date.

"We should go get Kenny before he causes a scene," he said with a wry grin.

Hannah smiled, picturing Kenny going off on the nurse to get information from her. "Yeah," she said, getting to her feet. "Let's go save him from himself."

Hannah followed Marcus down the hall, both jogging in the hope of catching up to Kenny before he got himself in trouble. They turned the corner that led to the office and heard Kenny's exasperated voice.

"I'm not asking for her medical history; I just want to know if she's okay!"

Hannah smiled at Marcus and opened the door, stepping into the office and grabbing Kenny by the shoulder before he could continue his rant. "It's okay," she said softly. "Mr. Holman just called back."

Kenny turned, red-faced and sweaty. "She's all right?"

Hannah nodded. "He said she gets migraines and she tried to push through instead of staying home. She's at the hospital, they're waiting for some test results."

Kenny opened his mouth to say something, then blinked, as if remembering where he was. He turned to the administrative assistant, Mrs. Fountain. He gave a slight bow, back in normal Kenny mode.

"Thank you for your assistance, you've been a font of information. And I apologize, I didn't mean to spout off. My friends and I are going to jet. Hope springs eternal."

Hannah laughed as she and Marcus dragged him out to the hall. Mrs. Fountain had been Principal Meadows' assistant since dinosaurs roamed the earth. She was known for many things; a sense of humor wasn't one of them. Hannah had seen color rising in her cheeks just before she pulled Kenny away. One more fountain joke and he might have ended up in detention anyway.

"Did he say anything else?" Kenny asked once Hannah had got her giggles under control.

"No, that was it."

"Well, I'm going to the hospital to make sure she's okay," Kenny said, heading for the door.

"Whoa," Marcus said, grabbing his sleeve. "We just saved you from getting detention, now you're going to leave school and end up in trouble anyway?"

Kenny gave him a humorless smile. "What would you do if it were Hannah?"

Marcus started to say something, then nodded and let go of Kenny's sweatshirt. "You're right," he said. "I'm coming with you."

chapter
fifty-six

HANNAH WAS TORN. She'd never been in trouble at school, and leaving without permission was certainly going to end that streak. But she wanted to be there for Dawn.

"Hold on," she said. "I'm going, too, but maybe we can go without getting in trouble. Wait here." She bolted down the hall and knocked on Mr. French's door.

"Come in," he called.

Hannah opened the door and stepped inside. Mr. French was in the middle of lunch; a huge salad and a Tupperware container of what looked like plain chicken. She frowned, then shook her head. "I'm sorry to interrupt your lunch," she said breathlessly. "Remember you said to keep being a good friend?" She waited a second until recognition crossed his face. "I'm going to do that now. Marcus, Kenny, and I have to go see Dawn at the hospital. I know it's against the rules, but ..." She shrugged, smiled meekly. "If you can help, I'd really appreciate it." Before he could answer, she'd left the office and closed the door behind her.

She hustled back to Marcus and Kenny. "Let's go."

They got outside and stopped on the top step. Hannah saw her confusion mirrored in their expressions. "Ummm," she began, feeling foolish. They'd been working on emotion and adrenaline instead of brains. They had no way to get to the hospital.

Kenny snapped his fingers and pulled out his phone. "My parents set me up with an Uber account. For emergencies. I think this qualifies." He tapped madly on his phone, then looked up. "Victor will be here in nine minutes."

Marcus slapped him on the back. "I'm glad one of us is thinking."

"We should wait somewhere else," Hannah said. "If a teacher comes out, we might not be going anywhere."

Kenny nodded. "Now *two* of us are thinking. When are you going to contribute something to this effort, Diaz?"

Marcus rolled his eyes and started down the steps. "Let Victor know we'll be at the flagpole," he called back.

Hannah snaked an arm around Marcus's waist and followed. A beat-up Dodge Caravan pulled in seven minutes later.

"Victor, I presume," Kenny said to the harried-looking man behind the wheel as they piled in. The man didn't smile, just nodded and watched them in the rear-view mirror until they all had seatbelts secure, then pulled out.

His eyes kept darting to the mirror as he drove toward the hospital. Finally, while idling at a red light, he turned and said, "Shouldn't you kids be in school?"

Hannah had been getting nervous about the way he'd kept looking at them. Would she ever stop being suspicious of new people? Afraid that they might be one of Mama Bayole's followers? Then she realized he was the nervous one. He probably thought he was going to get in trouble for driving minors around during school hours.

"It's okay," she said. "We have permission to go visit one of our teachers who just had surgery. They allow three students each day, you know, so everyone doesn't show up at once after school."

The man visibly relaxed. "Oh, that's nice," he said. "Is your teacher going to be all right?"

Kenny leaned forward, all in on the story. "We are praying he pulls through," he said, keeping his voice low. "You see, it's sort of our fault that he's in there."

Hannah bit her lip, afraid she'd burst out laughing when she heard whatever nonsense Kenny was about to roll out. She glanced at Marcus, but he'd turned to look out the window, no doubt for the same reason.

"Oh?" Victor said, eyes at the mirror again.

"Yes, I'm afraid so," Kenny went on. "We presented our class project the other day. It was a reenactment of the survivors of the USS Indianapolis. You know that story Quint tells in *Jaws*?"

Victor's eyes brightened. "Yeah, yeah, the ship that delivered the bomb!"

"Right," Kenny said gravely. "But Quint's story is only part of what they went through. I—" Kenny swallowed hard as if he was struggling to go on. Hannah coughed into her hands to hide a giggle. "Anyway, I guess we got a little too graphic with the shark attack, and poor Mr. Curly, well, I'm afraid the strain was more than he could bear."

Hannah leaned forward, out of Victor's sight, shaking with laughter. Marcus made a sound that she recognized as his attempt to conceal laughter. Somehow, Kenny held a straight face.

They reached the hospital and the three tumbled out of the car, holding their gales of laughter until Victor had driven away.

"Dude," Marcus said, "where do you come up with this stuff?"

263

"What do you mean, 'come up with'," said Hannah, "everything he just said was stolen from a movie!"

Kenny feigned shock. "My dear, *stolen* is such a harsh word. I'm merely paying homage."

This sparked fresh howls from Marcus and Hannah. "You could have at least stuck to one movie with your *homage*," Hannah said. "The *Jaws/Tombstone* mash-up was a bit much."

Kenny held his hands out wide, palms up. "Why limit myself when I have such incredible range?"

Marcus punched Kenny on the arm. "Let's go pay homage to your girlfriend," he said with a wicked grin.

Kenny's face reddened. "Who said she was my girlfriend?"

Hannah rolled her eyes at Marcus and started toward the entrance.

"Wait," Kenny said, jogging to catch up. "Did Dawn say she was my girlfriend?"

Marcus caught up to Hannah and took her hand, still grinning.

"Come on, you guys," Kenny said, his voice bordering on a whine. "Are you messing with me?"

Once inside the hospital, Kenny stopped pestering them. They approached the information desk and Hannah inquired about Dawn.

"She's in room 423," the woman told them, and pointed toward the elevators.

They rode in silence. Hannah couldn't stop thinking about the last time she'd been in the hospital, to visit Jake. It was in the middle of the whole Mama Bayole thing, and she realized she now associated the hospital with the incident. *File that away for therapy*. Big Jake was doing just fine, but Hannah couldn't shake the bad feelings.

Marcus tightened his grip on her hand. "You okay?"

She gave him a curt nod but didn't answer. She didn't trust her voice. The elevator seemed smaller than it had when they'd piled in. *What if it gets stuck?* Her cheeks and hands suddenly grew warm and tingly. Marcus was saying something else, but it sounded like it was coming from far away. She stared at the numbers on the elevator's display, positive that the car would lurch to a sudden stop, alarm ringing. Or worse, it would stop, and the power would go out, plunging them into silent darkness.

When the elevator did stop and the robotic voice told them they were on the fourth floor, Hannah moaned. The doors slid open, and she leaped out into the corridor, gasping for breath.

chapter
fifty-seven

"HANNAH!" Marcus's voice was panicked, that much got through the buzzing in Hannah's head. She was flexing her hands open and closed, trying to get rid of that tingling sensation. Her breath came in short gulps.

"Take a deep breath, Hannah. You have to slow down your breathing and that weird feeling in your hands will go away."

She turned to see Kenny calmly trying to talk her down. Marcus stood next to him in a state of panic. It was the combination of Kenny's poise and Marcus's terror that helped her level off. She finally managed a deep breath, and when she let it out, she burst into tears. Marcus stepped in front of Kenny and took her in his arms.

"It's okay," he whispered, repeating it until she was able to regain her composure.

After a couple of minutes—or hours, Hannah wasn't sure —she pulled away, wiping her face.

Marcus handed her a tissue. "What happened? I mean, what caused that?"

She blew her nose. "I don't know," she said at last. "I just started thinking about the last time I was here, then ... but I'm okay now, thanks guys. I'm just going to find a restroom to clean up. I'll meet you in Dawn's room?"

Frown lines creased Marcus's face. "Are you sure?"

She nodded and gave his hand a squeeze. "423, I'll be there in a minute." She turned and scanned the hall for a restroom, seeing the sign just a ways down. She washed her face and blew her nose again, then stared at herself in the mirror. *What just happened?* She heaved in a breath and let it out slowly, then went to join the others to check on Dawn.

When she entered room 423, all conversation ceased, and four concerned faces turned to her. "Wow," she said, wearing a humorless smile. "Very subtle." Three of the four faces reddened.

Mr. Holman stepped toward her, unabashed. "Yes, we were talking about you. Your friends are very worried. Are you all right?"

She smiled—a real smile, this time—and nodded. "Yeah, I just freaked out. Hospitals do that, I guess." She craned her neck to see around Mr. Holman. "Hey, Dawn. Sorry to steal your limelight." To her surprise, Dawn laughed. Hannah didn't know what she'd been expecting but her friend looked like herself. If a little pale. "How are you?"

"I'm fine," Dawn said, giving her father a look that Hannah couldn't read. "I get migraines and I tried to push through this one and just got dizzy—"

"You didn't 'just get dizzy'. You passed out," Mr. Holman said, not unkindly but with an edge. He turned to Hannah. "The doctors ran some tests to be safe. The bottom line is, Dawn needs to take these migraines seriously and heed her body's warnings."

"Dad ..."

Mr. Holman whirled and stepped to the bed. "Don't 'Dad' me," he said gently, taking her hand. "I can't stand the thought of anything happening to you."

Dawn paled more, her eyes filling with tears. "I'm sorry. You're right, I wasn't thinking."

Mr. Holman patted her hand. "You're okay, that's the important thing—"

"Excuse me?" They all turned to the voice. It was an older man dressed in doctor's scrubs. "May I have a word, Mr. Holman?" He smiled at the others. "Sorry to interrupt, kids."

Mr. Holman gave Dawn's hand a squeeze and followed the doctor out of the room.

Kenny looked shaken. "Are you really okay?" Even though Dawn appeared to be all right, Hannah knew it was a shock to see anyone in a hospital bed. Her heart went out to Kenny, considering the feelings he had for Dawn.

"I'm really all right," Dawn said. "I'm sorry to scare everyone like that. I just ..."

Kenny moved closer to her. "What is it?"

"I knew the migraine was coming, I should have stayed home. But I wanted to talk to you guys—" She stopped suddenly, looking around. "Where's Ashley?"

"Oh, she has a different lunch, she was in class when we ..." Hannah suddenly realized she hadn't thought of her best friend once since stepping into the cafeteria. She'll understand, Hannah thought, but still feeling like the world's *worst* best friend.

"... Ditched school," Kenny finished with a wink.

Hannah noticed Marcus's serious expression. He said, "What did you want to talk to us about?"

Dawn's gaze moved from Marcus to Kenny, finally landing on Hannah. "Derek Campbell."

Hannah slapped a palm to her forehead. How had they forgotten to fill Dawn in on their Halloween plan? They quickly brought her up to speed; Hannah noticed her friend looked better already after hearing the plan.

"ASH, is everything okay? You sound off." Hannah sat on the edge of her bed, rubbing Scout's belly with her free hand. She'd just finished telling Ashley about ditching school and the visit with Dawn.

"Fine," Ashley said, in a tone that screamed anything *but* fine.

"Come on, Ash, it's me." Hannah switched the phone to her right hand, grimacing as she wiped the sweat from the left one. She knew what was bothering Ashley. She'd preemptively apologized but it didn't appear that was going to be enough.

"What happened when Mr. Holman came back? You were about to tell me that part."

Hannah knew Ashley was still upset, but she also knew her well enough to understand she wasn't going to get a straight answer on the phone. "It was really weird," she said. "When the doctor asked to speak to him, Mr. Holman had been very quiet. Subdued, you know? Clearly worried about Dawn. But when he came back, he was practically giddy. Talking loudly and laughing at stuff that wasn't funny ... I don't know."

"It sounds like the doctor gave him good news," Ashley

said. "He was probably relieved and that's why he was actually different."

Hannah thought about it, picturing Mr. Holman when he stepped back into the room. "Yeah, I guess you're right. It just seemed odd."

"I don't know," Ashley said. "Maybe you just misread him."

"Maybe," Hannah said firmly. "If you were there—"

"Well, I wasn't," Ashley snapped.

Hannah recoiled, holding the phone away from her ear and staring at it as if she'd be able to see her friend. "Ashley ..." Hannah had known she was upset but had never imagined she would lash out like that.

"I have to go," Ashley said.

"No, Ash. It all happened so fast, and it was a spur of the moment decision to go—"

"I have to go," Ashley repeated. Her voice was low but sharp. "I'll see you at school tomorrow. *Maybe.*"

"Wait—" Ashley hung up. Hannah put the phone down on her bed and stretched out next to Scout. He nuzzled her and whimpered a little. "I know, buddy," she whispered to him. "It will be okay." She wondered if that were true. She picked up the phone and punched in Marcus's number.

"Hey, Hannah," he said. He always sounded genuinely happy to hear her voice.

"Hey," she said.

"You okay?" The concern in his voice was unmistakable.

"Yeah. No. I don't know." She sniffed. "Ashley is either mad at me, or just sad that she wasn't with us today."

"Why would she be mad?" Marcus sounded confused. "I mean, it's not like it was something fun."

"I know, it's just ..." Hannah paused, not sure she could explain it. "I guess we've been through so much together, it feels like we should go through *everything* together. Does that make sense?"

"Yeah," Marcus said. "I get it." Hannah could almost hear the smile in his voice.

"It's like that for you and Kenny, isn't it?"

"I guess so."

Hannah could hear the wheels turning. "What is it?"

"Do you think Ashley is jealous of Dawn? Like, she thinks of her as a threat to your friendship?"

Hannah considered it. Ashley's vitriolic tone echoed in Hannah's head: *Well, I wasn't.* She understood the statement could mean that Ashley was upset for more reasons than just not being there.

"Hannah?"

"Yeah, sorry." She felt worse knowing that Ashley might be concerned she was losing her best friend. "I'm sure that's what it is."

"You guys will be fine," Marcus said brightly. "It's like you said, you've been through a lot together. Compared to last summer, this is nothing."

"Yeah, you're right," Hannah agreed, but *was* he right? She wasn't so sure.

HANNAH HAD BEEN SITTING in Dr. Moore's waiting room for fifteen minutes agonizing over what to talk about. So much was going on that she didn't think forty-five minutes would be enough to even get started. Did she dare talk about Derek, suspecting that Dr. Moore had treated him? And what if he was *still* treating him, and he was telling Dr. Moore his twisted side of the story? Her panic attack on the elevator at the hospital? Then there was the complexity of having two besties.

What about Mom? The thought had hit her with an almost physical force. Knowing that her mother was alive, that she had been part of Mama Bayole's cult, was weighing on her terribly, and probably caused her the most stress. Then there was Dad and Rick Benson's relationship. She scoffed at the relative normalcy of that topic. No, given everything else, that was the least of her worries.

When the door to Doctor Moore's office opened and he gestured for her to come in, Hannah's stomach tightened. She still hadn't decided what to focus on. As she moved past him, he gave her a curious look, then shut the door after her.

Once she was settled in the chair and they had exchanged a

few pleasantries, Dr. Moore's visage tightened, and he went into what Hannah called therapy mode. "I couldn't help but notice how upset—no, that's not right—how *confused* you looked in the waiting room."

Hannah smiled to herself. Dr. Moore rarely came out with direct questions. His therapy mode consisted of his making observations and waiting for her to comment. She had conjured up the memory of an old Seinfeld rerun and a quote by Newman. *You really think you can manipulate that beautiful young woman like the half-soused nightclub rabble that lap up your inane "observations"?*

"Did I say something funny?" Dr. Moore was smirking a bit.

Hannah felt her cheeks heating up. "No, it wasn't you. Just something I was thinking about. Sorry." She tried not to picture Newman in Dr. Moore's chair, fingers steepled, talking in that haughty tone of his. She began to giggle, and slapped both hands to her mouth in shock, as if she could stuff the giggles back where they'd come from. Dr. Moore had gone from smirk to full smile. He waited calmly while she got herself under control. He handed her a tissue—the ones reserved for crying patients—and she used it to wipe the tears of laughter from her face. "I'm sorry," she said again.

"Don't apologize," Dr, Moore said. "It's not often enough I hear laughter in this room."

"I'm really, really sorry," she said. "But I needed that. All right," Hannah said, sitting up straighter, as if it gave her a more serious demeanor. "I'm ready."

Dr. Moore raised his eyebrows and Hannah realized she'd never responded to him. "The truth is," she said, "I was all worried about what to talk to you about, then I came in and wasted half the session laughing."

This time it was Dr. Moore who laughed. "Well, it is the best medicine," he said. "Or so I read somewhere."

Hannah smiled, realizing she actually liked talking to him. Even more, she trusted him. "There's a lot going on at home, with my friends, with ..." She hesitated. Did she trust him enough to mention Derek again? Yes, she decided. "With Derek, too."

"Hannah," Dr. Moore said, his face going back to serious therapist mode again. "You don't have to worry about talking about Derek with me."

Hannah looked at him for a long time, then nodded. "Okay. The truth is I'm scared of him. All my friends are, too. Not just in the way I'd be scared of a bully."

"Can you elaborate on what it is about him that scares you?" Dr. Moore's voice was steady but when Hannah looked at him, his unease was unmistakable.

"I think you already know the answer to that." Hannah forced herself to hold his eyes. She felt an odd sense of victory when he looked down and jotted something in his notebook. Or pretended to, she thought.

"If you're not comfortable speaking with me because you suspect I've treated Derek Campbell, this isn't going to work."

This time it was Hannah that looked away first. "We spoke to Emma Gould," she said softly, raising her eyes to gauge his reaction. To his credit, Dr. Moore's expression remained placid.

Hannah sighed. "Maybe you're right. Maybe this isn't going to work." She realized the thought was jarring. She'd come to look forward in a way to the sessions with him. She thought they were helping. She wanted him to help her deal with whatever lasting impacts the events with Mama Bayole were causing. And more so, her feelings about her mother.

"You look like you want to say more," Dr. Moore prodded.

Hannah steeled herself, feeling like she was under a magnifying glass. "I want to keep coming, but I don't think we can talk about Derek Campbell." Dr. Moore began to speak but Hannah cut him off. "I need to be able to trust you in order to … to tell you the things I tell you. You having knowledge about Derek that you won't—*can't*—share is going to weaken that trust for me. So, I won't bring him up again, even if that is what I need to talk about most. I know what he said to Emma, I just want you to know that much."

Dr. Moore wore the ghost of a smile before speaking. "I can live with that," he said. "Under one condition. If you ever feel like you're in real danger—I mean *imminent peril*— you must tell me."

Hannah nodded curtly, again feeling that sense of victory. What, exactly, she'd won she wasn't sure, but it was still a good feeling.

"So," Dr. Moore said, glancing at the clock, "what should we talk about?"

chapter
sixty

ASHLEY SAT IN THE LIBRARY, staring at the computer screen. She'd entered the words "Holman, Hartford, death" in the search engine. Her finger hovered over the ENTER key. Did she really want to do this? The conversation with Hannah the night before still stung. "*No way, if you were there—*" She glanced furtively around the room, feeling silly. She'd skipped soccer practice and had ridden her bike to the West Meadow library so she wouldn't have to look over her shoulder like she would in Hopedale.

It had been harder than she'd thought. Locking her bike to the bike rack had given her a chilling sense of déjà vu. When she'd stepped into the building, memories of her previous trip there had assaulted her. The meeting with the person she'd thought was a blogger who might help them. *We have Hannah.* She'd managed to push those thoughts away. She needed answers. If Dawn was hiding something, Hannah might be in trouble.

Then why not just go to the Hopedale library, Ashley? She couldn't shake the nagging voice in her head. Probably because she didn't like the answers to the questions it was asking. Hot shame coursed through her. She knew her face had gone beet red and was glad nobody was there to see it. Especially Mrs. Cheevers. She chewed the inside of her cheek, staring at the words in the search window. It took all her self-awareness to admit to herself that she was here because of her anger and jealousy at being excluded, not because she was concerned for Hannah's safety. Still, she hit the ENTER key. Yes, she'd come for the wrong reasons, but the possibility existed that Hannah was in danger. Maybe that was an exaggeration, but perhaps Dawn wasn't who they all thought she was. She scanned through the search results—and there were a *lot*—looking for a reputable source without a paywall.

Ashley read the first story from *The Hartford Courant.* It described the breaking news of the suspicious death of an infant. Details were sketchy but an autopsy was being requested and both parents were being questioned. The baby's older sibling was being held in child services until more information was available.

Ashley sat back and exhaled deeply. The rumors from earlier in the school year swirled in her head. Could Dawn have had something to do with it? And the article mentioned parents—plural—so where was Dawn's mother? Ashley returned to the search results and was about to click on the next link, then stopped. She pictured herself hunched over the computer, reading all the lurid details of the case. The weight of what she was doing, the *indignity* of it, brought a knot of chagrin to her gut. She clicked out of the browser and stepped back from the table shakily, her stomach threatening to betray her and expel her lunch all over the library's carpet. She turned and fled.

It took her three tries to get the right combination to unlock her bike from the rack, her hands were shaking so badly, her vision blurred by tears. Who was she? What kind of person was she? Trying to sabotage her best friend's relationship with Dawn out of petty jealousy? She climbed on her bike and started pedaling toward Hannah's house. She knew Hannah had therapy but hoped she'd be home by the time she got there.

When she'd gone into the library the day was cool and clear. Now, thick clouds hung low in the sky, bloated with rain. A light drizzle pelted her face as she rode. The soft breeze that had been at her back was now a stiffening headwind making the ride more difficult. The temperature had dropped, too. She hoped she could get to Hannah's before the skies opened. *It's what I deserve*. She glanced up, pedaling faster under the darkening clouds.

Thunder rumbled in the distance as she turned onto Hannah's street. The drizzle had become steady, pasting her hair to her neck and soaking her jeans and hoodie. She passed the empty lot where Mama Bayole's farm had stood, the smell of burnt wood lingering even after all this time. She shivered, partly due to the weather but more because of the memories that haunted her. She pedaled faster, wondering if she'd ever be able to forget the way she'd felt locked in that basement room, sure she was going to die. Her breath came in heaving gasps. Her legs felt suddenly powerless, and she feared she would lose control of the bike.

She skidded to a stop at Hannah's and jumped off her bike, stumbling as she tried to run up the steps. She began simultaneously ringing the doorbell and pounding on the door. The door opened and she fell into Brian Green's arms, sobbing and dripping wet.

chapter
sixty-one

"ASHLEY, what's wrong? Did something happen?"

She clung to him desperately, a life preserver in a stormy sea of emotion. What was happening to her? Hot tears soaked his shirt as he led her into the living room. Scout rubbed against her legs, whimpering. She was vaguely aware of a door opening and footsteps approaching.

"Ash!" Hannah was next to her on the couch, pulling her into a hug.

"I'll put on some tea," Brian said, uncertainty in his voice. "Ashley, should I call your folks?"

She shook her head against Hannah's shoulder as violent tremors ripped through her.

"It's okay, Dad," Hannah said gently. "Tea would be great."

Ashley felt Hannah grab her even tighter and it brought a fresh round of sobs. She couldn't control the shaking and was unable to speak. She had so much she wanted to say, but her throat was closing, making it hard to breathe, let alone speak.

"It's okay, Ash," Hannah said softly. Ashley focused on those three words, clung to them, wanting to believe them. The teapot whistled in the kitchen and Ashley focused her attention on the sounds of Mr. Green getting mugs and pouring tea and adding heaps of sugar. *Normal* things. When he brought the tea in, she had managed to compose herself, at least to the point where she felt coherent.

"Ash, what happened?"

Ashley thanked Brian for the tea but didn't respond to Hannah. After an awkward moment, she glanced up at Brian.

"Oh," he said. "I better go check on ... the thing." He started back toward the kitchen, then paused. "Ashley, you are okay, right?"

"Yeah, Mr. G, I'll be fine. Just ...I don't know. A panic attack, I guess." He held her gaze for a long beat, then nodded and disappeared into the kitchen.

"When you're ready to talk, I'm here," Hannah said.

The combination of warmth and disquiet in her friend's voice brought another wave of deep shame, and with it, fresh tears. She sipped her tea, trying to form the right words in her head. "I'm sorry, Hannah." It wasn't enough, but it was a place to start. She watched Hannah's face cloud with confusion. "Let me go on, okay?" Hannah nodded and Ashley took a deep breath. "I haven't been a very good friend," she finally said, and proceeded to tell Hannah about the trip to the West Meadow library and how she was about to dig into Dawn's history in Hartford. She stared into her teacup, unable to meet her friend's eyes. "I stopped when I read the first article, I swear. I was just so upset that I wasn't there to help Kenny and visit Dawn. And, I guess, I was jealous that you are Dawn were getting so close."

"I get it," Hannah said.

Ashley was finally able to look her friend in the eye. "You do?"

"Well, yeah. I know it's been hard because I spend time with Marcus that used to be *our* time. And then the whole group of us ditch school without Ashley Wallace?"

Ashley smiled for the first time all day. "Thanks for understanding. I feel like a witch." She shook her head at the poor choice of words.

Hannah was staring at her. *Examining* her. "Is that all? You were really upset?"

"No," Ashley said. "When I left the library, I kind of freaked out. I don't know what happened. I was thinking about the last time I was there, then when I was riding home and I passed Mama Bayole's place and smelled the fire …"

Hannah leaned in and hugged her, practically spilling the rest of her tea on both of them. "That stuff is going to happen," Hannah said, "Dr. Moore told me there could be triggers for years to come that set off that kind of reaction."

"Wow," Ashley said. "I have all *that* to look forward to." She grabbed Hannah's hand. "I'm really sorry. I feel like I betrayed you and Dawn."

Hannah shook her head. "We're good, Ash, I promise."

"One more thing," Ashley said. "While I was still debating over whether or not to look up Dawn's history, I googled Michael Gaines." Hannah frowned. The name rang a bell but she couldn't place it. "Remember? The guy Mrs. Cheevers was with on Black Hill Road?" Hannah nodded. "He killed himself. Based on the date, it probably wasn't long after that night on Black Hill Road. Do you think it was because of Lonesome Amie? Remember Mrs. C said he felt like the ghost was marking him."

Hannah recoiled. "It could be a million things that led to that. But, still…"

Ashley noticed something in Hannah's expression: what she saw on her friend's face signaled something else was bothering her. She made a 'spill it' gesture, twirling one finger. "Come on, I bared my black soul to you. Now you need to tell me what's eating you."

"I'm really worried about Dawn," Hannah blurted out. "I know it's the last thing you want to hear, but—"

"No," Ashley said. "Don't do that, okay? If we're good, then you need to know it's okay to care about Dawn."

"Thanks, Ash."

"Why don't we go check on her? I owe her an apology anyway."

Hannah stood and pulled Ash to her feet. "Great idea. Dad, can you—"

Brian walked in jingling the car keys.

"Really, Mr. G?" Ashley said.

"I only heard the tail end, I swear," he said, blushing.

chapter sixty-two

THE RIDE to the hospital was uneventful, if not a bit awkward. Hannah didn't know how much her dad had actually heard. Not to mention *any* trip to the hospital brought back painful memories of visiting Jake and the very adult conversation she'd had with him in private about Mama Bayole. Not to mention her incident on the elevator. She felt Dad's eyes on her as he drove.

"So," he said, "did the doctors give you any idea what's wrong with Dawn?"

"No," Hannah replied. "They were running tests, that's all we know."

"Do you know what kind of tests? I mean, does she have some sort of condition, or did this just come out of nowhere?"

Hannah squirmed in her seat. She really didn't want to talk about it. Truth be told, she didn't even want to *think* about it. She just wanted to make sure they were all friends. But her father's words had planted an ugly seed. *What if she did have something wrong with her?* The memory of the first day she'd hung out with Dawn. The weird trance-like thing in the pizza place, then the sudden mood change.

"Hannah?"

"Oh," she said, not realizing she'd gotten lost in her thoughts. "Mr. Holman said she has a history of migraines. I guess she has medication and if she takes it as soon as she feels one coming on, she's okay."

Her father looked like he was going to ask another question when Ashley perked up from the back seat. "Mr. G, where have you been hiding your better half? I haven't seen him around?"

Hannah smiled. Their friendship may have hit a rocky patch, but their mind meld was working perfectly. Ashley was trying to derail him from any further questions.

"He's been, uh, busy with a new case, I guess."

Hannah stared at her father. What was he doing? She remembered when he had lied about not knowing why her mom had left. What was he lying about now?

"What is it, some super-villain jaywalker in town?" Ashley joked. "Or is somebody mixing trash in with their recycling?"

Hannah watched her father field the question. She could tell he was uncomfortable even as he faked a laugh. "I'm not sure, he doesn't talk much about work."

Hannah turned back and gave Ashley a look. Sometimes their mind meld thing worked too well. Her friend's eyes were filled with sorrow. And something else. Something like fear. Hannah gave a barely perceptible shake of her head, signaling that particular line of conversation was over.

"Dad, did I tell you I scheduled another appointment with Dr. Moore?" Hannah cringed, hearing the near-panic pitch of her voice.

Her father didn't miss it either; he did a double take before turning his concentration back to the road. "Yes, you mentioned it. Is there something urgent you need to talk with him about?"

Hannah ground her teeth together. *Idiot.* Just the way her father had chosen his words, spoken them so carefully. As though they'd had sharp edges. As if they might hurt her. "No, I, uh, just wanted to make sure you could drive me." *Did that sound even vaguely convincing?*

"No problem," he replied slowly, eyeing her as he drove. "Honey, are you okay?"

She sighed, the concern in his voice nearly breaking her. "I guess so," she said, turning to look out the window. "It's just ..."

Her father had pulled up to the visitors' entrance to the hospital and put the car in park. "Ash, why don't you run ahead, I need to talk to Hannah for a minute."

"Dad—" She heard the back door open.

"It's okay, Hannah, I'll wait inside. Thanks for the ride, Mr. G."

The door closed and Hannah suddenly felt trapped. "Dad ..." she repeated.

"It's okay," he said. "I'm not going to sit here and grill you about Dawn or whatever's going on with you and Ashley." He took her hand and turned in his seat, leaning close. "I just want you to know I'm here for you if you need anything. *Anything*. And I'm sorry I was evasive about Rick. When the time is right, I'll tell you what's going on. It's nothing bad, I promise."

Relief coursed through Hannah, and she leaned in to hug her father. Whatever was going on between him and Rick suddenly felt less scary. "Thanks, Dad." She couldn't wait to tell Ashley there was nothing to worry about.

"I just need to know you're safe," her father said. "Promise me you're safe?"

"I promise," she said, tears welling in her eyes. "I love you." She gave him another hug, then jumped out of the car before she completely fell apart. *Why hadn't she told him about Derek?*

Ashley was waiting in the lobby and rushed over to Hannah when she spotted her. "What was that all about?"

"Sorry," Hannah said, wiping her face with her sleeve. "I don't want him worrying but *I'm* really worried about Dawn. Then when you tried to change the subject—thank you, by the way—I knew he wasn't telling me something. He just confessed that there is something going on with Rick and he'd tell me when the time is right."

Ashley gave her a quick hug. "Your dad is the best." They started walking toward the elevator. "Any idea what the big secret is with Rick?"

Hannah shook her head. "It has something to do with my mother."

"Oh."

Ashley gave her a tight-lipped smile and shrugged, pushing the button.

The elevator opened and Hannah pushed her friend into the car. "Let's go," she said, laughing.

The elevator ride was uneventful, making Hannah wonder why she'd freaked out the last time. Dawn looked up as they entered, and the room suddenly seemed to light up when she smiled. Hannah and Ashley went to the bedside and gave her a hug, careful to avoid the tubes and wires that still connected her to IV bags and monitoring gizmos. Hannah looked at it with suspicion. *Shouldn't she be off this stuff by now?*

"It's okay," Dawn said, her smile still radiant. "It's just a precaution."

"Sorry, this stuff makes me nervous, that's all."

"Well, don't be," Dawn said. "I'm out of here tomorrow and we'll be back hunting for Lonesome Amie and watching the wagon roll down Black Hill Road in a few nights."

"Whoa," Ashley said reverently. "I've been so distracted by everything, I'd forgotten it was almost Halloween."

Dawn clapped her hands. "I'm so excited for it!" she said.

Hannah couldn't help but smile. Dawn's mood was contagious. Then her smile slipped. *Is Dawn too happy? Manic? Faking?* She pushed the negativity away. More things to talk about with Dr. Moore.

"You're really getting out tomorrow?"

"Yes, Hannah. Pinkie swear." She held up a hand with just her little finger sticking out, the way she and Ashley used to do when they were younger. Hannah twined her own pinkie around it, then watched as Dawn repeated the ritual with Ashley.

Ashley took that moment to blurt out an apology, admitting she had googled Dawn but then hadn't read beyond the initial article. Tears spilled from her eyes as she told Dawn, their little fingers still intertwined. The moment stretched. Dawn remained silent. She'd looked stricken when Ashley had told her, then she'd closed her eyes. Hannah noticed she hadn't pulled her pinkie away and took that as a good sign. She glanced at the monitors, half-expecting them to start going crazy, lighting up and beeping, bringing a team of doctors running.

"Dawn," Hannah said softly, "please don't be mad. Ash was just looking out for me. There were all these crazy stories, and we didn't believe them, but ..."

"I can't tell you how ashamed I feel. I want to be your friend, want all of us to be friends ..." Ashley broke down, sobbing, unable to finish.

Dawn opened her eyes slowly "I get it," she said. "I'd probably do the same thing if I heard the stories."

Hannah turned away, unable to bear the agony on Dawn's face. *What had she gone through?* Hannah couldn't imagine the death of a baby sister.

"I promise I'll tell you all about it someday. The truth is, I don't remember a lot about that night."

"You don't have to tell us anything," Ashley said. "It was a dirtbag move and I promise I'll never break your trust again."

Dawn smiled, a lone tear slipping down her face. "You guys are the best friends I've ever had," Dawn said. Then she looked pointedly at Ashley. "Can I have my pinkie back now?"

The look on Ashley's face when she realized their pinkies were still entwined was priceless. They all cracked up, and just like that, everything seemed okay.

"Did the doctors say what happened?" The words were out of Hannah's mouth before she knew she was going to ask the question.

"Just a bad migraine," Dawn said.

Did she answer too fast? "Has this ever happen before?"

Dawn snaked out a hand and grasped Hannah's, squeezing it gently. "I'm fine, Hannah. And yes, this has happened before. Usually when I don't take my medicine in time, or even sometimes when I do."

Hannah held Dawn's gaze for a long moment, searching her friend's eyes for any hint of a lie. She found none. She nodded. "I'm glad you're getting out of here."

Dawn slapped her hands down on the sheets. "I wish I could leave *now*," she moaned. "We have a lot to do and not much time to do it."

"The wagon is done," Ashley said, walking around to the other side of the bed. "And we've got our costumes ready. Chill. We got this."

Dawn turned to Ashley. "What about Derek?"

Ashley made a dismissive sound. "We can deal with him some other—"

"No!" Dawn sat up too fast, nearly yanking out her IV. "We have to do it on Halloween."

Hannah watched Ashley's expression morph from surprise to confusion. "Why?"

"We just do," she said, turning to Hannah. "If we wait ... we might never get him. Not before something bad happens."

Hannah reached for Dawn's hand at the same time Ashley reached for the other. *Mind meld.* "You're right," Hannah said, "Halloween is the best chance we have. We need the guys here to work out the details—"

"What details?" a voice boomed behind them. Hannah jumped. She hadn't heard Mr. Holman approaching. Judging by the others' reaction, they hadn't, either.

"For the wagon," Ashley said.

"Ah, the mysterious burning wagon of Hopedale," Mr. Holman said with a grin. His face went serious when his eyes found his daughter. "We'll have to wait and see if Dawn is up for that kind of excitement."

"Dad!"

Mr. Holman held up his hands. "Please, Dawn, you've been through a lot and we're not going to argue about it here. Deal?"

Dawn seemed to shrink into the bed, resigned. "Deal," she muttered.

"Good," Mr. Holman said with forced joviality and a clap of his hands. "Who's up for some smuggled-in gelato?" He shrugged off a backpack and started unloading to-go containers of somewhat melty gelato.

They bartered good-naturedly about who wanted which flavor, then settled down to enjoy the unexpected treat.

Ashley broke the silence. "It's good, but pretty *soup*y," she said, looking pointedly at Hannah and Dawn. They all laughed, leaving Mr. Holman shaking his head. Ashley gave Dawn a wink and went back to her gelato.

chapter
sixty-three

ASHLEY TIPTOED down the stairs like a kid on Christmas Eve trying to catch a glimpse of Santa. She wondered if she'd end up just as disappointed as a little kid who'd caught their parents putting all the gifts under the tree. The sound of the television grew louder as she approached the bottom step, being careful to plant her foot all the way over to the wall side of the tread so it wouldn't squeak.

She stopped at the bottom, straining to hear what they were watching, but the sound was too low. Then she heard her parents talking in hushed voices.

What am I doing, sneaking around like a child?

With a shake of her head, she marched down the hall, then turned into the living room. The reaction was exactly what she'd suspected. Surprised faces and stumbling excuses, trying to cover up the fact that they'd been caught.

"Mom. Dad." Ashley made her way to the middle of the room and snatched the remote off the coffee table. With an exaggerated flourish she hit the power button, plunging the room into an ominous silence.

Her parents were next to each other on the couch. Ashley sat down on the coffee table in front of them. "So, what were you talking about?" Her words exuded sarcasm and she knew the smile she wore was more of an obnoxious smirk.

"We were just watching television," Jill said, fixing a confused smile on her own face.

Ashley had noted the *King of Queens* rerun that was playing before she'd shut the TV off. She grinned. "I didn't think you liked those CSI shows?"

"Well," Craig said, clearing his throat, "sometimes we switch it up—"

"Stop," Ashley said harshly. She clicked the power button again and Kevin James was trying to talk his way out of some silly situation. She turned it back off. "Now, what were you talking about?"

Both parents sighed at the same time, exchanging a look that spoke volumes. It seemed to Ashley like they had an entire dialogue in just that look. Her father sighed again, rubbing his eyes with a thumb and forefinger. "Busted," he said. "We were talking about you."

As much as she already knew that, hearing her father saying it that way chilled her. She suddenly realized she didn't want to know why they were talking about her.

"We know you've picked up on your mother and me acting a little weird lately, and I want to apologize for not being honest with you. The thing is..."—He looked at Ashley's mother and she gave a curt nod— "...we haven't been honest with you for a long time."

This was so much worse than she thought. "Just tell me, okay? Which one of you is sick?"

Her father's head snapped back as if she'd struck him. "It's nothing like that," her mother said.

"Then what is it like?" Ashley screeched.

"Listen," Craig said gently, "nobody is sick, your mother and I are happy—"

Ashley shot to her feet, hands clenched into tight fists by

her side. She glared down at her parents. "Stop telling me what it *isn't* and just tell me what it *is*!"

"You're adopted," her mother blurted out.

Her father recoiled, giving his wife a look of abject horror. Of all the scenarios that had spun through Ashley's head, this wasn't one of them. Her legs went wobbly, and she sat down hard on the coffee table. Her parents were both speaking, she knew that because she could see their lips moving, but all she heard was air rushing through her ears as if she were standing next to a speeding train.

She opened her mouth to speak but couldn't form the words, wasn't sure what she even wanted to say. Instead, a series of images—memories—flashed through her mind:

Me and my parents at Hampton Beach for the day, both of them horribly sunburned by the afternoon while my skin had turned a deep reddish-brown.

A family photo shoot where the photographer comments on my "almond-shaped eyes" and asking where I got them. My parents mumbling something about recessive genes.

Me, telling my parents I wanted to do a family tree using one of those 23andMe ancestry DNA kits and my parents vehemently refusing, saying those things aren't accurate and who knows what else they do with your DNA.

"Adopted," Ashley whispered, trying the word out for size.

"We were never sure when would be the right time to tell you," her father said.

"You're our daughter, Ashley, in every way other than blood ..."

Ashley didn't respond. *Adopted*. The word echoed in her head, along with all the stigmas that go with it. Then, like a bolt of lightning out of a clear blue sky, the rest of it hit her. "Then who ... where are my—?" She caught herself before uttering the word 'real' which would have devastated her parents. "Where are my *birth* parents?"

"That's why this has all come back to the surface," Craig said.

"The truth is," Jill said, "We never knew who your birth father was. Your birth mother was a single mom—"

Ashley's head snapped up. "Was?"

"I'm afraid so, honey," her mother said. "We just found out."

"We were going to wait until you turned eighteen," her father said, sounding as defeated as Ashley had ever heard him. "That way you could be free to do whatever you wanted with the information. Your mother and I did a lot of research on the subject, and we agreed that was the best plan."

"We just never thought...she was so young."

Ashley tried to consider this, to figure out how she felt, but it was all too overwhelming. She wanted – *needed* - to talk to Hannah. Instead of studying her feelings, she decided to stick with the objective information. Just the facts, ma'am. "How did she die?" Another one of those parental glances.

Should we tell her?

I don't think we have a choice.

But it's so hard.

We can't lie to her anymore.

"Are you sure you want to hear all this now?" Her father's pained expression almost made her decline, but she had to know. She nodded. "Her death was ruled a suicide. She didn't leave a note."

Alarm bells went off in Ashley's head. "*Ruled a suicide* sounds like it's not clear. Could it have been an accident?" Another thought hit her and, somehow, she knew it was closer to the truth. "Or ... foul play?"

"Ashley—"

"Come on, Mom," she said. "I deserve to know, now that I'll never get to meet her." She hadn't meant the words to be so sharp, but her parents' reactions told her they'd cut anyway.

Her father's lips tightened to a thin white line. "That's not fair—"

"I'm sorry," Ashley said. "It wasn't fair. I didn't mean ..." *What did I mean?* She burst into tears.

Both her parents got to their feet, one on either side of her, trying to console her. She wanted to have an adult conversation about this, but her emotions overruled her brain. She decided it was enough for one night. She would put the conversation on hold, call Hannah, then go to bed. Tomorrow, she would have a clearer head and be able to discuss it further.

"I'm sorry, I really didn't mean to say it that way. I love you both so much and I know this isn't easy for you, either." She pulled away and wiped a sleeve across her eyes. "But can we finish this tomorrow?"

"Whenever you're ready," her mother said, wiping the tears from her own eyes.

"Is it okay if—"

"Yes, you can tell Hannah," her father said with a sad smile.

Ashley hugged them both then went to her room to make the call.

chapter
sixty-four

AS SHE WALKED IN, Hannah was greeted, as usual, by a bouncing, twirling Scout. "Hey, boy," she said, kneeling to give him some love in the form of a belly rub. When she was finished, she stood and walked into the kitchen, where her dad and Rick sat watching her with stoic expressions on their faces. Her legs went rubbery as all the different scenarios that could have led to them sitting there like that exploded in her mind.

Is Jake dead? Are Mama Bayole's followers around? No, of course that isn't it.

Her voice came out sounding like that of a little girl: "Is it Mom?"

Dad and Rick exchanged a quick look that confirmed it, and Hannah's knees buckled, and she fell to the floor. Scout whined and was at her side, nuzzling her neck.

Dad and Rick were there as quick as a flash, helping her to her feet.

"Hannah, are you okay?"

Dad's voice came from the end of a long, dark tunnel, all echoey and weird. Hannah blinked, wondering why he *looked* so close but sounded so far away. "Dad?" She was on the couch, unsure of how she got there, with a half-empty water glass in her hand.

Rick knelt in front of her. "Hannah?"

She closed her eyes, then opened them slowly. She took a gulp of water and handed the glass to Rick, not trusting her shaking body to hold onto it. "Dad, it is Mom, isn't it?"

Dad sat on the couch beside her and took her hand. "It might not be anything, but I don't want to keep things from you anymore. It's eating me up."

Hannah took a deep breath, letting it out slowly. "I'm okay. Did you find her?"

Dad's eyes shifted to Rick, who nodded.

Hannah wondered if they had the same mind meld that she and Ashley had.

"No, Hannah, but we may have a lead." He paused, letting the information sink in.

Hannah knew the day might come when her mother turned up—dead or alive—but how does anyone prepare for that day? "A lead that she's alive, or ..." She couldn't bring herself to say it.

"Alive," Brian said, his voice sounding like a rusty hinge.

Hannah closed her eyes, teeth clenched, and focused on her breathing. All of the nights she'd lain awake, wondering why her mother had left. Wondering what she did to make her mother leave. Wondering if she was dead, buried in some shallow grave in the woods. Or if she was in Vegas or Rio, drinking champagne with some old rich guy, never giving Hannah and Dad a second thought. All those nights ... and finally, she might get answers.

"Okay," she said, exhaling a breath that had begun to burn her lungs she'd been holding it so long. So much for focusing on her breathing.

Rick took over, speaking slowly and carefully, as if he didn't think Hannah could absorb too much. He was right.

"The information is coming from one of the cult members." Rick held up a hand as Hannah opened her mouth to protest. "So, we were skeptical, thinking it might be a ploy to plea bargain. But, so far, her story checks out. We don't know where your mother is, but based on this information, we do believe she was alive as recently as August."

Hannah nodded, her thoughts a runaway train screaming down a steep incline without brakes. *It was her in the clearing that night.* With the thought came an unexpected wave of anger. That meant her mother was willing to sacrifice Ashley, her daughter's best friend. And she would have known how deep an impact that would have had on Hannah.

"Did she say anything else about Mom, this cult member? Like how she became involved?"

"She didn't say how your mother became part of the cult, but she did say that—" Rick hesitated, his eyes again finding Brian. Hannah could see he didn't want to tell her. Didn't want to *hurt* her.

Dad sighed and let go of Hannah's hand, brushing a lock of hair out of her face. His face was the picture of pure torment.

"It's okay, Dad," Hannah said, taking a deep breath. "Knowing is better than not knowing. No matter how bad it is."

Her father's expression softened, and his eyes filled with tears. "This woman, she said your mother had been part of the cult when she joined a year ago." He paused, letting it sink in. Letting Hannah do the math. How long had her mother been in the cult? Had she already been visiting with Mama Bayole before she left? Those nights she said she was going to church? Yes, of course she had.

Her dad started to speak again: "Hannah—"

"Dad, it's okay. I told you, I need to hear this." Her words came out bitter and left an aftertaste of shame.

Her father let out a defeated-sounding sigh and went on. "Your mother was considered a senior member of the cult. One of the more trusted followers. Almost a ... a second-in-command."

Rick stepped in, taking the baton seamlessly, "The woman referred to her as a High Acolyte. It's like your dad said, she was highly regarded by Mama Bayole, and she, Bayole, often delegated some of the duties to your mother."

Something icy took hold of Hannah's heart and started to squeeze. Coldness descended on her chest and sudden tremors wracked her body. She looked down at her traitorous limbs trembling against her will. Her father practically lunged at her, wrapping her in a tight hug and whispering that he was sorry, that it would be okay. She had told her father she needed to know. That she was ready for this. And here she was, a shaking little baby needing her father to console her.

"I'm going to make some tea," Rick said, getting up and hustling to the kitchen. Scout began whining, probably scared for Hannah, and that only added to her sadness and helplessness.

Hannah tried to speak, to tell her father she was all right, but her body continued to defy her. The image that had set her off was that of her mother, standing over Ashley, stealing her youth. Her mother somehow growing younger as Ashley aged and shriveled and died. She let out a strangled cry as the quivering worsened to almost seizure-level. Scout stood, hackles raised, and began barking and growling.

"I have tea ready when you feel up to drinking some."

Even in her current state, Hannah recognized that Rick sounded uncharacteristically afraid. She tried again to speak, to comfort her dad and Rick and Scout, but all that came out was another choking sob.

She heard the clank of the teacup as Rick placed it on the coffee table. Everything seemed magnified. Sounds were louder, the lights were too bright. Her father's hug was that of a constrictor.

Rick said, "Did Susan leave any of her Ativan behind, by any chance?"

The name Susan echoed in her head, as if Rick had screamed it into an open canyon. Susan, who had witnessed a sacrifice in the clearing. Susan, who had escaped the cult. Susan, who had sat on this very couch having a panic attack just like the one Hannah was experiencing now. Susan, who had conquered her fear, mustering the courage to face Mama Bayole a second time, risking her life for Hannah and Ashley. The memory of Susan's bravery, her *heroism*, had a calming effect on Hannah. She clung to the image of the woman that night as they'd split up at the clearing. Susan's words, *I let them end one life while I stood by and did nothing. I can't let it happen again.*

The tremors were subsiding. She wondered where Susan was now. She had left Hopedale immediately after the events at Champlain Park, promising to stay in touch. Hannah had received an email from her just after school started, saying Susan was taking some time to travel before she decided where to settle down. Hannah had replied but hadn't heard anything since. She knew she would eventually. After what they'd gone through together, they had a special bond that neither time nor distance could weaken. She pictured Susan cruising the country in some sort of throwback car, maybe an old VW bug, and smiled.

"I think I'm ready for that tea now," she said, pulling away from her dad and wiping the tears from her face.

HANNAH STOOD at the top of Black Hill Road, clutching the flashlight the way a drowning person clings to a life preserver. She exhaled, watching the wisps of her breath snake away into the cool night. Suddenly, this all seemed like a bad idea. Hadn't she learned her lesson playing detective last summer? Firecrackers exploded in the distance, making her jump. They sounded too much like gunshots. She paced along the side of the road, head on a swivel, searching the mass of costume-clad bodies for a threat. For Derek.

A tall, bulky figure in a hooded robe moved toward her. The face was hidden behind a plain, white mask, the kind the villains wore in *The Strangers*. It chilled her, bringing back memories of the movie. She knew the real fear came from the hooded figures she'd seen in the clearing. Another person emerged from the shadows, small and agile, and fast. This one was dressed as a Stormtrooper or some other Star Wars character. It approached the hooded figure and grabbed it by the shoulders. Hannah pulled the whistle from her pocket but stopped short of blowing it when both figures burst into gales of laughter and pulled their masks off. She stuffed the whistle back into her pocket as Mr.

Jennings—one of the grammar school teachers from Hopedale Elementary—and his son high-fived and went on their way.

Back at the edge of the woods, she could see the whole street. The shadows swallowed her, and she pointed her flashlight into the darkness of the trees, just in case.

"Get it together, Hannah," she whispered, her voice barely audible above the scraping of bare branches and the rustle of dead leaves set in motion by a sudden breeze. She shivered, wishing she'd worn an extra layer under her costume. Hannah, Ashley, and Dawn were dressed as Winnie, Sarah, and Mary—the three witches from the old *Hocus Pocus* movie. They'd agreed on it, figuring it would be easy to find each other in the crowd—who else would pick such obscure costumes? The problem, she was beginning to realize, was that the elaborate dress wasn't the best idea if she needed to move fast. As in, run away. She wasn't sure if she was thinking about Derek or Lonesome Amie right then. One seemed just as likely as the other.

She looked around for Marcus and Kenny, who were also easy to find in their Blues Brothers outfits. She picked them out, standing by the wagon. Well, not standing … trying to do the dance that Belushi and Aykroyd did in the movie and failing miserably. She couldn't help but giggle and a now-familiar warmth spread through her body and her heart kicked up a gear. She wondered, not for the first time, if she was falling in love with Marcus.

Hannah pulled out her phone and looked at the display. It was just after eleven. Less than an hour to go before they would light the wagon and set it on its way down Black Hill Road. All the warmth of a moment ago faded, replaced by a bone-deep dread. Something was going to happen. She glanced back toward the wagon, wanting the sight of Jake and Elwood fumbling through their dance to relieve her of her foreboding, but they were gone. She scanned the crowd, but it was too dark, they'd become just two more shadows.

She pulled her phone out and posted in the group text they'd set up.

All quiet up here. Everyone okay?

Responses came back quickly.

Kenny: Marcus and me are good—circling the wagon. Ha! Get it?

Ashley: Dawn and I are freezing ... otherwise bored. Send the wagon now so we can get warm by the fire!

She smiled, then posted a smile emoji and put the phone back in her pocket, amazed as always that there was reception here but not at her house. Then she went back to her vigil, studying the crowd, looking for Derek. The idea crossed her mind that this might all be in vain, that he might not even show up. She dismissed it immediately. Between what she'd experienced herself and the conversation with Emma, she was sure he'd show up, full of bad intentions.

The crowd was getting thicker the closer it got to midnight. Hannah decided to make a loop of the area to get a better vantage point. *If only we knew what he is dressed up as.* It wasn't as though he had any friends they could have asked. The thought made her sad. What must it be like to be such an outcast? Ridiculed by your classmates and despised by your teachers. Your only way to combat the loneliness was with your fists. No, she decided, part of it was on him. He didn't have to be that way. Hadn't she tried to be nice to him that day at Champlain Park? It was all too confusing.

She reached the far side of Black Hill Road without seeing anyone that might have been Derek in costume. She perched herself on a boulder that stuck out of the ground just off the road. Maybe watching from this side would prove luckier. Her mind was running through synonyms for loneliness: alienation, desolation, seclusion, solitude, forlornness. As afraid as she was, she couldn't shake the sudden despair that had over-taken her. Instead of searching for Derek, she found herself trying to pick the Blues Brothers out of the crowd. She needed to see a friendly face. Needed to know she wasn't alone. When a branch snapped in the woods behind her, she *knew* she wasn't. She turned quickly, scouring the woods for whatever —or whoever—had made the sound. Thinking better of it, she ran toward the relative safety of the crowd that surrounded the wagon.

chapter
sixty-six

ASHLEY PUT her phone away and said, "That was Hannah checking in. All quiet." Dawn nodded but the way her eyes were darting around made Ashley nervous. She looked like one of those googly-eyed dolls. Ashley was beginning to wonder if this was a good idea. Dawn had only been out of the hospital for a few days. What if she relapsed? Dawn smiled weakly. To Ashley, it was more disconcerting than comforting.

"Are you okay, Dawn?"

"I'm fine, just nervous. This all seemed cooler when we were all together and it was daylight."

Something was off. It wasn't just the barely contained mania in her eyes. There was an odd, disconnected manner about Dawn. Her voice was monotone. It was as if she was going through the motions or playing a part. It was unsettling. She considered texting Hannah but decided to hold off. Maybe the atmosphere was freaking her out.

"Maybe he won't show," Ashley blurted out. She didn't believe it but wanted to gauge Dawn's reaction. She regretted it immediately.

"He'll show," Dawn said. The intensity in her tone chilled

Ashley, so different than just a moment ago. There was a hint of gleeful anticipation that wasn't right.

A couple of large groups of older kids arrived and were milling about, talking loudly and roughhousing. Ashley glanced warily at them, wondering if there would be any trouble. She knew there were a few cops mixed in with the crowd, but her disquiet had taken root. And it was growing.

"Yeah," Ashley said, slipping her hand into her pocket to get her phone. She was scared. Not for herself but for Dawn. "I'm going let Hannah know to call instead of text if anything happens up there, it's getting pretty loud down here." Dawn gave her a ghostly smile but said nothing. Ashley took a few steps toward the side of the road. She didn't want Dawn seeing what she was texting. She exited the group chat—not wanting Kenny to see it either—and opened Hannah's contact.

Hey, I think something's wrong with Dawn.

Her phone rang seconds later, and Ashley was relieved to see Hannah's goofy picture that she'd put as an avatar. "Hey," she said quietly.

"What's going on? Is she sick?" Hannah sounded as anxious as Ashley felt.

I can't explain it," she said, talking fast. "Something's not right." She glanced over to where Dawn was standing. She was gone. A coldness spread from her chest to her limbs. Hannah's voice was growing frantic down the line but to Ashley it was some distant noise. She forgot she was even holding the phone as her head jerked right to left and back again: a sudden commotion from the gangs of kids that had arrived earlier. The good-natured yelling and jostling had turned into angry shouts and aggressive shoving. A panicked scream from the phone brought her back. "Hannah, get down here."

"I'll send Kenny," Hannah replied.

Ashley ended the call and shoved the phone in her pocket, willing her legs to work. They felt like stone pillars. Like a stone altar. *Why did I let Dawn out of my sight?* It took every ounce of resolve and willpower to move toward the uproar. Ugly memories of being chained up in Mama Bayole's basement flashed in her head. Of being tied down to the altar in the clearing. She shambled zombie-like toward the ruckus on barely functioning legs. She had no idea what she would do in the middle of what was turning into a chaotic clashing of bodies, only that she had to get there.

A voice exploded over a bullhorn: "This is the Hopedale Police. Disperse immediately or you will be detained."

Kids began to spread out from the crowd, running past her toward where the cars were parked. Ashley moved steadily forward, like a fish swimming against a raging current. Her long dress was clumsy, and she tried to hold it up as she went, not wanting to take a header if she managed to get her legs tangled in it. She craned her neck, desperate to catch a glimpse of Dawn, but it was no use. The police continued to issue warnings over the bullhorn. The rush of fleeing bodies grew thicker, jostling her as she struggled to find Dawn. Police whistles screeched over the sound of the crowd and the cacophony of voices became a constant hum, like a swarm of giant insects. Ashley was afraid she was going to pass out before she reached the center of the melee, trampled by the mob. Then she spotted Dawn.

Someone had her by the arms. Then Dawn's body went limp, and the man picked her up, carrying her toward the side of Black Hill Road woods like a groom carrying his bride over the threshold. Ashley's near paralysis broke and she sprinted toward her friend, desperately trying to gain speed and hold the hem of her dress away from her pumping legs. In the few seconds she had before she reached them, she decided to run full speed into Dawn's assailant, shoulder-first, and hope she could break his grasp. She somehow managed to pull up before the collision when she saw "Hopedale Police" on the back of his windbreaker.

"Dawn!"

Dawn's head lolled toward her. Her eyes fluttered, unfocused. "Eden?"

Ashley's stomach clenched, the coldness that had gripped her turning arctic. "Officer! What is going on?"

The man turned to her, his expression one of grave concentration. "Are you with this girl?"

"Yes!" Ashley began to cry.

The man placed Dawn gently on the ground and pulled a walkie talkie from his windbreaker. "Unit seven to base, do you copy?" A staticky reply came back. "Requesting an ambulance ASAP at the bottom of Black Hill Road. Over."

Ashley gasped, unable again to hear the reply. "What's wrong with her? What happened?"

"Calm down, miss," he replied. "What's your name?"

"A-Ashley Wallace."

A hint of recognition crossed his face. "And you said you're here with this girl. What's her name?"

"Dawn ..." Ashley's panicked brain stuttered, unable to come up with her friend's last name for a second. "Dawn Holman," she said, finally. She knew the officer was trying to keep her calm with simple questions, but it wasn't working. Her whole body was thrumming like a live wire. "Dawn?"

"Please, Ashley. I need you to calm down. Is there anyone else here with you?" He scanned the road as he spoke.

Ashley followed his gaze; suddenly sure Derek was approaching. Or something worse. But there was nothing. Wait ... there was a figure running pell-mell toward them.

Ashley's heart tried to crawl up to her throat. She was unable to breathe, unable to speak. Then a voice rose above the din of the chaotic scene.

"Dawn! Where are you?"

"Kenny!" Ashley tried to stand but her legs betrayed her, and she collapsed to her hands and knees. "Over here!"

Kenny followed the sound of her voice. When he saw her on the ground and Dawn's prone figure nearby, he sprinted toward them, his Blues Brothers tie flapping almost comically behind him.

"Dawn!" He skidded to a stop in the loose dirt on the side of the road and went down on one knee. He looked wildly from the cop to Ashley. "What's wrong with her? What happened?" The sound of an approaching siren cut the night and Kenny's panic seemed to rise with its wail.

"I'm Officer Hawkins," the cop said, his voice steady, but not *completely* steady. This sent a new bolt of fear through Ashley. He was a police officer; he shouldn't be afraid. "There was an altercation—"

Kenny's head snapped toward Ashley. "Was it Derek?" He got to his feet, fists clenched. "Where is he?"

Red lights bathed the scene, turning it into a horror movie tableau. Officer Hawkins waved a flashlight to direct the ambulance driver to pull in next to them, and Ashley got to her feet shakily. Sobbing, she pulled Kenny into a hug. He held her tight, telling her it was going to be okay. His body was rock solid under his black suit, like a coiled spring, every muscle tense. The paramedics jumped out and began examining Dawn.

chapter
sixty-seven

"WHAT SHOULD WE DO?" Marcus held Hannah tightly, watching Kenny bolt down the hill.

Hannah had found them at the wagon just as Ashley's text had come in. She'd immediately sent Kenny on his way, trying not to panic him but failing miserably. She hoped he would make it down the hill without face-planting. Nothing like a nice case of road rash to spice up your Halloween. She almost laughed out loud at the thought. If that was all that happened tonight, they'd be getting off easy.

"I think he's here," she said. "In the woods." She motioned to where she'd heard the twig snap. Marcus went rigid, and his eyes bored into the trees. He started to move in that direction, but she held him back. "No. I think that's what he wants. Let's wait. Stay near the crowd."

"Okay, but we came here to get him, right? We can't let him get away tonight, or ..."

"Or this will never end," Hannah finished for him.

"Is that—"

"A siren, yeah," she said glumly. Their whole plan was falling apart and now maybe something was wrong with Dawn. She knew Marcus was right. If they weren't able to snare Derek, he would win. And he'd get them eventually, one by one. The things Emma had told them came back to her vividly and she cringed. She and Ashley had agreed not to tell the boys the details of that conversation, and now she wondered if that had been a mistake. Maybe it had left the boys unprepared for what Derek was really capable of.

Why isn't Ashley calling me back?

"Have you recognized any of the cops up here?"

"I thought I saw Officer Ramirez, you know, the guy that's usually at the football games? But it was hard to be sure, he had on a costume and his face was painted. He was dressed as an escaped prisoner, ball-and-chain and everything."

"Let's find him," Hannah said. "If he's dressed up, Derek won't know we're talking to a cop. We need help, Marcus. I'm scared." The siren screamed from the bottom of the hill, and she realized with a flash of cold dread that it was coming from an ambulance, not a police car. "Dawn," she whispered, pulling out her phone.

"There he is," Marcus said, pointing to a figure in black-and-white stripes on the other side of the wagon.

Scenes of last summer at the concert—the jostling crowd, the cloying press of bodies, the darkness—suddenly exploded in her head. Her legs froze, refusing to move. Her vision narrowed, going dark around the edges. Strange black birds began to dart back and forth. She felt Marcus pulling her arm, vaguely aware that she'd stopped walking. Also realizing with an electric horror that she couldn't breathe.

Marcus was now facing her, those lunatic birds swarming in front of him. His mouth was moving but she couldn't hear the words. She tried to reach for him, but her hands were two stones at the end of wooden sticks. Her phone slipped from her hand. Her vision narrowed further until it was as if she were looking through two pinholes. Her heart was beating staccato, and she knew she was going to die here. The headlines flashed in her head. *Halloween tragedy on Black Hill Road*. She saw her father, broken at the news, nobody left. She pictured him standing over her coffin. He opened his mouth to speak. *First your mother, then you*, he said. *I couldn't save you. I failed you both*. She tried to close her eyes, willing the darkness to take her so she didn't have to listen to her heart explode. So she didn't have to see her father's pain. But it was no use, even her eyelids were paralyzed. Something shifted in her vision. Behind Marcus. The irony of what she was seeing almost made her laugh. Lonesome Amie glided at the edge of the woods. A ghost, she thought, just before she would become one herself.

chapter
sixty-eight

WITH A SATISFIED SMILE, Derek listened to the chaos he'd created. The sound of the siren at the bottom of Black Hill Road was music to his ears. Sirens would be the sound-track to the rest of this night if he had his way.

It had been almost too easy. Causing a distraction at the bottom of the hill by paying some drunk kid twenty bucks to pick a fight. Splitting up those assholes so the two he wanted most were left alone at the top of the hill. Most of Hopedale's police force would be down there. Too far away to help. He glanced in the direction of the siren but all he could see were the treetops, bathed in the lunatic strobe of the ambulance's lights.

"If only the fireflies were here to see," he whispered.

He turned his attention to Hannah and Marcus. They were on the opposite side of the wagon from Ramirez. Derek had scouted the area, unrecognizable in his costume, and knew Ramirez was dressed as a prisoner. He slid from the edge of the road, moving in the path of Hannah and Marcus before they could get around to the cop. He stopped when he saw Hannah freeze. Marcus turned back to her and was saying something, but Derek couldn't make it out over the din of the excited voices preparing to light the wagon. He edged closer, then stopped again. It looked like Hannah had fainted. Marcus was holding her up, but her body was as loose as a rag doll. Derek couldn't believe it: Marcus was dragging Hannah toward him! He stepped back into the shadows of the trees at the side of the road, knowing his dark outfit would make him almost invisible.

As they approached, Derek was able to make out Marcus's panicked voice, talking to Hannah, telling her he would get help. That everything was going to be okay. Derek snorted a laugh, slapping a palm to his mouth to cover the sound. Everything isn't going to be okay, he wanted to scream, it's going to be too late for help. But the fireflies had taught him patience, hadn't they? Yes. Better to be silent. To wait. Let them come to him. Like flies to a spider's web. Something rustled in the woods behind him: a deer, maybe, but he remained focused on Marcus and his useless babbling.

He barely suppressed a giggle as Marcus pulled Hannah to within ten feet of where he stood. Marcus let her down gently, leaning her against one of the mature pines that bordered the road.

"Hannah," he said, looking around wildly. "C-can you hear me?" He patted her face gently, trying to rouse her. When Marcus reached into his pocket and pulled out a cell phone, Derek made his move. Three long strides were all it took. He swatted the phone out of Marcus's hand, this time unable to control his laughter when he saw Marcus's shocked face. Then Marcus's expression turned to fear, and Derek knew. Even if the idiot couldn't see who he was, he knew.

"Not now, Derek," Marcus said. His voice was even, but Derek detected a note of uncertainty.

Derek sniffed loudly, savoring the smell of fear coming off Marcus in hot waves. He began to laugh. Marcus bent to retrieve his phone and Derek pounced. He raised his foot and used it to shove Marcus down and send him sprawling to the road with a grunt. Derek stepped forward and brought a booted foot down on the phone, giggling again when he heard it shatter into an unusable pile of glass and plastic.

Marcus was up, charging. He slammed Derek in the gut with his shoulder, driving him backward toward the trees. Derek was able to wrap both arms around Marcus as they crashed to the ground. He hit hard, Marcus landing on top of him, driving the air out of his lungs with a loud *whoosh*. Derek held on, keeping Marcus in a bear hug despite his squirming. Marcus's wiry frame was no match for Derek's meaty muscle. He held on, squeezing, picturing himself now as a boa constrictor. He had Marcus's arms pinned but Marcus was trying to kick Derek. It wasn't working. Derek could withstand the blows that were landing on his shins and thighs. It was only a matter of time until Marcus's oxygen-starved body gave out.

Pain erupted in Derek's head. He lost his hold on Marcus and his hands flew to grab his head, where fireworks were exploding with machine-gun rapidity. He barely noticed Marcus crawling away on hands and knees. His face grew warm, and he realized with a sickening feeling that it was blood. His nose was gushing again. He tried to stand but a nauseating wave of dizziness pulled him down. He rolled onto his back and pulled off his mask, pressing his hands to his nose to try to stop the hot flow of blood that streamed down his face. A rustling in the bushes beside him caught his attention. He turned his head, watching the figure in white disappear into the trees. He took a few unsteady steps in pursuit, then everything went black.

chapter
sixty-nine

DAWN PUSHED the paramedic's stethoscope away and sat up, ignoring his protests. "I'm okay," she said, staring him down.

"Miss," Officer Hawkins cut in, "you were pretty out of it and in need of medical attention. Have you been drinking? Or taking anything?"

Dawn clenched her teeth and took a breath before responding. "No, I have not been drinking," she said evenly. Coldly.

"Drugs?" Hawkins persisted.

"Only what I'm prescribed." Icicles clung to her words. She saw Kenny and Ashley exchange a look. She knew they were wondering what prescription drugs she was on. "Can I get up? I feel better, honestly. I was recently hospitalized for a severe migraine; you can call and confirm. I think I just tried to do too much too soon." Squinting, she scanned the woods but saw nothing.

The second paramedic had gone to the ambulance after Dawn mentioned being hospitalized. She came back now and gave the other one a nod. The first paramedic pulled Officer

Hawkins aside and they spoke for a minute in hushed tones. All the while, Dawn remained vigilant, searching the tree line.

It was Hawkins who came back to talk to her. "All right, Miss Holman, the hospital confirmed you were released a couple days ago. I'm not going to force you to go to the hospital, but I think you should probably call it a night. Do you have a ride home?"

"My dad is coming to get us," Kenny blurted out. "We have two other friends at the top of the hill, too."

She somehow knew he was lying and was thankful for it. It saved *her* one lie. "Thanks, Kenny," she said. "I don't want to worry my dad by calling him." She gave him a grateful smile and Hawkins seemed satisfied.

"Very well," Hawkins said, giving the paramedics a thumbs-up. "Be safe." He gave each of the kids a long look, then strode away.

"Thank you all," Dawn called. "I appreciate your help." When they were out of earshot, she said, "Kenny, you really didn't call your dad, did you?" She waited for a response, but he remained silent. He crossed the distance between them in two long strides and pulled her in for a hug. She gasped, taken completely by surprise. Over his shoulder, Ashley was smiling.

Kenny pulled away, keeping his hands on her shoulders. "You scared me," he said.

A strange warmth spread from her chest, enveloping her in an odd feeling of happiness. Of comfort. "I'm sorry," she said. "I'm okay. Really." She saw Ashley texting madly, probably updating Hannah on The Hug.

Ashley put her phone away and moved closer. "What happened?"

"I thought I saw Derek," Dawn said. I was going to confront him." She gave a short, humorless laugh. "I don't know why. It wasn't the plan." She shook her head, feeling a tear burn a trail down her cheek. "I like it here. I like … you."

She let her words hang in the air before continuing: "And Marcus and Hannah. I like Hopedale. And I just got so mad that he was trying to ruin it. I don't even know what I was going to do when I got to him. Anyway, before I could reach him, people started fighting. I don't know why. The kid I thought was Derek ... someone pulled his mask off, it wasn't him." She laughed that somber laugh again. "It wasn't even a kid, it was, like, a forty-year-old dude."

"But what happened? To you, I mean. If it wasn't Derek that upset you ..."

Dawn tried to swallow the lump that had grown in her throat. "I ..." She took a deep breath and blew it out slowly between puffed cheeks. Her gaze returned to the woods. "I thought I saw Lonesome Amie." In her peripheral vision she saw Ashley and Kenny's heads snap towards the trees, following her line of sight.

"Where?" Kenny said, his head swiveling back and forth between the woods and Dawn. "Was it like the last time, with the fire and everything?"

"No, it was just a figure, a girl, all dressed in white. Then..." She reached up and touched the back of her head. A lump the size of a golf ball had already formed. "Someone hit me on the back of the head." Ashley and Kenny exchanged a worried look. "It wasn't on purpose. I heard someone apologize. I think I caught an elbow from one of the kids involved in the fight." She started toward the other side of the road. "Come on, I'll show you where I saw Lonesome Amie." She moved quickly, ignoring the pain in her skull and the mild lightheadedness she was feeling. *No time for that now.* She stopped walking when she reached the edge of the road. She heard—no, *felt*— Ashley and Kenny come up next to her. "There," she said, pointing. "It was just kind of gliding through the woods." Dawn clicked on her flashlight app and stepped into the underbrush.

"What are you doing?" Kenny cried incredulously.

Dawn ignored him and kept pushing through the brambles. She knew she was probably ruining her costume, but it seemed important for her to do what she was doing. It crossed her mind that she might have a concussion and not be thinking clearly, but she was going on instinct rather than brainpower. She heard Kenny and Ashley talking behind her but couldn't make out their words. A minute later, two lights joined hers and she heard her friends crashing through the undergrowth to catch up.

Dawn was eerily calm as she tried to pinpoint the exact spot where she'd seen Lonesome Amie. She stopped several times to get her bearings, ignoring the pleas of Ashley and Kenny to get back to the road. When she was confident she was in the right area, she realized she was standing on a game trail. She nodded to herself. Would a ghost follow a trail? Unlikely.

"This is it," she said as the others stepped onto the trail.

Ashley said, "Okay, so what now? It's not like there's going to be a trail of ectoplasm. This isn't Ghostbusters."

Dawn rounded on her, fury rising. "If you saw her, what would you do? I'm not looking for *ectoplasm*, I'm looking for exactly the opposite. Broken branches, footprints, cigarette butts ... something to prove it *wasn't* a ghost." She raised her phone so she could see their faces and was shocked by their reaction. Ashley and Kenny had both taken a step back and wore identical expressions of confusion and something that looked like fear. *What do I look like? What did I just sound like?* "I'm sorry ... I ..." She lowered the phone, unable to bear their looks any longer. "I have to know, okay?"

"Sure, Dawn," Ashley said, sounding cautious.

Kenny stepped closer. "Dawn, are you sure you're all right?"

She closed her eyes, willing herself to keep her temper in

check. She gritted her teeth, knowing it would only give her a headache, but she was unable to stop herself. "I don't know, Kenny. That's what I'm trying to find out."

He put a gentle hand on her arm. "Hey," he said softly, "we're on your side, okay?"

Dawn relaxed a little. *Am I overreacting?* "Then help me," she said, hating the desperation in her voice.

"We're here," Ashley said, moving next to Kenny. "We'll help you look. And if we don't find anything, then you saw Lonesome Amie." Ashley's smile was visible even in the dim light.

A phone buzzed and they all looked at their devices. It was Ashley who had an incoming call. "Unknown caller," she said. "I guess the spammers don't take Halloween night off." She declined the call.

"Thanks," Dawn said, trying to hold back tears. It seemed like all she did lately was cry or pass out or somehow make a mess of things.

They searched the trail and the underbrush surrounding it for the next twenty minutes, finding no signs that anything other than deer had passed through. No footprints or other evidence that a human had used the trail. They were interrupted by the roar of the crowd from the top of Black Hill Road. It was almost midnight. They would be sending the wagon down soon.

chapter
seventy

HANNAH OPENED her eyes and was staring at the concerned face of Marcus hovering over her like a ghost. *Lonesome Amie*. She came to with none of the grogginess or confusion of someone regaining consciousness. Everything that had occurred just before things went dark was there in her mind with an eerie clarity. Fear returned, not with a slow, creeping sensation but like a hammer blow. Had she really seen the apparition in white, or had that just been part of the panic attack, like the fluttering black birds? *No,* she decided, she had seen it.

"Hannah, thank God," Marcus said. "Can you sit up?"

She noticed he was constantly looking over his shoulder then back to her. "I saw her," Hannah said. "I saw the ghost of Lonesome Amie."

Marcus frowned. "Hannah, please, sit up. I need your phone."

She let him help her up, then reached into her pocket.

"Where is it?" She checked her other pocket. "Where's yours?"

"Derek smashed it," Marcus said; his voice had a high-pitched quality to it that Hannah didn't care for. Dread crept in like a thief when she realized she didn't have her phone. Had he smashed hers, too?

"Yeah, he jumped me after you passed out. I thought he was ..." Marcus stopped, his eyes dropping. He took a breath then continued, "I thought he was going to kill me."

Hannah scrambled to her feet, the infusion of adrenaline making her need to move. "What happened? Where did he go?"

"I don't know. Please, we have to warn the others! I need your phone."

"I can't find it," she said. "Either I dropped it or Derek took it, I don't know."

"Shit," Marcus barked. "Let's go find Ramirez."

Marcus took her hand and they turned toward the wagon, stopping short when they saw the burgeoning crowd. It was five or six people deep, all surrounding the wagon. "We'll never find him in time," Hannah said. "You—"

Her words were silenced by the *whoomp* and the sudden explosion of orange light. The wagon was lit. The crowd roared and began chanting "*Send it down! Send it down!*"

"Marcus," Hannah started, but didn't know what she wanted to say.

"You find Ramirez," he said over the roar of the crowd. "I'll get to the bottom of the hill and find the others."

Before she could protest, he was gone. She watched in dismay as he sprinted past the crowd and out of sight down the hill. Hannah glanced into the darkness of the trees where she'd spotted Lonesome Amie, then turned and began pushing her way through the crowd, desperately searching for the black-and-white stripes of Ramirez's costume.

She jostled her way through the mass of cheering people, pushing back that gnawing, clawing anxiety that was trying to take hold. The crowd had grown significantly, and Hannah realized with a desperate sinking feeling that she wasn't going to find Officer Ramirez in time to do anything. She considered begging someone for a cell phone but decided to make a run for the bottom of the hill. *I should have gone with Marcus. We know better than to split up.*

She shoved her way out of the mass of bodies and started running, wary that her long dress was threatening to trip her up. She got a grip on it with one hand and yanked it up above her churning knees. As she got farther away from the top of the hill, the darkness became complete, a physical presence that threatened to slow her down, to stop her. She knew it was only a short distance until she would crest a steeper part of the hill and be able to see the lights—*the ambulance's lights*, her mind shrieked— at the bottom, but that was no comfort as she fought the creeping sense of panic that seemed to sense the darkness and strengthen.

A loud cheer erupted behind her — *the wagon must be on its way.* Hannah had been staying close to the middle of the road, partly because she believed it would be less likely to have cracks and frost heaves that could be almost deadly at her pace, but mostly because she was afraid to get too close to the edge of the road. But now, the prospect of being run down by a burning wagon careening toward the bottom of the hill forced her to the side.

She reached the top of the rise and began the even steeper downhill section of Black Hill Road. The scene in the distance below her was an odd juxtaposition of joy and tragedy. The road was bright with temporary lighting, illuminating a cheering crowd, enthusiastically awaiting the arrival of the wagon to cap off the festivities. Behind them, a police car and ambulance sat, their blue and red lights casting an eerie, unsettling aura on the scene. Hannah said a silent prayer to whoever might be listening that Dawn was not in that ambulance and was fine, cheering along with the others.

She had slowed down as she moved to the side of the road,

afraid of the loose asphalt and litter of rocks and branches that could trip her up. Also, she was winded, and her legs were on fire. She was moving at a slow jog when movement ahead caught her eye: a barely perceptible shadow emerging from the trees. For a split second, she thought it was Officer Ramirez coming to save her when she saw the black-and-white stripes. Then she realized the stripes were wrong. This was someone dressed up in a Beetlejuice costume. Not someone. Derek. She tried to stop, too concerned about the plummeting ball of fire that was the wagon to consider veering into the road. *Two more steps and I would have made it,* she thought as the shape slammed into her. The momentum carried them into the road, and Derek landed on top of her, knocking the wind out of her.

"Diaz isn't here to save you this time," he hissed in her ear. "*Nobody* is here to save you. I am Lord of the Fireflies."

chapter
seventy-one

HANNAH DESPERATELY TRIED to get air in her lungs, but Derek's impact and his crushing weight on top of her made it impossible to get more than a shallow breath in. *Did he say lord of the flies?* Something warm fell on her neck in a steady drip. *Blood,* she realized; his nose was bleeding again. This made her think of Dawn, maybe down in that ambulance. If Derek had been at the top of the hill, what had happened to her? Another migraine? She began to buck and thrash and squirm. Anything to get his suffocating bulk off her, at least enough to breathe.

"Stop trying to fight it, Hannah," Derek said. "I'm too powerful now. I have *become*. The fireflies showed me the way and I've been baptized in blood."

The night grew brighter, and Hannah wondered if she was going to pass out again. Then she realized that the flickering orange glow was coming from the wagon. She shifted her eyes and what she saw filled her with a sudden cold terror. They were in the middle of the road and the wagon was heading straight for them. She tried to warn Derek, but didn't have enough air in her lungs. She snapped her head forward, hearing the meaty thud as her forehead connected squarely with his nose.

He grunted. "Bitch." But he didn't release her. Streams of hot blood splashed onto her face, into her eyes.

The wagon was bearing down on them, a blazing inferno, Hell on wheels. Hannah gave a final adrenaline-fueled thrust but was still unable to move him. She could almost feel the heat from the wagon, could hear its roaring flames. Something rushed toward her from the side of the road, a pink apparition. She thought she was hallucinating until it clicked that it was the blood in her eyes tinting her vision. The figure wore *white*. Lonesome Amie.

chapter
seventy-two

ASHLEY FOLLOWED Dawn and Kenny out of the woods and immediately turned to look up Black Hill Road. There was no sign of the wagon yet, but it wouldn't be long. She squinted. *Is that someone running down the hill?* Ashley stopped, watching the shadow as it grew closer. She could make out a flash of white and, for a second, thought she might be seeing the ghost of Lonesome Amie. A few strides later and she realized the white was just a shirt. It was Marcus, dressed in his Blues Brothers costume. Her chest tightened. *Where is Hannah?*

"Guys, wait up," she called, unwilling to take her eyes off Marcus. She started jogging toward him, waving. She opened the flashlight app on her phone again and began waving it as she called his name. He veered toward her, giving a burst of speed.

When he reached her, he was so winded he was unable to answer her frantic question. She craned her neck, searching for Kenny and Dawn. They were both bent over, hands on their knees, talking to a little girl dressed like a princess. Ashley frowned, shaking her head in confusion, and turned back to Marcus. "Where's Hannah?"

"Top of the hill," he managed between breaths. "With Officer Ramirez. Derek was up there. I think he came down here. Have you seen him?"

Ashley instinctively swiveled around as another roar of the crowd carried down the hill. "The wagon's coming," she said, unsure why it carried such a sense of dread.

The others came over, the little princess in tow, Dawn holding her hand. After Marcus had told them what had happened—including that both his and Hannah's phones were gone—Kenny and Dawn introduced the girl. Her name was Lisa and she'd been separated from her mother.

Ashley studied Dawn's drawn face as she told the story. Her eyes were filled with fear and concern, and Ashley knew she was thinking of her little sister. The crowd erupted and surged forward. Ashley turned and spotted the eerie orange glow on the horizon. The wagon was still out of sight, but its hellish halo was clearly visible.

She waited for it to appear on the rise, filled with foreboding. "Oh my god," she screamed. Just as she'd spotted Marcus a few moments ago, she saw another figure streaking down the hill. "Hannah!" The figure slowed, then was hurtled into the middle of the road by an unseen force.

"The wagon!" Marcus exclaimed. "Kenny, let me have your phone." Once Kenny had given it to him, Marcus began sprinting up the hill. Ashley watched in horror as the wagon, flames whipping behind it, sped towards Hannah and the other figure. "Derek," she said, seething, sickened by how this had all come to be. Their stupid plan had failed and now Hannah was in peril. Marcus was never going to get there in time. It wouldn't even be close.

"Mommy!" The little princess tore herself from Dawn's grip and ran toward her mother.

The fiery wagon roared toward Hannah as Ashley let out a

primal scream of rage and frustration. The wagon bounced as it struck something and its course changed slightly, angled diagonally down the hill now. Ashley collapsed to the ground, knowing that the jounce and the explosion of sparks was the wagon either striking or running over Hannah.

chapter
seventy-three

LONESOME AMIE BARRELED into Derek with the force of a linebacker, knocking him off Hannah and eliciting a bellow of pain and rage from him. *Can ghosts tackle people?* Hannah scrambled backward; crab walking as fast as she could. The sound of the wagon was deafening as the wheels hummed on the ground and the inferno roared. Hannah felt the intense heat as the wagon passed. It caromed as it struck Derek, sending fireworks of orange embers into the sky before continuing along its new course down the hill.

Hannah sat up, dazed by the adrenaline rush and the relief that followed. It sucked the energy from her, and she glanced stupidly at the scene that the wagon had left in its fiery wake. Derek lay motionless, his clothes smoldering. The other figure —*Lonesome Amie,* Hannah thought, awestruck—rose to her feet, the hem of her white dress on fire. "You're safe now," Lonesome Amie whispered, then vanished into the woods on the other side of the road. The figure didn't glide as she expected but moved in a loping kind of run. Hannah watched until she disappeared, then returned her gaze to Derek. She saw a small burst as his costume caught fire.

Hannah stood and shuffled toward him. The flames were

growing brighter as whatever his costume was made of fed the fire. Without thinking, she ripped her dress over her head, thankful she'd put on yoga pants and a long-sleeved t-shirt underneath, and began beating the flames, finally throwing the heavy dress onto the flames and spreading herself on top to smother the fire.

ASHLEY WATCHED, dumbstruck with anguish and terror as the little princess ran across the street directly in the path of the raging wagon. It would crush the girl, then continue right into the crowd that lined the side of Black Hill Road.

Suddenly, a figure glided across the road, a blur of white, and sent the little girl flying toward the side of the road. The wagon struck, but instead of crushing the figure and barreling into the helpless crowd, it exploded in a blinding conflagration of hellfire. The crowd screamed and Ashley realized she was screaming right along with them. She heard Dawn behind her, just one word that carried her friend's pain. *Eden.*

A siren wailed as the fire truck that had been waiting blared its horn to get to the wagon. Ashley had lost sight of the little girl in the firestorm, and now she pulled away from her friends and sprinted past the fire truck. When she got to the other side, she saw the little girl clinging to her mother. "Is she all right?" Ashley said, moving next to them and reaching toward the girl, as if she could do something.

The girl's mother was nodding, hysterical with relief, as a police officer—Officer Hawkins, Ashley realized, with that weird, giddy feeling you get when you recognize someone—

arrived, barking orders for the ambulance into his walkie-talkie.

The little girl turned to Ashley, a brilliant smile on her face. "Did you see her? Did you see Lonesome Amie?"

Before she could answer, Kenny's voice rose above the commotion. "Dawn!"

Ashley turned to see Kenny catch Dawn as she collapsed.

chapter
seventy-five

HANNAH HEARD what sounded like an explosion and jumped to her feet. The blinding orange glow and shower of embers was dissipating. *The wagon must have veered off course and hit a tree.* She peeled the remains of her dress off the smoldering bulk that was Derek Campbell and tossed it aside. She had no idea if he was alive or dead and realized with a deep, burning shame that she didn't really care. She rummaged through the pockets of his costume until she found his cell phone. Even if it was locked, she'd be able to make an emergency call, but she stared with dismay at the shattered screen. It wouldn't power up. With a last glance toward the woods where Lonesome Amie had vanished, she began to trudge down the hill.

Sirens were wailing and people were still screaming and scurrying around in panic. She was so distracted by the commotion that an approaching figure took her by surprise.

"Hannah!"

It was Marcus's panicked voice. She squinted into the darkness, her eyes unadjusted after looking at the inferno below. Then she saw him, sprinting toward her. He pulled up just in time before bowling her over and pulled her into a bear hug. Hannah winced, the aches and pains of her tackle starting to announce themselves.

"Thank God you're all right," he whispered in her ear. "We saw the wagon and thought—" The rest was choked off by a relieved sob. Hannah didn't need to hear the words to understand the sentiment.

"I'm okay," she said, not wanting the hug to end despite the discomfort of her battered body. "Lonesome Amie saved me."

Marcus pulled away; head cocked. "What ..."

Hannah didn't wait for him to get his thoughts together. "Never mind that now, we need an ambulance for him."

Marcus stared at her for a beat then remembered he had Kenny's phone. He made the call. Hannah watched in dazed amazement as one of the numerous police vehicles started up the hill. It was like watching a true crime show on split screen.

After Marcus ended the call, he put an arm around her. "Are you really all right?"

"Fine," she said. "What about Dawn?"

Marcus quickly explained that Dawn had recovered and seemed okay.

The police car pulled up, followed by an ambulance. Hannah pointed at Derek and told the officer and the paramedic he'd been struck by the wagon. She showed the office her dress and explained how she'd used it to extinguish the flames when his costume had ignited. He took down her contact information and joined the paramedic at Derek's side.

"You really did that?" Marcus's voice held a note she couldn't identify.

"What?"

Marcus glanced back at Derek; his face hard. "I think I would have let him burn," he said, ice in his voice.

"I don't believe that," Hannah said. "You would have done the same thing I did."

"Yeah, probably."

Hannah leaned in and kissed him; there were words on the tip of her tongue, but she bit them back. *Not here. Not now.* "Let's go," she said, and started down the road.

chapter
seventy-six

"HANNAH!" Ashley ran toward her and Marcus as they approached the smoldering remains of the wagon. The police had sent most of the crowd home, but a few diehards were hanging around, filming the fire department's efforts or trying to get selfies with the wreckage of the wagon.

Ashley and Kenny both grabbed her in a fierce three-way hug. Ashley was sobbing with relief and when Kenny pulled away, Ashley hung on tighter. "I was so scared, Hannah," she said.

Hannah had no words, and even if she did, they wouldn't get past the enormous lump in her throat. Instead of words, she tightened her grip on her best friend. They stayed that way for a long time.

When Ashley pulled away, Hannah noticed Marcus and Kenny were talking quietly a few steps away. At first, she assumed they were giving the girls some privacy, but then it hit her. "Where's Dawn?"

Ashley took her hand. "She's on her way to the hospital—"

"Marcus said she was better—"

"She was," Ashley said. "Then when the wagon—"

"Listen," Hannah said. "I don't know what happened down here, but Lonesome Amie saved me up *there*." Her eyes shifted to the spot up the hill where the ambulance was now pulling away from. "Derek was on top of me, and the wagon was coming. She ... she knocked him off me and the wagon hit them instead of me." Saying it out loud hammered it home. She could have been mangled up there, permanently injured or disfigured. She could have been killed. Her knees went rubbery, but Ash was there to steady her.

"We can compare notes later," Kenny said. "My dad is on his way to take me to the hospital to make sure Dawn is okay.

Hannah looked at him, closely, for the first time since getting down the hill. He was pale, his eyes sunken. *Haunted*. As if on cue, Kenny's father's Audi turned onto Black Hill Road and pulled up next to them. Kenny gave them a hesitant wave and ran over.

"Wait," Ashley called, "Can we come?"

Kenny leaned into the driver's window for a second, then gestured for them to get in.

The ride to the hospital was strangely quiet. Other than giving Kenny's dad short and somewhat vague answers to his questions, nobody really spoke. Hannah realized with a deep ache in her heart that it was because they were kids and had "kid stuff" to talk about. Kenny's dad would never understand, in fact, he'd probably think they'd all lost their minds. *How many years am I away from that? Of losing my ability to believe in things like ghosts and supernatural cult leaders who perform arcane rituals to live longer?* There were exceptions, like Big Jake, who somehow carried whatever it is that makes childhood so wonderful into their adult life. She thought it might be because he'd seen it firsthand and had never let it fade. Could she do the same?

"Are they even going to let you see her?"

Mr. Driscoll's voice pulled her from her thoughts, and she

was surprised to find they were at the hospital's emergency entrance.

Kenny was already halfway out of the car. "If they don't, her dad will tell us how she's doing."

Mr. Driscoll made a noise, half scoffing and half something else, that sent Hannah back to her thoughts of how bleak it must be to an adult. "Text me when you're done," he said. "I'll find a spot in the parking lot."

Hannah mumbled her thanks as she scrambled out of the car. Her entire body screamed at the movement. She'd stiffened up during the ride and wondered just how much pain she'd be in tomorrow.

She followed the others into the lobby, ignoring the stares of the desk nurse and the other people waiting. It occurred to her that it was sometime after one o'clock in the morning and they probably had no business being there. Deal with it, she thought, and perused the lobby to see if Mr. Holman was there. A young mother held a crying baby in her arms. The baby's face was red and feverish, the mother's lined with concern bordering on fear. An older couple, probably in their forties, sat talking quietly while the woman held an icepack to her face. A pair of teenage boys that Hannah didn't recognize sat in the corner, different parts of them bloodied and amateurishly bandaged while an older man—*one of their fathers?* —stared impatiently at the desk nurse. No Mr. Holman.

Kenny had already approached the desk and was gesturing wildly as he spoke to the bored-looking woman. Hannah cringed. Why hadn't they talked about letting someone else—*anyone* else—be the one to do the talking?

She came up behind him and was surprised to hear him explain things in a calm tone in spite of his in-constant-motion hands. He thanked the nurse and stepped away, out of earshot. Hannah and the others followed.

"She won't tell me anything but she's calling the ER nurse to ask Mr. Holman to give us an update."

Hannah nodded, noticing how stressed Kenny looked. It made his demeanor at the nurses' desk even more impressive. He must have wanted to leap over the desk and search the emergency room beds for Dawn. *Because that's what I'd want to do if Marcus was back there.* She shifted her gaze to him and felt that now-familiar warmth spread through her. She loved him. It hit her with such suddenness, such sureness, that it almost unhinged her knees. Marcus glanced up, catching her stare, and her face burned. She tried to smile but it felt like her face was contorting. *Oh, God, what am I doing?* Marcus gave her an odd little half-frown, half-smile. He started toward her, and Hannah's heart skipped. Her tongue felt too big for her mouth. She'd never be able to speak. Why was this happening here? Now?

The door to the emergency room opened with a *ding* and Mr. Holman stepped out. *Saved by the bell.* It struck her that she'd thought that very same thing recently. It was the night at the diner when Officer Ramirez interrupted the fight. It seemed like forever ago.

She shook her head, returning to the present. One good look at Mr. Holman and all her mushy thoughts about Marcus evaporated. He looked like he'd aged ten years since she'd last seen him. His skin was a waxy pale, his eyes hooded by deep, black caverns. His expression was grim but seemed to brighten when he saw his daughter's new friends.

"Kids," he said, "thank you for coming. The others are down the hall, we can talk there."

chapter
seventy-seven

HANNAH SAT NEXT TO MARCUS, clinging to his hand so tightly her fingers had lost all feeling. Ashley was next to Kenny, and she had a tentative arm around him. They had all called their parents when Mr. Holman had asked the hospital if they could use a small private room to tell them about Dawn.

"First," Mr. Holman said, "Dawn is going to be fine. She suffered a concussion at some point this evening and..."

Hannah realized that Mr. Holman was about to give them terrible news. The *worst* news.

"Do you know about Dawn's sister?" He didn't wait for a response, just plowed ahead, as if he had to get the story out while he could. "She died last year. Before we moved to Hopedale. Dawn was babysitting so my wife...*ex-wife* and I could celebrate our anniversary. When we came home, and..." He sobbed, pausing to wipe his eyes. "It was what they call crib death, or Sudden Infant Death Syndrome. It was just a...a terrible tragedy. My ex-wife, couldn't cope and she...she blamed Dawn."

"That's so sad," Hannah said. "She never said anything..."

Ashley was looking down, her face a portrait of shame and regret.

"Between losing her sister and being blamed by her mother, Dawn had a sort of breakdown. She's recovered well, the move has helped and..." He choked up again but seemed to will himself to continue. "And you have been such good friends to her...she may never get over Eden's death—"

Kenny sat up straight. "Did you say Eden?"

"Yes, that was my daughter's name. Why?"

"She said that name," Ashley said, staring at Kenny. "You heard it, too?"

Kenny nodded. "But it was when—"

"She saw Lonesome Amie," Ashley finished.

"Hold on," Kenny's dad said, his voice taking on a note of disbelief. "Are you talking about a *ghost*?"

"We all saw it," Kenny said, his voice firm.

Mr. Driscoll rolled his eyes and stepped away from the table, running a hand through his thinning hair. It confirmed Hannah's suspicions about why they'd kept silent on the ride to the hospital.

"Have you kids been drinking? Or smoking pot?"

"Dad!" Kenny stood, face flushed. "Please. You know better than that."

He threw his hands in the air. "What am I supposed to think?"

"Mr. Driscoll," Dawn's father said, "can we discuss that part later?"

Mr. Driscoll seemed to remember where they were and why. He mumbled an apology and leaned against the wall, head down.

"Please, go on," Kenny said, looking at Mr. Holman.

Mr. Holman gave Kenny's dad another look, then continued. "Dawn's mother was sick. I believe she suffered from anxiety and depression, though it was never diagnosed. I tried to get her help..." He took a deep breath to compose himself. "She was never the same person after what happened to Eden. She began drinking all the time, *self-medicating,* the doctors called it. She was hostile. Mean. Lashing out at either me or Dawn every chance she got.

"She came home drunk one night, and I'd had enough. She started ranting about Dawn. I was frazzled. I screamed at her. Called her terrible names. I'd never raised my voice to her before that. Never responded to her taunts or insults. She went crazy. Dawn had woken up and Margo tried to attack. I fended her off with one hand, trying to push Dawn out of the room with the other. Margo was like a wild animal, scratching and clawing at me."

He rolled up his left sleeve and Ashley gasped at the sight of his disfigured arm. Hannah recalled seeing them the first time they'd met. Thinking he'd survived an animal attack. *Maybe he had*.

"She tired after a while, leaned against the dresser, her eyes were half closed. I thought she was going to pass out. I relaxed — No, that's not right. I let my guard down. Dawn was standing in the doorway. I turned to comfort Dawn and Margo leaped at me. I think now, looking back, she'd feigned her weariness, the way she'd slumped against the dresser ... it was to shield me from seeing what she was doing.

"My best friend from college had sent a beautiful snow globe that depicted the castle from The Wizard of Oz as a gift when Eden was born."

Hannah stared, something cold and hard forming in her gut. She knew where all this was going. Not the exact details, but the end result, sure. She swallowed hard, tasting the bile that had crept up her throat.

"She blindsided me. Dawn yelled a warning, but it was too late. She fractured my skull, shattering that globe against the back of my head. The pain shocked me. I remember distinctly thinking, how could Dawn's scream cause me so much pain—

"Dawn tried to intervene. Margo was going to kill me, but she managed to fight her somehow. They both fell. Dawn struck her head on the crib. Margo landed on the broken glass of the snow globe. It ... I don't know ... sobered her up enough to realize what she'd done."

"How ...?" Kenny let his question fade, like he didn't really want to know the answer.

Mr. Holman smiled. It was a ghastly thing. "How do I know if I had a fractured skull? Margo told me everything that happened after she hit me. Including that she was going to kill me. She even showed me how. There was a shard of glass she'd spotted on the floor, shaped like a karambit because of the curve of the globe. Deadly. She planned to cut my throat. I have to take her word on that part. I was unconscious and Dawn doesn't remember anything."

"Was she knocked out, too?" Kenny asked.

Mr. Holman frowned. "Margo insists that she wasn't. Dawn had a nasty bump on her head but Margo swears she was conscious. I can't think of a reason she'd lie about that part."

Hannah gaped at him, unable to grasp the pain he must be in. The agony he lived with every day. She pictured him at their first meeting, his dazed expression, his empty eyes. After a moment, Mr. Holman picked his head up. A fresh dagger of pain jabbed at Hannah's heart. *How many times must he have to pick himself up? Just to go on.*

She waited for Mr. Holman to continue, but he seemed far away, lost in his memories. "So," she said, "could this concussion...be bad because of her previous injury?" Mr. Holman blinked, looking around the room as if he'd forgotten where he was. He's so lost, Hannah thought, so broken.

"I'm sorry," he said. "I guess I went away for a minute. I

didn't mean to go on such a tangent. Yes, the doctors were concerned about that, especially where she lost consciousness tonight and due to her migraine the other day. They'll be running more tests but they're confident there will be no long-term effects."

"Okay, kids," Mr. Driscoll said, clapping his hands together. "I think it's time we call it a night. He pulled his car keys out of his pocket. "It's late. I'm tired. Mr. Holman has had a very trying night. Let's let him spend some time with his daughter."

Kenny was about to object when there was a soft knock on the door. Mr. Holman rose and pulled the door open. The desk nurse was there. "A couple more folks to join you," she said quietly.

"Dad. Rick." Hannah stood and ran to her father, wrapping her arms around him. He returned the embrace and Hannah felt Rick's hand on her shoulder. All the despair and confusion she'd felt lifted just a bit. "Thank you both for coming," she said. "Come on in, join the p— Join the gang."

"We'll make room," Mr. Driscoll said, "Kenny and I are leaving—"

"Dad, please," Kenny said, his voice pleading. "Let me stay."

"I'm happy to take everyone home," Brian offered. Hannah could tell he sensed the tension in the room and was trying to help.

"Please, Dad?"

Mr. Driscoll sighed. "Fine." He turned to Brian. "You're sure you don't mind?"

Brian and Rick assured him they'd get everyone home safely. Mr. Driscoll turned to Dawn's father and said, "I'm sorry for your troubles. My wife and I will be praying for Dawn." His face softened as he glanced at Kenny. "My son thinks quite highly of her." He smiled. "Never stops talking about her, actually."

Kenny groaned. "Thanks, Dad." His father smiled vaguely, glanced quickly at Brian and Rick, then left.

Hannah sat, then realized neither Brian nor Rick had moved from their spot by the door. She looked at her dad's face and all the bad feelings that had lifted upon their arrival settled on her again. Both men's faces were set with hard lines, their eyes unable to hide their stress. *Mom*, Hannah thought.

"Hannah," her father said, "Rick and I need to talk to you alone for a few minutes." His tone, though sad, left no room for debate.

Mr. Holman seemed to sense something else was going on. "I think it's time we took a break, anyway. I'd like to get a drink of water and look in on Dawn."

"Can I come?" Kenny asked, getting to his feet.

Mr. Holman offered him a smile. "It's probably against the rules but let's see what we can do."

Hannah told Marcus she'd be right back and followed her father and Rick out the door. Once they were in the hall, Hannah grabbed her father's arm. "Dad, what's wrong? It's Mom, isn't it?"

He gave a nod. "She was there, on Black Hill Road. She was injured at the Wagon Burning. An EMT treated some burns on her hands and face but she refused to go with them."

Hannah's hand dropped from his arm, and she staggered a step back. Rick was by her side before she could fall.

"Injured?" Hannah said. "How?" Then it was clear. *You're safe now.* The way the figure in white had run off into the woods, not ghost-like at all.

"We're not really sure what happened," Rick said.

"She saved my life," Hannah whispered, awestruck.

"Hannah?" Dad moved closer. "What do you mean?"

"I thought it was the ghost," Hannah said. "I guess it was,

just a different one." Her dad and Rick exchanged a worried glance. "Don't worry," she assured them. "I'm okay. Let me guess, she was wearing a white dress, partially burned?" She enjoyed the dumbstruck look on both their faces, then quickly filled them in on what had happened and how the figure in white had saved her from being struck by the wagon. This time, she didn't enjoy the look on either of their faces.

"You mean this boy assaulted you and Marcus? When did you plan on getting around to telling us? And reporting it?" Her father's complexion had gone dark red.

"I guess so," she said, unable to tell if he was mad at Derek, or at her. "I wasn't trying to hide it; we were all just so worried about Dawn. And I'm fine, really. Derek isn't going to be a problem, an ambulance brought him here, too. He was in pretty bad shape, I think."

"I'm going to check on this Derek kid and make sure he's not going anywhere tonight."

"Campbell," Hannah said, anticipating his next question. "Dad, will you come with me to find out how Dawn is?" Her voice hitched, the rest of what she was going to say stuck in her throat. Her father was there, by her side, holding her.

"Of course," he said. "Rick, you know where to find us."

chapter
seventy-eight

HANNAH and her father got back to the conference room at the same time as Mr. Holman and Kenny. Hannah stopped, shocked by the change in Kenny. He looked somehow smaller, diminished. His face, pale to begin with since they'd been at the hospital, was now a chalky white that made the dark circles under his eyes even harsher. His eyes were puffy, he'd been crying. All of this added up to more bad news, she knew.

"Are you all right, Kenny?" Instead of waiting for an answer she hugged him. Kenny returned the embrace, clawing at her as if desperate for human contact. She felt his body shudder and knew the tears weren't done.

"Let's go inside," Mr. Holman said gently. "I'd like to finish up here so I can be with Dawn."

Hannah followed him into the room. Marcus gave her a questioning look, but she shook her head and mouthed '*later*' as she took her seat next to him. Once everyone was settled, Mr. Holman spoke. "I just want to update you on her medical condition," he went on. "But first, I wanted to thank you all for making Dawn feel so welcome in your town. She's never been happier, and I have no doubt I owe that to each of you for being such good friends.

"Now, about Dawn. I mentioned the breakdown and the concussion. She is prone to extreme migraines and occasional nosebleeds. In some cases, the headaches cause dizziness and fainting, which is what happened at school the other day."

"But she's going to be all right?" Ashley's voice was more of a plea than a question.

"Yes," Mr. Holman replied. "It's just so hard to see her like this. Did you know she used to be a great athlete? She was an all-star pitcher for her softball team back in Hartford."

Hannah and Ashley exchanged a wide-eyed look. *The football.*

Hannah filed that bit of information away for later.

"You really are the best friends she's ever had." Before anyone could speak, Mr. Holman turned and hurried out of the room. Nobody said anything for a long time. Hannah glanced around and saw the dazed looks that no doubt mirrored her own.

Her dad broke the pain-filled silence. "I think I should get you all home," he said, getting to his feet.

chapter
seventy-nine

THEY RODE IN SILENCE, Hannah lost in her thoughts. She assumed the others were, too. They still hadn't had a chance to compare notes and piece everything together, but there would be plenty of time for that. Especially with Derek out of the picture, at least for a while. She thought she should feel guilty for the relief she felt about his injury but reconciled it in her head that he'd got what he deserved.

One thing about the night was still bothering her. She realized now that the figure that had saved her from the wagon was her mother, but... "Ashley," she said, turning to her friends in the back seat. Ashley jumped, startled by the sudden break in silence. They all laughed, though a bit nervously. "When you saw Lonesome Amie save that little girl, it was obviously after my mother saved me. But there's no way she could have gotten down the hill in time, even if she *wasn't* hurt."

"Yeah," Ashley said, "I've been thinking about that, too. It was really her."

"Hey," Marcus said, "I bet everyone there had their phones out to record the wagon coming down. There should be tons of video showing Lonesome Amie is real."

They began to talk excitedly about it. The possibility that they might have actual proof of a ghost, right here in Hopedale. It could mean all those ghost hunter shows would come to investigate, maybe someone would make a documentary, even a movie. But the conversation petered out quickly. Kenny hadn't spoken, he was staring out the window, concern for Dawn etched on his face. Hannah's dad didn't join in, either. Hannah assumed his head was spinning worse than her own with thoughts of her mother and what Derek had tried to do.

Silence returned to the car and Hannah turned to face the front. As her father dropped each of them off, she got out to hug them. By the time they pulled into the driveway of her own house, it was almost sunrise and the exhaustion hit her all at once. She wanted to close her eyes and sleep in the car, her bed seemed so far away.

"Come on, honey," Dad said, "let's get you inside."

They were both met by Scout, whining and spinning in his crazy circles, alternately licking each of their hands as they tried to pat him.

"This is all going to look better after some sleep," her father said, giving her a hug.

"Thanks Dad, for everything. Goodnight." She trudged off to her bedroom, Scout at her heels. But after changing into her pajamas and getting comfortable in bed, she couldn't sleep. Birds began to sing outside, and the sky began to lighten as she tried to process everything that had happened. She didn't know what to think about her mother. Had she been the one following her around, dressed in an overcoat and floppy hat to disguise herself? It seemed likely. Now she was in the hospital because she'd been following Hannah. *She saved my life.* That led to Derek and his deranged ramblings. He'd been talking about fireflies and some other nonsense. She pushed those thoughts away; it was all too crazy.

That left Dawn, and Hannah felt the weight of her new friend's past threatening to crush her. Tears soaked into her pillow. Scout, somehow sensing her sadness, squirmed up closer. She wrapped an arm around him and finally, sleep came.

chapter
eighty

HANNAH WOKE up when the angle of the sun was just right to blast her eyes like a laser. She blinked, shading her face with one hand and rubbing her eyes with the other. It didn't make sense, the sun never— She noticed the time on the clock and leapt out of bed, suddenly wide awake. She was late for school! Why didn't Dad— Then she remembered the night before in shocking clarity, and just as suddenly was exhausted again.

She shuffled out into the kitchen, not really surprised to see her father and Rick sitting at the table drinking coffee and eating bagels out of a Dunkin' Donuts box. Scout, of course, sat close by, ready to pounce on any fallen morsel — accidental or intentional. "Morning," she muttered, and plopped down, grabbing a plain bagel and pulling small chunks off to eat.

"That might taste better toasted, with some cream cheese. Or maybe some cinnamon butter?"

She smiled wanly at Rick and kept plucking and eating. She had a headache, probably from the combination of stress and lack of sleep. Or, she thought, maybe getting tackled by Derek Campbell had rattled her brain. "So," she said, between bites, "where do we begin?" Before either could answer she said, "It was rhetorical. Did you find Mom?"

"No. The EMT is sure it was her, though. He suspects she may have been hurt worse than she let on."

Hannah pictured the figure in white tackling Derek. Had she been hit by the wagon, too? "Can we call—"

"Rick already called all the hospitals in the area. No luck," Dad said.

Hannah started to get up again, tossing the rest of her bagel to Scout.

"There's something else we need to talk about," Rick said.

Hannah looked at him, not liking the stern, cop-like demeanor. She sat back down. "Okaaay."

"It's about Derek Campbell," Rick started. "First, you don't have to worry about him bothering you or your friends anymore."

"Is he dead?" Hannah asked, feeling the sleep around her eyes stretch when they widened.

"No," Rick said, "but his mother is." Hannah frowned, waiting for him to continue, the pieces falling into place before he did. "The hospital had been trying to contact Mrs. Campbell all night with no success. They finally requested a wellness check, and..." He took a breath. "They found her half-buried corpse in the basement. It was starting to decay. Until the autopsy is complete, we won't know how long she's been there."

"He killed her," Hannah whispered.

"That's the indication, yes. Again, nothing is sure until the autopsy, but we found an empty bottle of painkillers and evidence that they'd been ground up. There was a bowl of chili on the kitchen table. It was likely what he ground the pills into."

Hannah closed her eyes. The reality of what could have been washing over her like a cold wave. She jumped when her father wrapped her in a hug. "It's okay, Hannah," he said, "you're safe."

"I know," she said, "it's just…" She struggled to find the right words. "I'm sitting here wondering where Mom is, how hurt she is because of him, and meanwhile he had already murdered his own mother. It's so…unreal."

"Clearly he's a very disturbed individual." Rick said.

"I've known that for a while," she said, then realized her mistake. Too late.

"What do you mean?" Her father's tone was beyond suspicious. It was more along the lines of, *what now, Hannah?*

She sighed, knowing she'd have to tell him everything, but too overwhelmed to even begin. "It's a long story," she said, "can we leave it at that for now? I want to visit Dawn."

She was surprised when her father smiled and said, "Go get dressed. I already walked Scout; we'll go as soon as you're ready."

Hannah dressed quickly, throwing on jeans and a sweatshirt, pulling her hair into a ponytail and sticking it through her Red Sox cap. She was back in the kitchen in under five minutes — most of that time spent brushing her teeth.

"Wow," Rick said with a laugh, "I thought women took forever to get ready. I was all set to grab another cup of coffee."

"Make it to-go, Benson," Hannah said, "we're burning daylight."

"No offense, Hannah," Dad said, "but you burned most of it in bed."

She stuck out her tongue at him, then stopped. She hadn't really looked at him since she'd been up. "Have you slept at all?" she said, horrified.

"I'll get plenty of sleep when I'm dead," he replied, then winced. "Sorry, probably not the best time to be joking about that."

Hannah laughed it off. "Just remember what happened to

Wade Garret after he uttered those words." She gave Scout a pat and walked out the front door to the sound of Rick and her dad laughing.

chapter
eighty-one

HANNAH SAT in the back seat, anxiously waiting for her dad to turn onto Route. 33. That was the first spot she'd get any cell service. Once he started into the turn, he yelled, "Go!" Hannah smiled and started texting. Before she could hit 'SEND,' a message from Ashley showed up.

We have to talk. Important.

Hannah started responding, then called instead.

"Hey," Ashley said, "you're alive."

Second death joke of the day, Hannah thought. "Barely," she replied, "what's up?"

"Not over the phone, okay? Are you at the hospital?"

"On our way now," Hannah said, "are you all right?"

"Yes...no...I don't know," Ashley said. "I'll meet you in the lobby."

To Hannah's shock, Ashley ended the call. She had sounded more than just tired, she sounded sad. She knew Ashley had been worried about her parents' weird behavior, that had to be what this was about. She sighed, and shifted gears, steeling herself for more bad news.

. . .

To Kenny and Marcus: *Any update on Dawn? On my way to the hospital now.*

From Kenny: *She was stable overnight. Her dad is in with her now. Waiting...*

Hannah*: Be there in a few minutes.*

After what seemed like an eternity, her father pulled into the hospital lot and promptly found a parking space. As they walked across the lot, clouds moved in front of the sun, throwing everything into shadow and casting a chill. Hannah looked up, noticing the heavy clouds gathering, a sure sign of a cold, autumn rain. November rain, she thought, thinking of that sad Guns N' Roses song. Followed by a colder winter, she thought with a shiver.

Rick was telling her father that he was going to check in on Derek Campbell while Hannah was visiting Dawn. "Dad, I'm going to stop in the lobby to talk to Ash for a minute before I see Dawn, okay?"

Her father gave her a quizzical look before saying, "Sure. I'm going to tag along with Rick."

She confirmed it with him as they went through the revolving doors, then they split up, Rick and her dad heading for the elevators while she made her way to the main lobby.

It wasn't hard to spot Ashley. She was the one pacing back and forth at top speed, one hand raised to her mouth in an effort to destroy her fingernails. "Ash?"

Her friend didn't even look up at the sound of her voice, just changed direction like she was using echolocation, and speed-walked to Hannah. No greeting, no eye contact. Instead, she grabbed her in a fierce hug. Hannah couldn't return it; her arms were pinned to her sides.

"Ash, what's wrong?" After a long minute, Ashley pulled away and finally looked at Hannah. She wasn't crying, she seemed all cried out, if that was possible. Her normally bronze complexion was drained, sallow. Her eyes were puffy and red but also somehow sunken. She looked haunted...no, hollowed out. "Have you slept at all?"

Ashley tried a wan smile. "Thanks, you look great, too."

"I cannot tell a lie," Hannah said, "you look like poop on burnt toast." No reaction. "Okay, spill it." Hannah knew it was the only way to help. Begin the bloodletting, then heal. Still, she dreaded hearing anything that could make her best friend look like this. Ashley mumbled something but she couldn't make it out. "What?"

"I'm adopted," Ashley said.

Hannah blinked, for a split-second thinking this was one of Ashley's pranks. But she was looking at Hannah so helplessly it broke her heart. And confirmed immediately this was no joke. This was why the Wallaces had been acting so weird. "Oh," Hannah said, feeling stupid. "I mean, okay..." Why was she such a bad friend, she couldn't find a single decent thing to say to make Ashley feel better about this? While she knew Ashley must be feeling a rollercoaster of emotions, the thing that struck Hannah was that it didn't really matter. Sure, there were questions Ashley needed answered. *Who are her biological parents? Why did the Wallaces wait until now to tell her? But...she's still the same Ashley. And the Wallaces are still her mother and father.* "We'll figure it out," she said. Maybe it was her tone, maybe just those simple words of friendship, but Ashley smiled. A real Ashley smile. "Me and you, and your mom and dad. Together."

"Yeah, we will."

"Now," Hannah said, returning the smile, "Let's go see Dawn."

Hannah gave Ashley the Reader's Digest version of everything — her mother, Derek, Derek's mother, then gave her a hug and headed for the elevators.

epilogue

HANNAH LOOKED AROUND THE HOUSE, unable to keep a goofy grin from spreading across her face. Thanksgiving dinner had been a smashing success. The food had been great and everybody she loved was gathered to celebrate. Well, she thought with a pang of guilt, almost everyone. Her mother was still missing. Nobody had seen her since Halloween night. She still couldn't believe her mother had been following her around ever since that night in the clearing.

She tried to push thoughts of her mother away and focus on the moment. Big Jake arrived late after a long day of serving dinner to homeless people in New Hampshire. After hearing of their adventures on Black Hill Road, he'd regaled them with stories he'd heard about the identity of Lonesome Amie. How she'd been killed by the original burning wagon sent down the hill by the loggers.

During his story, he'd mentioned a name that had caused Hannah, Ashley, and Dawn to exchange a wide-eyed look. Jake had called out one of Vancleave's as being the real mastermind behind the attempted massacre of the loggers. Wesley Gaines. Hannah recalled Mrs. Cheevers' story about the boy she'd been on Black Hill Road with that night. *He said it felt like she was marking him*. Michael Gaines.

Later, Marcus, Ashley, Kenny, and Dawn had moved to the living room to watch football with Hannah's dad, Rick Benson, and Ashley's parents. Mr. Holman had lingered behind, helping Hannah clear the last of the dessert dishes. He approached her now, glancing back at his daughter. She followed his gaze and smiled. Dawn sat on the couch, cuddled in with Kenny, and Ash sat on the floor next to them. Even from where she stood in the kitchen, Hannah could see the grin on Dawn's face.

"She's doing great," Hannah said.

Mr. Holman turned, swiping the back of his hand across his eyes. "I'm sorry," he said, laughing, "I don't know if I'll ever be able to talk about her without crying. There was a time I never thought she'd bounce back after what happened to Eden."

Hannah didn't know what to say. She snuck another look at Dawn. Kenny was barely paying attention to the football game. He was spending more time sneaking his own peeks at Dawn, his expression a mix of concern and adoration. Dawn had changed him. He was quieter, introspective. There were still flashes of the old Kenny — his manic storytelling and inappropriate jokes — but those came less often. It was as if he saved all his energy for Dawn.

This time, Mr. Holman's smile was genuine, touching his eyes and smoothing out the wrinkles. Hannah saw the resemblance to Dawn then. "Hannah," he said, "you are the best thing that has happened to Dawn. You and your friends. Hopedale." He looked back again at them. "I think she might have given up without you."

Hannah tried to push back the lump in her throat. "She's a special person, Mr. Holman," she said, her voice strangled with emotion. "And you're a special dad."

He nodded. "Yes, she is," he said, running a hand through his long gray hair. "But I think the jury is still out on me."

Jury. The word chilled her. Even though she might not have to testify against Mama Bayole's followers, it was very likely she *would* have to testify against Derek Campbell. He was being tried as an adult, assuming he was able to stand trial at all. While he was recovering from most of the injuries he had received that night, he was still convinced he was some sort of god. *Lord of the Fireflies.* She shivered.

"Hannah," Mr. Holman said, pulling her from her thoughts, "do you think it's strange that none of the footage of that night was clear enough to show anything?"

She knew exactly what he was talking about. Despite the countless cell phones aimed at the wagon that night, there wasn't a single clear video. None that showed what most people there claim to have seen: Lonesome Amie. In the ones that were clear enough to make anything out, the little girl appeared to leap out of the way just before the wagon exploded. There were white flashes in some, weird blurry spots in others, but nothing conclusive. It had definitely struck Hannah as being, well, impossible. "It is weird," she agreed.

Mr. Holman said, "Maybe Lonesome Amie didn't want to be seen anymore. Or, maybe," he went on, "there's something about these ghostly appearances that has some science behind it. Something that interferes with technology. Dawn told me about the woman at the library, Mrs. Cheevers, and how her car had stalled the night she was in the presence of Lonesome Amie."

Hannah nodded.

"I may have been spending time reading a few of Dawn's books," Mr. Holman said, then smiled. "But there are a lot of things in this world that can't be explained,"

"Especially here in Hopedale," she said, and they both laughed.

acknowledgments

I wish I could personally thank everyone who has helped me on my writing journey. Whether it was a simple word of encouragement, the purchase of a book, editing, leaving a review, or stopping by to chat at a convention...all these things keep me going.

Specific to the book you're holding...

Thank you to Linda Nagle for her editing prowess. She takes every story and makes it better with her red pen. *The Ghost of Black Hill Road* is no exception.
A shout out to the Monday Night Writing Group for all their helpful critiques on the prologue.
Thank you to my formatting department, Sheila Deady, for the wonderful interior design.
The horror writing community is a special place. Whether I chat with folks online or meet up at conventions, they are always wonderful and supportive.
Thank you to my readers, old and new. Without you, this would be a (more) lonely endeavor.

As always, my family deserves all the thanks. Your love and support are everything.

about the author

Tom Deady is a Bram Stoker Award winner (2016) for Superior Achievement in a First Novel, and has since published several novels and novellas inspired by his love of horror.

Tom was born and raised in Massachusetts, not far from the historic town of Salem.

He resides in Arizona, where he's working on his next novel.

Shop for signed copies and more at
https://www.tomdeady.com/
Subscribe to my newsletter to get exclusive updates!

facebook.com/tomdeady

instagram.com/tom_deady

tiktok.com/@tomdeadyofficial

bookbub.com/profile/tom-deady

also by tom deady

Shop for signed copies and more at

https://www.tomdeady.com/

Subscribe to my newsletter to get exclusive updates!

Hopedale Mystery Series

The Witch of Hopedale

The Ghost of Black Hill Road

Novels

Haven

Eternal Darkness

Those Left Behind

Novellas

Weekend Getaway

Of Men and Monsters

Collections

Tales from Circadia

The Edgewater Chronicles